SNUFFLING
UP
B⚠NES

SNUFFLING UP BONES

UP

B💀NES

THE PIG AND I MYSTERIES

DONNARAE MENARD

LEVEL
BEST BOOKS

Author Photo Credit: Klementovich Photography, North Conway, New Hampshire

First edition

ISBN: 978-1-68512-777-0

Cover art by Level Best Designs

This book was professionally typeset on Reedsy.
Find out more at reedsy.com

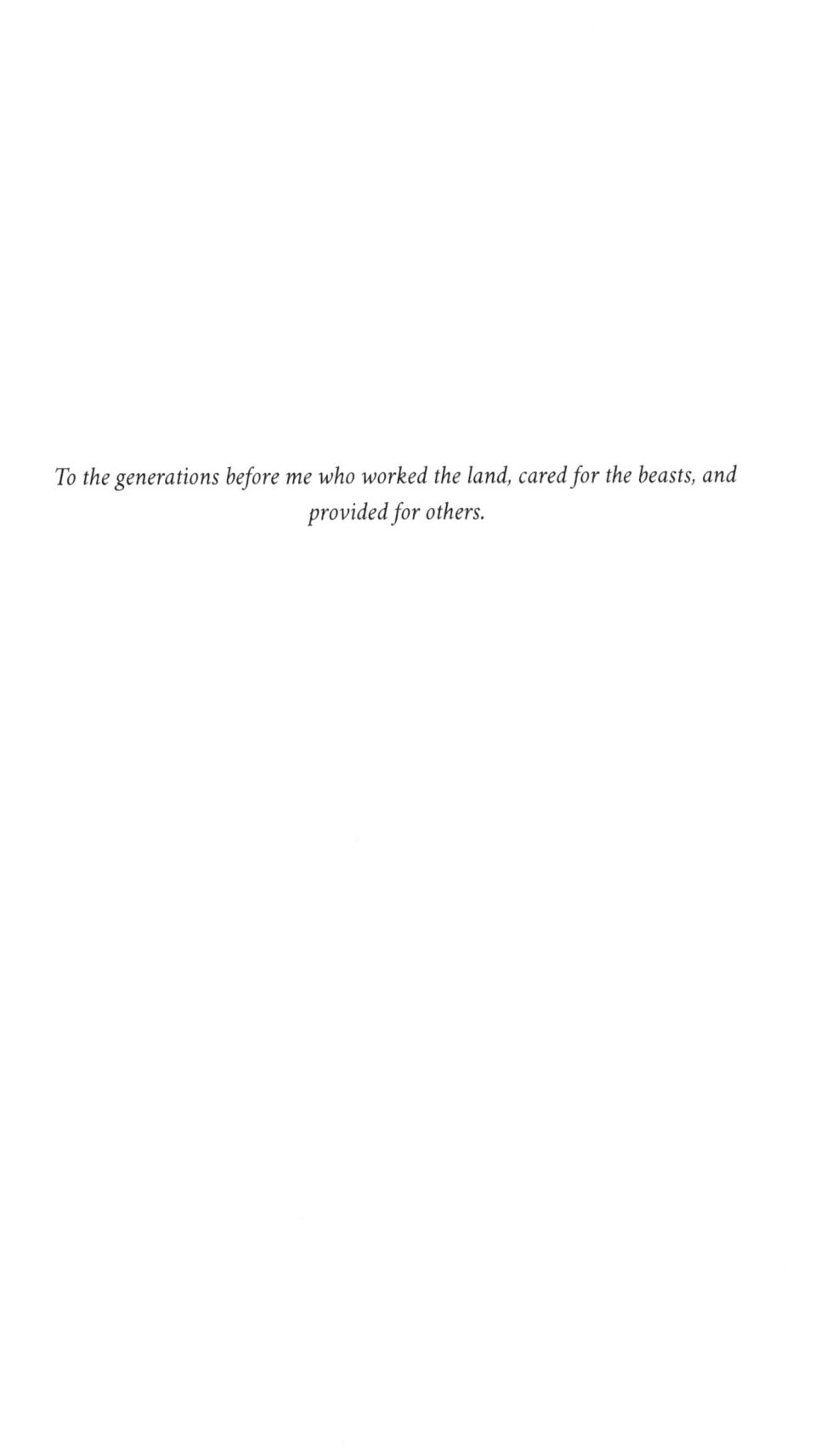

To the generations before me who worked the land, cared for the beasts, and provided for others.

Praise for Snuffling Up Bones

"DonnaRae Menard's evocative writing brings Vermont to life and introduces Doris Flynn, a sharp and fearless farmer and amateur sleuth with an irresistible 450 lb. porcine sidekick. Whether Doris is rescuing animals in need or searching the woods for clues to a murder with snuffling pig Buttercup at her side, readers will be glad they journeyed with the duo through the Green Mountain State's majestic but sometimes dangerous landscape."—Ellen Byron, *USA Today* bestselling & Agatha Award-winning author of The Golden Motel Mystery series

"DonnaRae Menard always has something humorous to relate regarding her pet pig. In *Snuggling Up Bones*, she shows us that her 450-pound baby girl is not only funny, but smart, dedicated, and relentlessly devoted. Elderly cats, re-homed dogs, and a feisty pig! Not to mention the hunky sheriff trying to keep Doris Flynn's nose out of his investigation."—Darlene Dziomba, author of *Clues from the Canines*

Chapter One

I wrapped my hands around the edge of the kitchen counter, forcing my elbows to lock. Below my t-shirt sleeves, I could see my arms extending down to tightened fists. They looked like rigid poles, skinny and brittle. My head lolled forward, and the screen of my brown hair with its ever-multiplying gray strands blocked out the world around me. I allowed myself to droop further.

Is it possible for my neck muscles to lose all their strength? Will my head bounce if it hits the counter? What if it rolls out of the house like the meatball in "On Top of Spaghetti," and I can't catch it?

Sometimes, my give-a-crap meter seems stuck on zero. Other times, it just ships me to the funny farm.

I tried not to, but I had to laugh at myself. There was nobody else around. And here I was in the kitchen with a big bag of kibble and cans of stinky cat food, having a private pity party while chirping, barking, yowling, and oinking voices called out for their evening's rations. I could answer in kind, imitating the critter voices around me. Would they stop and wonder exactly what I was trying to say, or just go on telling me what to do? This was one of those moments I cracked myself up.

The largest critter, Buttercup, was closest, making soft little noises. She wanted to be fed first for a change. It took an effort to shake off my confused meanderings and focus on the three-by-five index cards taped to the front of the cabinet door. But my thoughts kept wandering back into that no-man's-land of memories.

Within the space between my ears, I could still hear that short conversation from less than a year ago. I had been standing right here, doing the same thing. Now, no matter how hard I swallowed, I couldn't push down the solid lump that filled my throat, making me feel like I had eaten too much food too fast. Maybe I was going to throw up.

I tried to turn, in the event an out-of-control rush to the bathroom was in my future, but my way was blocked. My big girl was right behind me and gave me a solid thump behind the knees. If I let go of the counter and she did that again, it would surely prove to be my downfall. Literally.

Pressing my lids together as tight as they would go, I counted to five, opened my eyes, and refocused. I was okay, I really was, I told myself.

"Memories will warm your heart," I said aloud, repeating what the reverend had said. *Or drive you crazy.*

The list taped to the cupboard door became readable. Each color photograph of a cat was attached to an index card bearing pertinent information. On this one, a gray/green tiger with a pink nose was identified as Shay Shay. Eight years old, surrendered, spayed, no seafood, Bowl # Six.

I poured one-quarter cup of dry cat food into the gray ceramic bowl with SIX painted on the side. Buttercup gave a resigned little woof, the equivalent of a critterly sigh. She could tell by the sound it wasn't for her. The cat food rattled around for half a second, then settled into place. I added a tablespoon of wet beef bits and two tablespoons of water, mixed them together well, and moved the bowl to the plastic tray that had at one time been the property of a McDonald's. When the red tray had shown up among Melanie's things, she had explained it had accidentally fallen into the backseat of the car. Melanie, my daughter, my one child, had inherited my father's ability to turn a word, any word, to her advantage. Because she couldn't remember which McDonald's the tray came from, it wouldn't be fair to return it. Yup, it was hard to find fault with the reasoning of a young adult who owned wheels and had been given authorization to drive by the State of New Hampshire. I got another nudge.

"Okay. In a minute," I said, smiling down at the whiskery nose now raised to my thigh. Tray in hand, I headed for the door to the cattery.

My companion gave an impatient sigh, but settled on the floor, having long ago been taught immediate access was strictly denied to all but the cats domiciled there and the humans who served them. Just inside the pocket door, an old-fashioned bike bell was screwed to the wall. I gave the thumb-push one shove. At the jingle, every feline not already secured in the two-room wire condos came galloping from throughout the house. None of them gave the sulking bulk on the kitchen floor a second glance. Those who did not run fast enough were jumped over.

I dispensed the evening meal and provided fresh water. As soon as the appropriate cat entered a wire condo and dove nose-down into their food dish, I secured the door. Those identified as house cats had mats lining the wall. They also knew their places and were not friendly to any who got it wrong.

"Okay," I said, passing Buttercup. "Dogs are next."

On the door of a different cupboard, the canines were listed. Two residents, one guest in the outside kennels. This time, when I left the house with the bowl for Rex, the kennel dog, my knee-thumping friend, who had doubled up on the attention requests as I was working, trotted along beside me. She knew it was almost her turn. It was the same every day. Right after the dogs, she knew she would be first. But Buttercup hoped against hope that one day she would be served before all others. The few times I had taken pity on her and fed her first, she had finished while I was still dishing up and returned to my side, demanding seconds. Getting extra food would not help with her weight control issue. More than once, I'd thought somebody should step forward and restrict my caloric intake in the same manner I controlled Buttercup's.

I covered the ground between deck and barn quickly. Even at fifty-three, I can move along. After I fed Rex, I turned my attention back to Buttercup, the four-hundred-fifty-pound lap pig who had been thumping my knees since I had started putting the dinners together.

With my focus now on her, she reacted like any other four-year-old. Every happy little squeak was accompanied by the lifting of her front feet off the ground. There was a wiggle in her rump, and her tail thrashed back and forth, snapping like a whip. The whole world knew it was time for her supper, and she was *so* excited.

"You know, Buttercup," I said, mixing grain, water, and a bag of fresh green snap beans into her bowl, "you're not being a very good hostess. You live here. These other babies are homeless orphans. You could be more generous."

Buttercup snorted as if to say, "Yeah, sure. Feed me."

When I picked the bowl up from the counter, she deserted me and ran into her home pen. She knew the drill. I closed and latched the gate, went outside, and closed the barn doors behind me. Then I poured her meal into the trough in the outdoor pen. Buttercup had run through the home pen, out of the weather flap, and was already waiting on her side of the trough. I watched her eat for a few moments, pushing mush around while searching for the snap beans before fetching the small wooden flowerbed rake that hung on the barn wall. The garden tool was a perfect back scratcher for my porcine friend. I gave her a good rub. Her tail continued to rap back and forth against her rear quarters, and her happy little grunts expressed her pleasure. There was no stopping my smile at her happiness while listening to her little piggy giggles. After all, she was my big girl, the rescue that never got to leave. The one no one voted to keep, but none of us could let go.

That's what I did: I took in rejected dogs, helped them get over their angst, and got them ready to go to new homes. The cattery was the same, though it had evolved to caring for felines who were older, sickly, or semi-feral and possibly tamable. But Buttercup was a different story. I knew in my heart she had to have been someone I knew and loved from a previous life, because even though she and Melanie were good friends, my bond with her had been instant and absolute.

"Good night, pretty baby," I whispered.

Dusk was just settling in. The bird calls of robins and mourning doves had changed to the weeping solos of nightingales and the honking of a homeward-bound flock of Canada Geese. In these few days between the end of spring and the start of summer, it was warm enough for windows to be open until suppertime. But when the sun, still winter-weak, began to fade, it was time to button the house up against the chill again.

CHAPTER ONE

Back in the farmhouse, I had one last dinner to prepare. When I had been mixing up Rex's, I had mixed the bowls of supper for the two dogs who lived permanently in the house. Each had their own mat, and when everything was in place, I released them from the confines of the sitting room. If I hadn't kept them restricted while putting together the feline dinners, I would have tripped all over them. Not to mention how the dogs' excitement spread and sparked a four-hundred-fifty-pound pig like a keg of gunpowder. I would have been trapped against the kitchen cupboard for heaven knows how long.

The dogs came across the aged linoleum now, sounding like a rushing horde of little old ladies in high heels. Royally was my boy, a red-headed Pembroke Welsh Corgi, and Lilo was Melanie's black Pug.

"Chill out, you two, or you'll choke," I cautioned.

I reached for a hand towel. The only ones left to feed were myself and my daughter. "Melanie? Omelet and salad, or tacos?"

A voice drifted back from the living room at the front of the house. "I'm not quite done. Another twenty minutes. An omelet would be fine."

I pulled ingredients from the refrigerator, glad to be cooking for two and not just my miserable self. After the unexpected heart attack and loss of my husband, Ian, Melanie had opted to come home from a brief time in the city to stay at the farm for a while. Her job as a resolution specialist with a major pharmacy company allowed her to work from home. It worked well for us while we were both adjusting, me from the loss of my heart-song and our future together, Melanie from the twist that her health had taken.

As I pulled open the refrigerator door, another sudden resurrection of that long-ago moment shared between me and Ian, the little duty that he and I had shared every evening, the memory that had stopped me cold earlier. I had done well for the past several days and yet, today I was an absolute mess. One year had proven not to be long enough. I never would have expected to miss him so much. He wasn't my first husband, and I wouldn't have classified him as my greatest love. But we had shared a harmony, a peace of mind that had been missing in my life before. And then we had Melanie. Her birth had pulled us tighter together, making what we had even more solid and giving weight to the memories.

5

* * *

Morning bloomed bright and cheerful, with the offer of a warm day in the making. I snapped a leash on Rex and asked Buttercup if she was interested in going for a walk with us. A purely rhetorical question. The national forest runs up the ridge to Calwin Mountain behind the farm. It was a good place to wander and work some of Rex's energy off before his first interactive lesson of the day. I'd been up there a gajillion times. Ian and I put up markers over the years so we or our guests wouldn't get lost on the wooded slopes.

I was intent on Rex and how well he was doing. There was also the wonder of the little bits of leaves bursting from the trees and tiny white or yellow spring flowers peeking out of last year's brown ground cover. Then I realized Buttercup was giving the scree-scree-scree call that meant she'd found something exciting.

"Buttercup?" I turned around.

The pig was nowhere in sight.

I frowned. She had gone silent.

I hurried back the way we'd come, pulling Rex with me. Fortunately, he had caught the excitement and, being more tracking-astute than I, dragged me in the direction of Buttercup's path. Ten feet back from where I had stopped to see what Buttercup had gotten into, he left the path and charged into the underbrush. All I could do was stumble along behind him.

We got a little tangled in a feathery stand of evergreens, which slowed us down. Bursting through, we found Buttercup on the other side. Just as when she was presented with food, her hindquarters were aquiver, and her tail lashed. She pawed at the ground, her grunting low and excited. Her strong frontal disc was buried in the leaves, rooting and upheaving everything in her way. A bone popped up, and then another. She had found carrion!

"Oh, disgusting!" Holding the pit bull-boxer back, I grabbed at the pig's halter. "Get back, Buttercup. No. Drop it!"

Like a dog, if Buttercup came across a dead animal carcass, she wanted to roll in it, no matter how offensive it smelt. With only one hand available, I was handicapped, and now Rex wanted in on the action. I let go of the pig and took a firmer grip on the dog's collar, holding him on my other side. Stepping around Buttercup, I bumped my knees into her shoulder, trying to push her aside, all the while repeating the verbal commands. I was going for stern but came off as grossed out.

It took effort, but Buttercup and I had spent many hours on her training. An important fact often pointed out by both the veterinarian and my other pig-owning friends was that, inevitably, my rotund friend would get heavier. Physically directing her would become increasingly difficult.

With a last, disgusted snort at my continual prodding, Buttercup finally turned away. I heard little grunts of anger, seeming like cuss words, as she slowly pressed back through the evergreens. I wasn't offended, but for some reason, even as I prodded Buttercup's backside with my knees, I cast one last glance toward the final resting spot of our lost forest brethren. The pig disappeared among the flapping greenery, and the dog tried to follow. But still holding Rex's collar, I was stuck, unable to lift my feet. And staring back at me from the leaves was a human skull, empty orbital sockets pleading with me not to desert it alone in the woods.

Chapter Two

"So, Ms. Flynn, tell me again how you came upon the remains."

Sheriff Everett Neddel had joined me on the wooded path. He was new to the area. I had never met him and felt slightly intimidated because, unlike his predecessor, this man was tall and physically fit. His uniform, which didn't have a single food stain on it, was freshly pressed. His deputy, with a face the same slightly faded shade of green as the shoots breaking the ground, stood guard at the spot in the evergreens my animal cohorts and I had exited from less than an hour earlier.

"*Mrs.* Flynn," I corrected him. My mouth felt as dry as a wood chip. I was exhausted. Maybe not so much from the second walk up the trail, but from the emotional hysteria that had overcome me as I rushed Rex and a sulking Buttercup home. The faster I'd tried to go, the slower the pig waddled.

"You were up here alone? With a pig? Where was your husband?" the sheriff asked, sounding disgusted.

"Ian is dead," I said. Not to be cold. Just stating the fact.

He looked a trifle embarrassed. That was okay, because I was feeling slightly offended. Did he think, because I was a woman, I couldn't walk in the woods alone with my dog? And pig?

I threw that thought off. I didn't need pity from some guy who had never known either of us. I had heard the gossip about how this new law officer was so good-looking. He was from away, which gave him a certain allure, and I had also heard he was unmarried. Apparently, there was already a herd of available women trailing him. If he thought he could cast me in with that lot, he had another think coming.

I looked away, in the event he was astute enough to read the displeasure on my face. My attention was drawn to the sound of voices—people approaching, possibly innocent hikers. Even though it sounded like they were right in front of us, they were not yet visible in the fresh, budding foliage. Half-birthed tree leaves and ferns, tender and green, surrounded us, yet in their midst, beyond the screen of firs, was a dark hole, this place Buttercup had found of death, I knew dropped all the way to Hades.

Neddel shot a look back toward the evergreens that were keeping the lost soul out of sight. His dark eyes shriveled into tight lines beneath scowling brows. I almost laughed at the realization he was probably wondering if the remains could be Ian, like I had returned him to nature and forgotten. I was sure I looked disheveled, but hopefully not demented. Neddel caught my look. His eyes widened, and the guessing game went up another notch. His reaction allowed me to suddenly feel his equal, because I, too, could read thoughts through facial expressions.

"I was just walking my dog. Buttercup, the pig, came with us for the exercise." I moved backwards to a fallen mossy log and plopped down. My legs suddenly felt too exhausted to hold me. Even my shoulders and chest wanted to curl up. I just wanted to be left alone.

"Ah-huh. Well. Most people don't take a hog on a hike." Neddel's mouth pinched.

I felt the color in my face drain south.

"Are you alright?" Neddel asked. "The EMTs are on the way."

"She's not a hog." I ignored his questioning my abilities and struggled back to my feet as the EMTs and the county medical examiner, Burt Kennett, came up the path. "She's a pig. And a pet." I felt a surge of heat flash across my face. I knew I had been rude, but right then, I didn't care. This idiot presented himself as a chauvinist and someone who thought he was better than me. I hated it when some guy wanted to pat the little woman—me—on the head while the big, strong male took over. Made me want to spit.

"Right."

After that, Neddel ignored me. He spoke briefly with the medical examiner, pointing the way toward the remains. I could tell by Burt's attitude that he didn't care for the new sheriff who had replaced his old high school buddy. The deputy with the chalky-verdant coloring stepped aside, obviously not eager to pass through the evergreen barrier.

While the men talked, I began drifting down the path. They didn't need me, and finding remains almost within sight of my home had unnerved me. I felt the need for caffeine and chocolate.

I made it down the hill without being called back and stepped out of the tree line near the end of the dog runs.

Rex was where I had left him, in his kennel. His brow was wrinkled, and he looked like a worried soul as he stood at attention with his nose against the wire. His tail gave a single limp wave, and his golden eyes followed me to the end of the kennels. I heard the weather flap smack as he ducked inside to see if I would go in the barn.

On the other side of the wide building, I could hear Buttercup's angry complaints. It was a nice day. She didn't want to be penned up, even in her outside enclosure. Besides, there were new people around, and she needed to investigate. Melanie stood outside the wooden barricade, trying to calm her down by offering carrots and a head of lettuce.

"That's our salad," I pointed out.

"You should have heard her," my daughter said, shaking her head. "I thought she'd bust down the walls." She nodded behind me, alerting me that I had been followed. Then, picking up the woven basket and her cane, Melanie moved slowly over the rough ground.

Without looking back, I said to the person trailing me, "I'll be right back." It was a command to sit and stay.

I walked beside my daughter, matching her steps. As we moved ahead, Melanie pointed out that, besides the police cruiser and second deputy, who Sheriff Neddel had left posted at the end of the driveway, an SUV and a large van had also arrived and parked. Both had vomited out a reporter and a cameraman. Currently, one reporter was harassing the deputy, undoubtedly looking for newsworthy information. The second newshound had spotted Melanie and me walking toward the house. That woman, with blond hair that cascaded down her back, had the pinched look of someone twenty pounds underweight. She yanked her cameraman around with one hand and discreetly waved in our direction with the other. Her discretion was in vain. The other reporter picked up on the movement and shifted her focus. Fortunately, the deputy was on it, forbidding either from advancing up the dirt driveway.

"Don't make eye contact," I said to Melanie, moving to block her from the cameras. "And watch what you're saying. If they're recording, they might be able to read your lips at the playback."

"You're kidding, right?" Melanie asked.

"No, I am not," I said. "When your father and I were part of a no-kill picket line in Concord years ago, the cops always seemed to know what our group was doing, even as we did. We learned later they were filming the conversations between the rally organizers and deciphered from the film."

"And it worked?"

"Yes, except for Paul Murphy. Too much facial hair." I couldn't help grinning at the memory of my redneck, chew-spitting friend.

When I went back out to the pen, I wore barn boots.

"I have more questions," Neddel said.

He had left Burt Kennett and followed me, but hadn't moved much since I'd walked off. Now he stood where Rex couldn't see him, which kept the dog quiet. But the sheriff wasn't aware that the animal in the barn capable of doing math, being able to figure out problems, was not the dog. Behind him, with her chin between two slats of the fence, Buttercup was assessing. I wasn't sure why. Then I realized she and the sheriff hadn't been introduced. She didn't like strangers.

"Hold that thought." I stepped inside the barn door and returned with a three-prong dung fork, square-tip shovel, and work gloves. Buttercup edged closer, keeping her eye on Neddel. She was hoping to squeeze out before I stopped her. Instead, I climbed over the heavy wooden slats and dropped down beside her.

"Is that safe?" Neddel asked, never taking his eyes off the big pig.

Buttercup and I both looked back at him. "Of course it is. Well, for me. You, maybe not so much."

11

Removing one work glove to dig the large dog cookie out of my pocket, I offered it to the pig. Buttercup's disc wiggled up and down. She snuffled, then gently reached out, lips surrounding the snack and the tips of my fingers. When she withdrew, the cookie was gone, but my fingers were all intact. I pointed to her nose.

"That big flat piece on the end of her nose? That's referred to as a disc. I don't know how disc clues work on all pigs, but on this one, if it's wiggling up and down, it's good. If the disc rocks back and forth, she either doesn't like what you're offering, or she's not happy in general. In that case, my advice would be to back away."

Buttercup took her snack and, after one last warning look at Neddel, shuffled through the hanging weather shield back into the barn. I moved into her potty corner, scooping up waste and dropping it over the fence into the riding mower trailer. Neddel took a step back. I smirked.

I paused for a second before the next scoop, biting my lip.

Maybe this guy isn't really being an ass, and I'm projecting. It hasn't been a great day for me. Am I overreacting?

The answer was no. Facing the sheriff again, I started talking. There was a hard edge on my words that should have let Neddel know that, like the pig, I was not happy. He didn't react, which led me to believe he either had thicker skin than a Blue Hubbard squash, or he lacked something in the smarts department.

"I'm sure you've heard, even in whatever city you used to live in, that pigs are basically clean animals. If Buttercup has a choice, she will not poop in either her house or her pen. She prefers to use the place at the edge of the yard where the cockleburrs grow thick. And no, I am not cruel enough to send her into the prickles. It was her choice. It's like she knows it's not a place to be used for anything else."

I bent back to my task and threw a particularly wet shovelful over the fence. The splat sent droplets outward in several directions. Neddel fairly leapt out of his skin to get out of range. "Well, that should do it," I said.

Neddel followed me to the spigot, where I rinsed my tools before putting them away. I waited for the questions he had mentioned earlier, but nothing was forthcoming. When I turned to look at him, I caught him staring at the hand-painted sign nailed on Buttercup's house. It said: *135½ Calwin Mountain Road.*

"Melanie and Ian made that sign and hung it there when we first got Buttercup three and a half years ago." I opened the gate to her home pen, and the pig sauntered out. "Let's go down to the house if you still have questions."

Neddel moved to walk beside me, but with a disgruntled piggy woof, Buttercup took that place, forcing him away. Neddel followed.

Melanie had left a pitcher of iced tea and glasses on the picnic table. The small deck led to an even smaller back porch, half of which was screened. After kicking off my boots and opening the door so Buttercup could get into the kitchen, I went back to the deck and sat down across the picnic table from Neddel. He was still staring at the screen door that had closed behind Buttercup's ample derriere.

"Missing her already?" I asked with a laugh. "Don't worry; as soon as she realizes there's nothing lying around for her to eat, she'll come back out."

There was a soft woof-woof, and we saw her disc pressed against the protective Plexiglas shield at the bottom of the door. When the screen door swung outward, Buttercup exited and edged up to the table. When no treats were offered, she gave up and stretched out in a sunny spot.

"Who taught her to do that?" Neddel asked, shaking his head.

"Opening the door? She learned it all by herself. So, okay, what are your questions?"

Neddel produced a small tape recorder. After getting my permission and stating the information that identified us and what we were doing into it, he began.

"Tell me about your day prior to finding the remains," he said.

"I got out of bed, put on my slippers, walked to the bathroom—"

He cut me off. "Fast forward to where you decided to walk up the path."

"Rex has a lot of energy in the morning. I took him out to walk some of it off before I started his training sets."

The screen door banged open, and Royally and Lilo rushed out. I had left them with Melanie earlier, but they had probably worn out their welcome.

13

They ran over to snuffle around this strange new man. When Neddel said hello, Buttercup raised her head. If there were going to be treats passed out, she wanted to be ready to jump in line. The sheriff, however, did not offer the dogs either goodies or pets.

"No, Royally, Lilo. Down," I said. "Sit." Both dogs immediately parked their rumps on the deck. Though they neither moved away from Neddel nor stopped scrutinizing him, they sat quietly. Buttercup's head thumped back to the deck with a disgusted snort.

"You took only one of your dogs with you on the trail?" Neddel asked.

"Rex is not my dog. He's a boarder. These two are mine," I explained.

Before the sheriff could ask anything more about my private life, I continued with the story of our trek up the mountain. I had reached the part where I rushed back to the farm to retrieve my forgotten cell phone and call 911 when a line of men trooped out of the wood line. Rex gave a bark. With surprising agility, Buttercup leapt to her feet. I reached out, grabbing the pig's tail.

"Stay," I ordered in my I-am-alpha voice. "Stay."

With my other hand, I grasped Royally's collar. Lilo wasn't a problem, as her bravery ended at the edge of the deck. Neddel excused himself, telling me he'd be back in a moment, and then walked across the yard to join the men standing beside the medical examiner's vehicle with its blacked-out windows. I had taken Buttercup's harness off and had nothing to hold on to except her tail or ears. She wanted to go see what was happening. With Royally in my arms, it took an effort to get all three of them into the house.

"Melanie," I called urgently. "I need you to watch these guys so I can go see what's going on."

Having heard us trying to get inside, Melanie was already coming down the hall.

"Here pig, pig," she called.

After shooing Lilo inside, I closed the heavy wood door and rushed toward the knot of men. One of the EMTs closed the rear door of the ME's SUV. The other, sitting in the driver's seat, shut off the flashing lights.

As I approached, Neddel held up his hand, stopping me. I didn't step closer, but I felt my ears stretch forward as I tried to eavesdrop. The medical examiner was speaking. The few clear words that came across the gravel driveway let me know the remains had been lying there since at least the previous fall.

My senses whirled. I think I might have actually staggered. I'd gone up and down the mountain all through the year, though maybe not as much these past months since Ian's death. There were half a dozen trails leading back from the house alone. The one Rex and I had climbed that morning was actually one of the easier ones.

When was the last time I was up there? I wondered.

On the far side of the SUV, at the bottom of the driveway, the reporters worked in tandem, trying to get around the deputy standing guard to keep them out. Flanking the deputy on either side, one pair after another inched ahead every time the other set distracted him.

Neddel called out, "If any of you advance further, I guarantee you will not be allowed entrance at the briefing."

The sheriff was as new to them as he was to me. I was willing to bet they didn't know whether to take him at his word or not. Though the news people stayed in place, they continued to film. To their credit, the rescue personnel who were getting ready to pull out had worked quickly, limiting the amount of footage garnered.

After the ambulance and medical examiner left, with the two street-side vehicles following, Neddel and I walked back to the deck. This time, we were the only two sitting under the picnic table umbrella. The sheriff asked me to repeat my recollections twice more, asking questions for clarification. At least once, he tried to trip me up.

"I never said that." I shook my head, unwilling to play his game.

Over his shoulder, I could see one or two cats in every window. Periodically, Melanie looked out as well. To have her keep checking on us made me nervous. It was bad enough that some gene she had inherited from either me or her father had raised its ugly head to make her life difficult. My very athletic daughter was having to learn to cope with the fast onset of MS, as well as deal with her father's death and returning home. And now, another evil had been dumped in our backyard. I knew stress caused her symptoms to jump into hyperdrive. I was worried.

Neddel opened his mouth.

"No more." Suddenly, I was all done. "I can't do this right now. I just can't." The hand I was holding up trembled.

The recorder clicked off. "That's okay. Go have something to eat and relax," said Neddel. "I'll be here for a while, working in my car. OCME has already sent the medicolegal death investigator out. I was instructed to wait on site."

"OCME?" I started to rise, but hesitated.

"Office of the Chief Medical Examiner," Neddel explained. "Burt Kennett's boss."

Without inviting him to wait in the house, I went inside. Melanie and I sat at the table speaking in whispers while I drank orange juice and tea, then shared half a sandwich with Buttercup.

"I'll put her back in the pen, then lay down for a few minutes," I said, feeling stronger with some substance in my belly.

My lie-down ended up being a nightmare-filled nap, which ended when a hand grasped my shoulder. Melanie moved back, startled, when I jumped up and called out.

"Mom?" Concern tightened her face. "Are you okay?" At my nod, she added, "There's a mess of people out in the dooryard."

* * *

The mess of people consisted of the tall, and not bad looking, Sheriff Neddel; Shane Davis, an assistant to the local medical examiner who was also a neighbor down the road; the two EMTs from earlier, and a dark-haired damsel. She was reading every one of the men the riot act.

"I'm sorry, ma'am. Burt Kennett sent me a message that he wouldn't be able to get out here again this afternoon. Thumbs in his waistband, Sheriff Neddel looked more chagrined than imposing.

"No." The woman's tone evoked a burn, like laying a wet tongue on a frozen pipe. "It's not that he *can't* get out here; it's that he *won't!* He knows he screwed this up. All those fossilized old farts should be forced to retire, like eighty-year-old senators. They've been sitting in their seats for so long they can't see the real world and don't have a clue. Burt was notified to leave those remains in situ, but did he do that? Of course not. That would be too damn easy. He's gotta go all alpha and get his underwear in a tightwad. He knows he overstepped the boundaries. He's not out here because he doesn't have the hardware." She ran her fingers impatiently through her wavy chestnut hair.

All the guys except Neddel inched away. The woman pulled two backpacks of gear out of the back of her vehicle. They hit the ground with a solid thump. This was going to be fun. I walked between the EMTs, holding out a hand.

"Doris Flynn, property owner," I said, hand still extended and grin still in place. "That's a lot of gear you have. We could use the wagon to haul it all up onto the ridge, or the lawn tractor and trailer. Which would you prefer?"

The woman paused before her cherry lips curved up. Reaching out, she grasped my hand in a solid, unladylike shake. "Rose Ann Lombard. The tractor would be awesome."

"Shane." I turned to the young man I had known for all of his life. "Go get the tractor. Make sure you hook onto the trailer that isn't half full of poop. Keys are in the ignition."

"I know," he said, taking off at a fast trot.

The medicolegal death investigator added more equipment to the pile. While we waited for the tractor, I asked, "Ms. Lombard, would you care to meet the pig?"

"I beg your pardon?" Ms. Lombard's brows rose to her hairline.

"The pig that found the remains. Buttercup, my big girl."

Ms. Lombard's grin grew. "I would be delighted. And please, call me Rose Ann."

"Doris," I said.

Stepping away from the men, who all looked a little shocked, and Neddel, busy studying the tips of his boots, I led the way to Buttercup's house. Rose Ann went directly over to the railing of the outside yard.

"She's in here. In her house. It's time for her nap," I explained.

"In her house," Rose Ann said in wonder, following me into the barn.

Neddel let the woman pass, then followed us inside.

"Wake up, baby girl. You have company," I crooned. I never use baby talk, but she can tell by my tone if what is going to happen is good or not-so-good. And she knows what v-e-t spells.

Buttercup gave a couple of quick grunts. When I jangled her harness, she clambered to her feet. This was going to be good.

"This is not a baby!" Rose Ann leaned over the pen wall and laughed.

"She really is." I released the safety latch and opened the gate so I could enter the home pen. Buttercup stood still, waiting for the heavy leather harness to be fastened in place around her.

"Where did you find such a big dog harness?" asked Rose Ann.

"It's actually a miniature horse harness. Buttercup's farrier is also a leather smith. He modified this for her. For a while, she outgrew them about every three months. Hopefully, this is the last one."

"She has a farrier?" Rose Ann lifted her eyes from Buttercup to me.

"Yes. You have pretty decent fingernails, so you probably spend time fussing around with them, right?" At the woman's nod, I went on, "Buttercup needs the same attention. Her hooves are made of keratin, like fingernails, and they need to be trimmed on a regular basis. She gets brushed daily. We give her two or three baths a week and sunscreen as needed."

"Unbelievable," said Rose Ann.

When I pushed the gate open, Rose Ann and Neddel stepped backwards. Buttercup exited the pen, with me following. I gave her a moment to sniff at the medicolegal death investigator's rubber boots, then snapped a short, heavy leash onto the harness.

"Heel," I said.

Buttercup immediately moved into position. Across the way, Rex sat on his haunches and watched the show. When it was evident he wasn't going to join us, he gave a little whine.

"Sheriff Neddel." I pointed toward the back wall. "In that mini fridge hanging over the counter are some soup bones. Could you give Rex one?

Thanks."

We left the barn with Buttercup in the lead like a prom queen, head high and prancing in a new dress and sparkling red stiletto heels. I didn't have to give her any directions. She walked right over to the guys waiting at the wood line where the tractor idled. Once we were on the path, I let Buttercup range ahead slightly. Though the sheriff had used orange plastic tape tied on tree branches to mark the way, Buttercup would let us know when we should turn off to where she had found the remains.

"She does tricks like a dog?" Rose Ann asked.

"Not really. Oh, she knows some tricks, but most of those she taught herself. When we first got her, she was unruly. I decided if I was going to get her adopted, she needed to be better behaved. I ran her through the same paces I use with the dogs, teaching her simple commands. She knows about ten."

"I don't understand," said Rose Ann. "She isn't your pet?"

"It gets a little sketchy right there," I said. "Originally, Ian, that's my late husband, and I worked with the local animal shelter and at-risk dogs. German shepherds, Dobermans, rottweilers, pit bulls—breeds that can't be kept at the shelter. We brought them here and worked with them until they were adoptable. We also took in overflow cats. Technically, they don't belong to us."

"So, you rehabilitate," Rose Ann said.

"I'm not licensed to do that. We were just good with dogs. Ian was like a dog whisperer. There didn't use to be so many, and we only took one at a time. Then it got worse. The local veterinarian, Dr. Rhoades, and Ian came up with a plan. The doctor set up a trust and asked his patients to donate five dollars for runs and housing for the dogs, so they didn't have to be euthanized. He matched dollar for dollar. We had the barn and the land, and there weren't many houses out here. Now we have room for four dogs. I have a permit for up to seventeen cats on the premises. The cattery holds eleven. Then there are my personal pets.

"Huh," Rose Ann said.

"The road ends about a mile further up. People see the barn and assume this is a farm and, you know, all farmers want all the cats and dogs they can get."

Rose Ann rolled her eyes.

I continued, "Outsiders were forever slowing down and throwing out dogs, kittens, and crates with white rats or gerbils. But Buttercup was different. The shelter called and said somebody had dropped off a potbellied pig. They had nowhere to keep her and needed to move her until they figured out what to do. I went down to pick her up, thinking I could house her in one of the dog runs. Well, when I got there and took one look at her, I couldn't stop laughing. She is not a potbellied pig. As I told the people at the shelter, she's a Hampshire. The folks who dropped her off said she was already too big, and she was only about twenty-five pounds."

"They should have gotten a guinea pig," Rose Ann said.

"Exactly. Anyway, I put her in the back seat of my car and brought her home. She was so darn cute. Melanie was afraid she'd freeze in the barn, so we brought her into the house. It was supposed to be only for that first night. We called her Buttercup Belle. Ian house-trained her. Even potbellied pigs can get to be over one hundred and fifty pounds. It's all in the feeding. I control Buttercup's intake. It's like Weight Watchers for porkers."

Rose Ann laughed aloud. Behind us, I even heard Neddel chuckle. Buttercup made a scree-scree noise and diverted from the path.

"This is where you want to go." I set my feet and held tight to Buttercup's leash. "She can still smell the remains, so I'm going to take her back down to the farm."

Rose Ann looked at the pig, straining to move forward and me trying to hold her back. It was easy to see she thought Buttercup was going to be ruining the site in another minute. But I had a secret weapon. I pulled a Ziploc bag from my pocket, ripped it open, and held out another dog treat. One smeared with goo.

"PEANUT BUTTER!" I yelled out. Buttercup's absolute favorite food.

That was all it took. I had the four-hundred-fifty-pound jiggling, jostling pig's undivided attention. Walking briskly back the way we had come, I held my hand high while she tried to block my way so I would stop walking and give it to her. As I went along, I sang, *"Doris had a little swine, little swine, little swine. Doris had a little swine as cute as cute could be."*

At the end of every verse, Buttercup woofed happily, and I started singing again. I'm sure everyone watched us go, and I caught a couple of remarks as we did.

"Can you believe that?" I heard Rose Ann ask.

"Only because I'm seeing it with my own eyes," said Neddel.

Chapter Three

The last EMT left about an hour later. He had been roped into helping Doctor Lombard. I think he was willing to stay because she kept dishing on Burt Kennett. The reporters who'd followed the medicolegal death investigator up the road to my house and gotten stopped at the culvert were also gone, defeated in their quest for informational tidbits.

I put off making supper for myself and Melanie. Instead, I fed all the furballs, checked the barn loft for bat poop, and put new straw in all the nest boxes. It was almost fully dark, and the barn chores were done. Buttercup and Rex, as well as the extra cats, were tucked in for the night.

I had seen the EMT and Shane make several trips back to the vehicles. With the kitchen door open, I could sit at the table and watch the wood line while I waited. Melanie had just asked if I thought the sheriff and the medicolegal death investigator had gotten lost on the side of the mountain when the glow of the tractor's dual headlights shone through the trees. I walked out to meet them.

By the time everything Rose Ann had collected and all her gear was packed into her jeep, Shane was ready to head for home. On the way up the mountain, I had heard Doctor Lombard tell him that if Burt wasn't coming back, Shane would have to stay. He had agreed with less enthusiasm than the EMT. Now, even Neddel looked downright wiped out.

"It took you a while to get here today," I said to Rose Ann as she leaned on her truck, limp with fatigue. "Where did you come from?"

"My office is in Manchester," she said.

I took about three chews on my bottom lip. "That's over two hours away.

Is your family waiting for you?"

"No family, just me." Rose Ann slammed the rear hatch on the jeep closed.

"Listen, that really is a long way through big woods and down a dark interstate. You look totally exhausted. We have American Chop Suey for supper, a hot shower, and plenty of room." I paused. She looked tempted. "Besides, I'm not done telling you about Buttercup."

"Will Buttercup be joining you for supper?" Neddel asked.

"Phfft." I laughed. "She's already gone to bed. Beauty sleep, you know." But to my trained ear, I could hear the soft snorts and grunts that bespoke her watching us through the slats of her outside pen.

I could see Rose Ann wavering. "Your decision," I said. "Goodnight, sheriff."

"Okay. If you're sure." Rose Ann gave a tired sigh. "This was my second site today, and they were at opposite ends of the state, so it was a long drive. I'd appreciate your hospitality."

* * *

"Okay, here we go." I pushed open the door to the extra bedroom, set under the eaves on the second floor. Scooping up a cat that tried to meander into the room, I added, "Bathroom down the hall, towels in the cabinet. That dresser has assorted sleepwear in it. Find what you need. I understand from my daughter that supper will be ready in about forty minutes."

"Thank you." Rose Ann turned in the doorway. "This is really very kind."

I nodded and went downstairs.

Melanie was working on a salad as I set the table when Rose Ann joined us. She was about my height, wrapped in a blue quilted robe that had been mine before it was replaced by one with pink rosettes.

"Thank you for this." Rose Ann blushed. "I didn't realize how tired I was until the hot water was dissolving me like a sugar cube."

"No problem, really. We're pretty informal, so pick a spot and have a seat. Unfortunately, this is a dry house, but I can offer milk, iced tea, or coffee?"

"It's not unfortunate at all." Rose Ann scooped American chop suey onto her plate. "I'll take iced tea, please. Now, about the pig?"

"Oh, my god!" Melanie threw herself back in her chair. "More about the pig?"

I ignored her. "Like I said, Buttercup came from the animal shelter. What they didn't tell me was that, having been run through their facility, she was now classified as a pet. So, we couldn't raise her for freezer food, which wasn't a problem. As soon as Melanie saw her, I knew Buttercup was safe. But it also meant finding her a forever home was going to be difficult. No one else could raise her to butcher, either. She went from piglet to shoat, which is like a teenage pig, and moved toward adult size. It became evident she might be here a while, and the shelter requires all their critters to be spayed or neutered. So, Buttercup was spayed."

"You had a pig spayed?" asked Rose Ann. "Is that normal?"

"If pets are spayed or neutered for their health, why not your pet pig?" I dropped a pod into the Keurig. "Having her spayed wasn't without its dangers, though. Doctor Rhoades said it had to be done before she got to be seventy-five pounds. Using anesthesia on pigs is dangerous. They don't handle it well."

"You must have been terrified," said Rose Ann.

"If I said I wasn't, I'd be lying. We work a lot with Doctor Rhoades and really trust him. He was right up front about what he was going to do and what could happen. The night before the surgery, Ian and I slept out in the barn to be near Buttercup. At seven the next morning, the doctor pulled in. The surgery happened right here on the farm, with Doctor Rhoades's assistant and Ian assisting. My husband was so nervous. When she recovered, he threw a party. Like a Bat Mitzvah with singing, dancing, and food."

"Yeah," said Melanie. "That's when we learned Buttercup loves singing. Not just music, which she enjoys, but she really loves vocals. There's a radio in the barn that plays the local country station all the time. You should hear her carrying on if there is yodeling. Mom has specific ditties she sings, pretty badly, that are clues to Buttercup about what's going to happen and how she should behave."

"She also likes opera." I peeled off another slice of garlic bread.

"But no punk?" asked Rose Ann.

"Not a fan," I replied. "When I do fifteen-minute training sets with the dog, I try to make time to do sets with her as well. She's already been through the training, but a refresher is always good."

"You were telling me earlier that potbellied pigs can get up to one hundred and fifty pounds. Buttercup looks like she weighs well over that. How old is she?" Rose Ann helped herself to the last slice of crusty bread.

I picked up dirty dishes and got out clean ones as Melanie cut into a coconut cream cake.

"She's four. At this point, she weighs four hundred fifty pounds, but could weigh up to six hundred soon, easily. Maybe as much as one thousand pounds, if she was kept penned and continually fed. If she got that big, I'd have to keep her contained all the time because she's been known to hike up-street. I control her diet, allow her to root around if she wants, and make sure she gets plenty of exercise. If we go for a walk, I keep her moving. I was busy with Rex when Buttercup scented the remains. She found them before I knew what she was doing."

"Yeah, that was a mess." Rose Ann sighed, accepting a cup of coffee. "And I don't mean just because the pig was in there."

"How so?" I asked. Then, realizing I might be asking about sensitive information, I held up my hand. "Don't tell me if it's classified."

"There's a very public posting about what I do. I can repeat it for you verbatim. It has to do with all situations similar to this one." Rose Ann grinned. "It's part of a public service announcement. Here goes: The Office of the Chief Medical Examiner created a position for a Medicolegal Death Investigator. The MDI function will be to thoroughly investigate *any and all* deaths deemed suspicious or that have fallen under the heading of not in a place or circumstance where medical attention was available." The grin disappeared. "Using that descriptive, the remains found in the woods, not on a path, and having been there for at least six months, would be a reason to call me *before* they were touched or moved."

"Oh." Both Melanie and I nodded our understanding.

"Yeah, but the good old boy circuit screws me up again," said Rose Ann.

"It's not so much about the position being created as the fact the person selected to fill it was under forty years of age, and a female. My education and experience didn't amount to a hill of squat to people who couldn't get beyond the physical me. There are a lot of elected coroners or medical examiners who have been sitting in their jobs for years. They aren't ready to admit they don't know it all, or might be too old to do their jobs. For Burt Kennett, the big bashed-in place on the skull was no indication death may have been foul play."

Melanie and I stopped nodding, and my daughter looked uncomfortable. She's pretty gentle, so I figured it had to do with the anger Rose Ann had for other people in her field. I, however, understood what she was saying. In my life, I had seen it when some guy wanted to say, have a cup of tea, I'll get that for you, honey. The Medicolegal Death Investigator had to be a highly trained woman, yet she found herself working with staid, older guys who couldn't get past the fact she was just that, a woman. Maybe Burt and some of his cronies had thought this was going to be a paper-pushing position, but it didn't sound that way to me. I had yet to hear Rose Ann say a word about an assistant, an office in the capital building, or a six-figure income. I could see her point and hear her frustration. And I agreed with her.

Chapter Four

When Ms. Lombard came downstairs the next morning, I was already dressed and mixing breakfast for the animals.

"Oh, that's heavenly." Rose Ann inhaled deeply the smell of fresh coffee and bacon on the human side of the kitchen.

"What would you like for breakfast?" I asked.

"I'm afraid I can't accept. I have to get on the road." Rose Ann looked disappointed. Then she looked out towards the barn and grimaced. "How does the p-i-g feel about you cooking bacon?"

"I thought you might say you couldn't stay for breakfast." I held out a foil-wrapped packet and a to-go drink container. "Bacon, egg, and cheese on a bagel, coffee black, fixings are on the table. She doesn't know what it is. She never gets any. Buttercup is the only pig I have, and cooked pork smells different from that on the hoof."

Rose Ann laughed as she accepted both. "How will I get your coffee container back to you?"

"Are you kidding? They're like rabbits. Every time I open the cupboard, there are more. I think the original two are breeding in there."

I walked my guest out to her car. I liked her and hoped we might become friends, even if it would be over a distance. Opening the car door, Rose Ann turned and looked up toward the barn, where Buttercup, still behind the locked gate, was already calling.

"Melanie is not an early morning person," I explained, thinking that's who she was looking for. "She won't be up for another forty-five minutes."

When Rose Ann looked back, a little surprised, and then at the house, I realized it was Buttercup she could hear and was looking for. I had to laugh. I was used to hearing the swine song and took it for granted.

"Should I let her out so you can say goodbye?" I asked. "It seems like you're going to miss that pig."

Rose Ann giggled, put her bag in the car, and hesitated for just a second longer.

"Actually, what I wanted to say," said Rose Ann, her eyes gone sad, "was that you might want to think about posting your property. I mean, a lot of signs. This, ah, event, hit the news stations last night. The media and the curious are going to start swarming out here. I know the site is actually within the national forest, but if the perpetrator got out there, then the public will try to find a way, too."

Gooseflesh ran up my arms. "How do you know it was foul play?"

"Like I said, the big bashed-in place on the victim's skull. Plus, the person who did this took the time to spread lye." Rose Ann got in her car. "Too bad for him that he only had one bag."

I found it hard to believe that with all the new technology available, some clown would resort to an old farmer's method of disposing of an animal carcass. It was a simple recipe. For one carcass, enough lye to cover it well, add natural rain and plenty of sun. Before you knew it, all you had left was a thick, oily residue to be absorbed by the dirt.

I returned to my feeding ritual, and when I'd finished, took Rex back up the path. Where the trampled growth showed the way in, I stepped into the brush, pressing through the young evergreens. There was an empty place on the ground where every leaf, twig, and the top three inches of soil had been removed. All that was left was the rich, loamy dirt, already drying to a crust on top.

I was right. This was a black hole to Hades. Standing on tiptoes, I looked closely, leaning over the edge while holding Rex back. Near the center were a few narrow bands of something that looked like rivulets of lard. Jerking back, I hauled Rex back out to the path, running down the hill. I had an idea what the lard had been, and I didn't like it. It would be a long time before we walked that way again.

* * *

Rose Ann Lombard had been right. Even before I finished with the morning chores, traffic rose significantly. Some vehicles idled past, but as I returned with the egg basket, one had the audacity to turn around right in the driveway. Even the rural mail carrier opted to hand deliver to the door instead of using the mailbox, and I had to remind him the box was in good working order. I tried to continue with my normal routine, but I was a bit unnerved each time I heard a car's engine. Buttercup and Rex responded to my tension by snapping and acting out.

"If I'm going to keep from flipping out every time I hear a car," I told the two, "I need to put myself in the driver's seat."

Leaving the animals, I went back into the house, returning with a notebook and pen small enough to fit in the pocket of my capris. Each time a car tooled by, I pulled out the notebook. Blue sedan, silver Tahoe, black pickup truck with Tonto cover. From where I was working, I couldn't make out license plates, but to be honest, I didn't believe they would be relevant.

Rex and I had just finished a set, and I was attaching him to the hundred-foot overhead run when a small blue car not only pulled into the drive but drove far enough up to be in sight of the back porch and deck. I hurried around the chicken coop, ready to give the invader an earful and send him on his way. The driver's door opened, and a young man about my height, five foot eight, stepped out. He had wide shoulders and narrow hips, with a wiry look that spoke of physical exercise.

"Mrs. Flynn," he called out.

"Oh, Noah." I sighed with relief. Here was a friend of Melanie's, a local boy whose family had lived in the village for many years. He and Melanie had gone to school together until Noah's family had moved during his junior year. There had been some scuttlebutt involving Noah's father, but the facts had never been clear. After college, Noah moved back to the area. "I was ready to jump on you and send you packing."

"I just heard what happened this morning. This is the first chance I've had to get out. Are you okay? And Melanie?" The young man took hold of my arms, holding me steady as he searched my face. "You look exhausted." Wrapping an arm around my shoulders, he led me back to the house.

I like Noah. He's always ready to help with lifting or hauling. When things were off-kilter after Ian passed and I had to be gone, he and his friends took care of the critters. He was someone I could trust.

Melanie came in from the hall as we entered. Lilo bounded forward, but Royally was less enthusiastic. He didn't like other people touching me and had always been standoffish regarding Noah, who didn't notice. Ever watchful, I motioned the dog forward. Kneeling, I gave him a good rub and a treat. The corgi didn't return to his bed but continued to follow me around the kitchen, ignoring any attempt to get him settled down.

"I'm on my lunch," Noah said. "But I had to get out here and make sure you both were all right."

He gave Melanie's hand a squeeze. I turned away to the refrigerator, giving the couple a moment. "I'll make you a sandwich," I said. "Chips?"

Noah left a half hour later, promising to return for dinner and bring No Trespassing signs with him.

"I don't dare leave and drive into town right now," I'd explained to him. "There are too many strange cars coming around. All I need is someone to walk into the barn and start messing around in there. It could be dangerous. With Rex still unsure and Buttercup being so nosy. Fingers could be lost."

Noah nodded in agreement and said goodbye.

"He's a good guy," I said to Melanie as the blue car disappeared.

"Yes," she said. "Too bad he's not the one."

Give him a chance, I thought, watching Melanie move carefully up the hall to her office. I had tried to point out Noah's good points. He had a good education, a solid job, and he was well-liked. Not to mention easy on the eyes, and attentive of my daughter's feelings and moods.

Her diagnosis of multiple sclerosis had come as a shock. My only child had immediately started closing people out of her world. The death of her father had further traumatized her. Maybe if Noah did not allow himself to be driven away, Melanie would soften toward him. I looked out the front window toward the pansy bed that had been trampled by the reporters.

Time, I thought. *Time might set the flowers back to right, but what would it take to raise a soul back up?*

Melanie had gone back to her computer and the work and the chore of making the world right for patients, druggists, and big pharmaceuticals, intent on correcting the issues computers couldn't see. I elected to try to save the pansies.

The sun was warm. It felt good to bury my hands in the narrow band of loam overfilled with multi-colored flowers, each with a cheerful face. The border ran at the edge of the front lawn, along the top of the roadside ditch. Not quite ready to roam free in the yard, Rex had his soup bone to gnaw on, while Buttercup enjoyed her yard privileges. Being the last house on a dead-end road meant little traffic, with the exception of hunting season. Buttercup had gone down the driveway and was checking out the drainage. I could hear her happy little chirps. She had found something to play with. She'd be back slimy, I was sure.

"MOM, TELEPHONE!" Melanie yelled through the open window.

I got to my feet, dusting off my knees. "C'mon, Buttercup. Let's go. Quickly, now."

Rushing toward the back of the house, I didn't realize she had emerged from the ditch with a brown paper grocery bag in her mouth. Between the ditch and the deck, the contents of the bag fell out through the damp bottom. The pig dropped the bag, scooped up the contents, and trotted along toward the kitchen door.

My telephone conversation was quick. Sheriff Neddel wanted to stop by later to discuss the remains again. Not what I wanted to hear, or how I wanted to spend my evening. Replacing the handset on the telephone base, I turned just as Buttercup went by—headed toward the hallway and Melanie's office. Buttercup reacted by dipping her head toward the floor. Her scuttling steps picked up the pace as she moved along.

"Whoa, right there, lady." I jumped forward, a knee against her shoulder. Grabbing hold of the closest ear, I pointed to the floor. "Drop it. Drop it right now."

One other time, Buttercup had brought in a live garter snake to share. It had been such a surprise, even Ian had jumped up onto a chair. I got ready to do so myself.

"Drop it right now!" My order was sharp, accompanied by a shake of her ear.

Buttercup spat out the contents of her bulging cheeks. A half-grown kitten, saturated in pig spit, rolled over and coughed. Before I could react, the feisty little fur ball jumped up, tail pointed straight up, hissed at Buttercup, and ran under the old mint green and cream-colored Glenwood cook stove.

"Where the heck did you get that?" I asked as Buttercup yanked free and headed after her plaything.

I went around the other side of the table and got down on my hands and knees, trying to reach the kitten. Buttercup also stuck her snout under the stove, only to have me push her away. Buttercup and the stove had a bad reputation. One time, when she was much younger, she and Melanie had been out playing in the snow. When they came inside to warm up, Buttercup tried to get behind the stove, which had a fire within. She'd gotten burned, not to mention the stovepipe had come dislodged, filling the house with smoke.

The kitten was all hiss and wicked-sharp bitsy claws when I dragged it out. After rinsing the spit off and wrapping the baby in a towel, I tried to dry him. I was still considering where he had come from when I remembered the pig playing in the ditch.

"Here, Melanie, dry this little fellow off and keep Buttercup here until I get back." I ran out the front door, knowing Buttercup couldn't open that one. She had learned early that, by inserting the top ridge of her disc beneath the old wooden door in the kitchen, she could rattle the wooden panel enough to release the cast iron latch. Only the deadbolt kept her out.

Rushing toward the ditch, I passed the paper bag on the ground. Lifting it by one corner, I calculated the size. There wouldn't have been room for more than two kittens, and the top was stapled shut. My fuse lit.

After several minutes scrounging around in the muck, and not finding any tracks, I decided the baby Buttercup had brought in had been the only one in the bag.

Thanks to Melanie's tutorials, I knew how to use my cell phone to take photos. Yanking it out, I recorded the drop site and the bag. Back in the house, I carefully folded the paper bag into a plastic grocery bag. Melanie stood beside the sink with Buttercup and both dogs crowding her. Each wanted to get closer to the kitten in her hands. The kitten didn't appear to want to make friends with the animals or Melanie either.

"Some moron threw that kitten out. In a paper bag that was stapled shut." I scrubbed my hands in the sink, unmindful that with every punctuating jab of my finger, water splashed the woodwork.

"Why are you keeping the bag?" asked Melanie.

"Like Rose Ann said, the good old guys wouldn't turn a finger to help for squat. Maybe the new sheriff will have an idea." Releasing a hard breath and peeling my clenched fingers off the edge of the sink, I continued. "Poor baby. Thrown away like garbage, mouthed by a pig."

Though I tried to make light of what had happened, I knew it could have been worse. Often, people reminded me that pigs are carnivores. They would eat people if need be. An old television program showcasing a murderer who disposed of his victims that way had caused people to shun Ian and me for weeks after we had entered Buttercup in a Fourth of July parade. She had been so cute pulling the decorated dogcart.

There had also been an event right after we'd gotten her where she chased a chicken around the yard. Incredibly funny, especially when the rooster took offense and chased the piglet back to us. But Ian had pointed out that Buttercup chasing smaller animals was a bad habit. Immediately, we had curbed the pig's enthusiastic chicken racing, teaching her that all critters, furred and feathered, were off limits. I needed to trust that Buttercup would know the poultry and rescued rabbits should be safe. We never offered her meat, but... no matter how much I tried to deny it, there was always a chance she might act instinctively.

"Well, I'm not finding any injuries," Melanie said. "A little skinny, maybe, and I don't think he's ever going to be a fan of pork. Do you want me to call the shelter and tell them we've got a newbie?"

"Yes, and call Doctor Rhoades to schedule a physical." Taking a carrot out of the refrigerator, I cut it into chunks, then sat in a chair and coaxed Buttercup over. With the pig's chin on my knees, I fed the carrot, one chunk at a time. "You are such a good girl, Buttercup. Such a sweetie. Yes, you are. I'm proud of you." She got a healthy rub before I let her back outside. Then, of course, Royally was waiting.

* * *

When Sheriff Neddel's cruiser pulled in at supper time, I was just closing the big barn doors. Normally I left them open during the good weather unless it was raining, but the medicolegal death investigator's warning was still hot in my ears.

"I'm just going in for a cup of coffee, Sheriff. Would you like a cup?"

"That would be kind, thank you," he replied.

At the kitchen door, I kicked off my barn boots. Without being asked, Neddel also removed his. I didn't tell him it was okay, that he didn't have to, but I hid a smile. It was nice, especially since the eight hens, which had come to me as rejected urban pets, and roamed loose in the dooryard during the day, were indiscriminate poopers. It also proved he had been exposed to farming hospitality at one time. None of Melanie's city friends bothered when they came to visit, unless the snow was deep. Even then, there had been a few times ski boots had clomped across the tired kitchen linoleum. I pulled squat ceramic mugs from the cupboard, square on the bottom but lighter in weight than they looked. Neddel hefted the mug as he took one, gazing at the design.

It took a few moments to collect sugar, milk still in the carton, and a plate filled with homemade, raspberry-stuffed shortbread cookies.

"Sorry, but I like real glass or pottery," I said. "I don't usually buy paper products."

"I was just admiring the shape," he said. "I have some nice big mugs, but they are all tapered near the bottom." He laughed aloud, a hearty male guffaw that had Royally lifting his ears and wiggling his tailless heinie. "I can't tell you how many times I've sent coffee sloshing all over everything on the table and floor."

"Been there, done that." I nodded. "Melanie and I like a solid mug, but it has to be lightweight, as well. My friend at Back Front-Door Pottery makes these for me." My eyes drifted to the hall entrance as I sipped.

Neddel caught the pause and waited. When I didn't expand on my thought he let it go. Instead, he selected a cookie and took a generous bite. Raspberry filling squirted out, and Neddel took a second, quicker bite to catch the sweet goodness. This time, there was no hiding my laughter.

"I should have warned you. I like a sufficient filling so you can taste the jam."

His mouth still filled; Neddel could only nod.

"I'm sure you didn't drive all the way out here for a chance at fresh coffee and snacks," I said. "But before you get started, I'd like to tell you about the incident that occurred today with Spitball."

Neddel listened attentively to my story, asked if I would forward the photographs, and told me he wanted to take the bag. "You never know," he said. "We might be able to at least issue a warning to somebody for animal cruelty."

"Thank you. So, what are you here for?"

There was a scuttling noise in the hall. Royally jumped up to investigate. Lilo's happy little yipping grew. It meant Melanie had closed down her computer, and feeding time was coming.

"I wanted to speak with you and Melanie about the remains," Neddel said.

Melanie moved quietly into the kitchen. Lilo's toenails tapped out a Morse code as she closed in on her person. "I didn't go up there," my daughter said.

Neddel nodded. "Actually, I need some local information that won't degrade into the kind of gossip-mongering I usually get from people who do their looking from behind their curtains."

"Well, that sounds only a little convoluted." Melanie opted to lean against the cupboard shelf, slightly behind Neddel, sipping her coffee. The dogs, realizing supper wasn't immediately forthcoming, settled on the floor.

"We haven't identified the victim," Neddel said. "DNA is going to be sketchy. Exposure, animal predation, and all that negatively impacted what we found. But we did discover the victim's teeth. Once we find the right dentist, we'll go from there. I haven't been here long. I'm sure you know I transferred in three months ago, when my predecessor was diagnosed with prostate cancer."

I blew out my cheeks. It had been a sad thing to learn that the life of one of Ian's good friends was in jeopardy because he had ignored the symptoms for so long.

"I'm working to build rapport with the people in the office. It takes time, and I'm still at odds with some of my staff. One woman called me Doug the other day. I'm from away. They want Doug back. I know several of the locals, but not well. A lot of people I talk to seem to have an interest in me checking out their neighbors, or some church member they aren't happy with. Or they want to know if maybe I'm in the market for a bride?"

Both Melanie and I smiled behind the rims of our coffee mugs. Typical small-town behavior.

"So, you'd like to know if we can help you without being prejudiced against the milkman?" I asked.

Neddel sighed. "Yes."

"Okay, but don't ask about the mailman." I remembered how, just a few days before, the rural carrier had handed over my flyers with a question in his eyes, hoping I would spill some juicy gossip about the remains Buttercup had found in the forest.

"It's a deal." Neddel lifted his empty mug in a toast. Melanie reached around him, refilling the mug.

"Thank you," he said. "Have either of you noticed the disappearance of a young male from around here, twenty to thirty years of age? Maybe he moved away. Or he's just out of town and hasn't been back to visit through the winter."

"No," we both answered. This was the first we had heard that the remains were identified as being male.

"How about somebody just drifting through? Doing seasonal work or just hanging around?"

Again, the answer was no.

"Okay." Neddel tapped his foot. "In this particular neighborhood, do you remember somebody camping out in the woods last summer and fall? Short-term, or for a while? Like a hobo or a vagrant?"

I sat back in my chair, aware a negative response was not what he wanted to hear. "You didn't find anything else? No identification?"

"Just what was left of the clothing," said Neddel. "Men's sneaker, size nine. Medium-sized sweatshirt. Wrangler jeans, size 34-30. Basically, we know from the bones the remains were male. And from what we discerned, of average size. The jeans were pretty well-shredded, but the waistband area was intact. Watch pocket just below the waistband. Inside, I found this." Neddel pulled a small evidence bag from his jacket pocket and laid it on the table.

"May I?" I asked.

At his nod, I picked up the bag, studying the exquisite piece of jewelry inside. Melanie came to stand behind me, also peering at the bag. I flipped the plastic container back and forth, pressing the contents against the clear sides to get a good look. The jewelry was obviously southwestern. It depicted a stylized bird adorned with blue and white stones. I felt Melanie stiffen before she moved back to the counter, leaning on it once again. Neddel's eyes followed her. My daughter had a thoughtful look on her face. I think both Neddel and I realized she was searching within her mind. There had been a spark, but where had it taken her?

"Anything?" Neddel asked the room in general.

"I've seen that before." Melanie sounded small and sorrowful.

Something had clicked, and the memory was making her sad.

"Are you sure?" asked Neddel.

Melanie gave a harsh laugh. "I've actually seen it several times since I moved back here, but not for a while. I can tell you it's an eagle made with Navajo silver and turquoise. The white stones are a type of jade the Navajo call *White Buffalo*. I was told the Navajo don't usually share it. It's big medicine. This was given as a gift from a woman so her true love could travel safely and return to her."

"Is it a brooch or maybe a pendant?" I asked my daughter.

"No. It's specifically a piece of male jewelry. A clasp for a string tie."

"Like cowboys used to wear?" asked Neddel with a frown.

"Like gauchos still wear," Melanie said.

Very carefully, I put the bag down. I had a fair idea of what Melanie was going to say, and if I was right, the words were going to hurt.

"I believe this clasp belonged to a guy named Juan, who was here with a group of Forestry Service Trainees for a while last year," said Melanie. "They all came from the southwest, mostly from New Mexico, I believe. I didn't think a lot about him being gone because the group was stationed here only temporarily, to begin with. But then some of them stayed here. The only one I see often lives in Bartlett. He still works in the forestry service. His name is Mike. He's a Navajo, but I think he actually has a different name. I don't remember. He married Laura Carpenter.

"We were told this guy, Juan,— she hefted the plastic bag, "gave up the idea of working in the northeast and returned home because people around here are so bigoted. If this was the same guy, though, he would never have given up the clasp. It was a prized possession."

"Do you know this man's last name?" Neddel asked.

"Juan Noche," said Melanie.

38

Chapter Five

We stayed exactly where we had been sitting or standing. Melanie's eyes stayed on the plastic-encased clasp, but her thoughts had gone adrift. Neddel watched her. He didn't know my daughter, or me either. I was concerned about what he would say. I knew this man Melanie spoke of, but only fleetingly. Melanie, ever curious about whoever she met, had obviously known him better.

After several moments, Sheriff Neddel asked, "How do you know all this? About the clasp and about the man as well?"

I could hear suspicion, skepticism. I didn't like it.

"Last summer, early in the season," Melanie began, "I went to a bonfire party at the cove. I was living down near the city and here visiting. I hadn't gone anywhere in town, really, since I found out I had MS. A couple of my old friends pushed me to go with them, hoping I would feel better. So, I said, what the heck? People who have never seen MS don't have a clue what it is. I swear, people have asked me if it's like having Mono."

She pulled out a chair, but then just leaned on the back. I wanted her to sit, but she didn't.

"Let me tell you upfront that, like a lot of these gatherings, there was plenty of booze and a quarter keg. My drug therapy had been updated recently enough, so the warning not to imbibe was still in capital red letters on my brain. That was fine. There was plenty of food and people having fun who didn't know about my diagnosis and weren't looking at me with pity." She paused, grimacing as if in pain.

"Something happened later in the evening that kind of erased a lot from my memory. But early on, one of my friends introduced me to this guy Juan, who had come up from New Mexico and was part of the forestry service training program. I thought it was rather bizarre that somebody from a place where there were mostly just cacti would be up here across the country in the woods. I think he was a little shy. Most of my friends have really big personalities. Anyway, we were sitting around talking. I asked him why he chose forestry, particularly here in the northeast. He wanted to move here. He and his fiancé back home had talked about it. It was their plan.

"I admired his string-tie clasp. He took it off so I could look at it and told me his fiancé had given it to him. It was a promise she would wait for him, like a reverse engagement ring. For a couple of weeks after the party, we ran into each other a few times, shared coffee. He came over here once for supper. That was all. I wasn't romantically drawn to the guy, but he was nice. Then, I heard he had just up and left. Rumor was, something bad had happened back home."

I remembered that meal. We ate out of the box tacos. He laughed and said one day he would make us real tacos and burritos. He'd talked about food that I'd never heard of.

Neddel swiveled his whole body to face Melanie. "So, other people knew this guy, too?"

"Yeah, he was pretty popular, especially with the girls. But he was always very clear that he had a girl, and he was not tempted."

"Can you remember who, in particular, introduced you?"

Melanie finally slid into the chair but stayed right on the edge.

"That's part of the cloudy stuff. I remember sitting on a log. There was somebody standing right here." She raised her hand to indicate her right. "And Juan walked up. The person introduced him, said we had a lot in common because Juan was dry, too. Heh, heh, heh." Her tone indicated sarcasm in the laughter. "Anyway, the two of us spent a while sitting there talking. He had a can of soda in his hand." She gazed at a point on the ceiling across the room. Neddel waited.

"A while later, somebody else handed me a glass of sherbet punch. Not the type of thing you usually see at that kind of get-together, but what the hey? I took a couple of sips, and within a few minutes, I felt really bad. Kind of barfy and disoriented. I thought the fruit punch base had spoiled. I didn't want to make a stink, but I definitely wanted to go home. Juan didn't have a car, but he sat with me while I called my dad. Most of the others were playing volleyball on the beach in the moonlight. My father told me it took both of them to get me into the car. I don't remember him arriving, or how I got out of the car when I got home."

I wanted to cut in and tell Neddel how angry Ian and I had been. How terrifying it was to see my child like that.

"Do you know who handed you the punch? Was it Noche?"

"No, to both questions." She paused. "I never would have thought somebody would spike my drink, but later, I wondered. I mean, no one was egging me on to have a drink or laughing at me because I wasn't. Just that one laugh, and I can't remember who that was."

"And you don't remember who introduced you?" Neddel sighed. "Who was there? Do you remember?"

"You know, it's the weirdest thing," Melanie said slowly. "I can sense them there now, so close I can feel the body heat. I want to say it was a guy. The words are clear, but not the voice. The illusion of the person isn't scary, but the feeling of not remembering is frightening. And I believe a woman gave me the punch, but again, I'm not sure." Melanie got up and paced in front of the counter. Lilo paced with her, while Royally watched. His brow was all puckered up.

Neddel had been leaning towards Melanie. As if realizing she might be reading the tension rippling off of him, he leaned back, lifting his mug. "How did you get to the bonfire?"

"Noah took me."

"Hey, what's going on?" The question came from the kitchen door, the screen settling silently back into place behind Noah.

All three of us in the kitchen jumped with surprise. Neddel rose to his feet. Lilo danced over to the young man, but Royally stayed beside me, the curiously cute wrinkles on his forehead deepening to something uglier.

"Oh, Noah," I said. "You gave me such a fright. You didn't make a sound."

To myself, I was thinking that either Melanie or I were going to have to share a little talk with Noah. No matter how casually we lived, he needed to knock before entering.

Noah moved toward Melanie, who stood with her hand pressed to her chest.

"I'm sorry." He sounded contrite. "I didn't mean to scare you." He reached out, laying his hand on her shoulder. "You all looked so intense I thought something bad had happened."

"Oh, my god, Noah!" Melanie cried out. "What did you do to your hand?"

His right hand was wrapped in a handkerchief. Fresh red blood seeped through the fabric. I jumped up, already unwrapping the cotton cloth while Noah spoke.

"I thought I'd do something to surprise you. Like catch some trout for supper." Noah flinched as I pressed his hand beneath the spigot flow. "I was going to do a little fishing. I wasn't paying attention, and I caught me instead of a fish. Ouch." He tried to pull away.

"It doesn't look terribly bad. Don't be a baby, Noah." I patted his shoulder. "Melanie will get you wrapped up while I walk the sheriff out."

"I suggest a tetanus shot," said Neddel.

Noah nodded in agreement, but continued to flinch as Melanie prodded his injury.

Standing beside the cruiser, Neddel said to me, "Why do I have the impression there was more to Melanie's story beyond what she said?"

I shrugged, rubbing my upper arms with my hands. I didn't think any of this had to do with the remains on the mountain. Even if they were in truth, Juan Noche. The episode at the bonfire had been something else, with people we had known and, until then, trusted. Juan was a bit player. I didn't want Neddel, who was from away, an unknown, and somebody who probably wouldn't stay in the valley, to be harassing Melanie.

"She's incredibly private about the MS, and her life in general. It took a lot for her to tell you that story. Myself, I can only answer to what happened, when Ian brought her home. We had to carry her into the house. She was totally out of it. Ian went ballistic. He thought she had ignored the doctor's warning and been drinking after she had been told not to. We didn't take her to the hospital, because her respiration and heartbeat were solid. In retrospect, if we had, maybe the doctors there could have told us what she had ingested.

"I sat with her, trying to figure it out, and I sniffed her breath, looking for an alcohol clue. When I told Ian I hadn't found anything, he got this weird look on his face. The next thing I knew, he was roaring down the road. He went back to the party, supposedly, he said, to tell those kids the punch was bad. While he was there, he talked to Lila Weathers. She's one of Melanie's good friends. Lila told Ian she didn't know about the punch. She hadn't seen anything that would suggest there was any in a cooler somewhere. Lila said she knew Melanie wasn't drinking alcohol. That she'd had a couple of beers and gone down to the volleyball game and hadn't even realized Melanie was gone until Ian showed up looking for answers. I don't know if he asked her more about the party. And I can't ask him now. He told me the next morning he was afraid somebody had slipped Melanie one of those date drugs you hear about."

"How was she the next day?" Neddel asked.

"Hungover, pukey, nasty to be around. It lasted through to the day after," I said. "That's when she told us most of her memory about the evening was just plain gone. By then, it was too late to take her to the hospital. We never found out what happened. She could have suffered an MS episode."

Neddel's eyes narrowed. He looked back toward the house. "If she was given a drugged drink, somebody she knew probably gave it to her."

"It could have been anybody," I said. "But Sheriff, those people were her friends. Still are."

"And yet, knowing she had MS, they left her sitting there by herself," he said.

I felt my anger rising. Not so much with Neddel this time, as with the cards my daughter had been dealt.

"Sheriff, at that time, Melanie had told very few people about the MS. Noah. Lila. But not many. The diagnosis was still new, the wound still raw. She didn't even want to talk to us about it. She kept saying she'd take care of it. Her doctor said to give her space. She was still learning to accept how this was going to change her life. I'm sure she pushed her friends off the same way she shut us out."

I paused. Neddel had a look on his face that was asking how I could accept that. If this would have been Doug, I would have had a meltdown. Neddel made me too angry. Who was he to ask about our private pain? I wanted him to leave.

"What are the chances we could get a list of who was at the party?" he asked.

"I can check with Melanie, I suppose. See what she remembers." Asking her wasn't something I wanted to do. I could tell Neddel was reading me on that.

"Do it," he said.

I took immediate offense at his tone and command.

"Do you have any other questions?" I asked coldly. "I have things to do."

"Do you know if Ian spoke with Noche?"

"I don't. A few weeks later, Melanie returned to her job out of town. And then Ian was dead."

* * *

When I went back inside the house, Noah and Melanie were sitting on the sofa. She was showing him the kitten Buttercup had yakked out. In one hand, she held an eyedropper filled with baby food.

"He's so skinny," she said. "We need to fatten him up. His working name right now is Spitball," she added to Noah.

"You mean Spit*fire*?" Noah laughed.

"No, when Buttercup hawked him up, he was pretty much just a ball of spit."

"That's disgusting," said Noah, but he was still laughing, sitting on the sofa, one arm around Melanie's shoulders. When she offered to let him feed Spitball, though, he declined.

I made supper while they canoodled with the kitten. That is, Melanie canoodled. I don't think Noah is as into cats as she is. Later, with his freshly bandaged hand, Noah promised to get a tetanus shot and went home. The stack of No Trespassing signs that I had asked him to pick up was on the counter. With or without help, I was going to need to get the farm posted. I hated the thought of building a fence, but I could see the wisdom in what Doctor Lombard had advised.

Chapter Six

The next morning, the sun was streaming in the windows, suggesting the line of cat snot eleven inches up should be washed away. In her office, Melanie looked up from her laptop, frowning. I stood in the doorway, dressed in a pair of Daisy Duke shorts over a black bathing suit. My flip-flops had big plastic flowers attached. I was also doing the cha-cha.

Dropping her head to her chest, she said with a whine, "But it's Sunday!"

"It's warm, and the black flies aren't out yet." I smiled. "The perfect day. I'll get set up while you change."

"I never agreed to do any more pigwashing," Melanie called out to my retreating footsteps.

My only answer was the slam of the kitchen screen door. Even from outside, I could hear two sets of clicking doggy footsteps race down the hallway towards Melanie's combination office and bedroom. Knowing those two hounds, I'm sure both Royally and Lilo stood waiting with sad and hopeful eyes. My guess was verified when I heard Melanie talking to them through the window screen.

"Aargh, let me get changed, for crying out loud!" Melanie exclaimed. "Move and let me find something that won't get ruined at the pig wash."

This time I heard a single set of canine toenails scooting back up the hallway, and yowling cats flying in all directions to get out of Royally's way. He couldn't get outside, but he could get onto the screened-in porch. Looking over my shoulder, I saw his nose pressed against the screen, watching me.

Five minutes later, when I exited the big barn doorway pulling an ancient red wagon, I could still see Royally's flattened black nose and hear Melanie's complaints as she searched for warm but serviceable clothing. So much drama!

On the southeastern side of the house, a grassy lawn stretched down to flower beds along the driveway on one side. On the other, the tender green leaves of lilacs filtered dust, which rose from the dirt road.

Time to get to work. First came the tarp. Once spread and ready, the deflated eight-foot pool was stretched in the center. There were soft scrub brushes, a loofah brush Ian had contrived especially for this chore, and bottles of shampoo and lotion lined up. From the front porch, I hauled the portable air compressor, dragging its extension cord. Then I brought out four five-gallon buckets of hot water from the house, since hose water coming out of the well would be icy cold. I made a quick trip for a lawn chair and finally stretched out the hose.

By that time, Melanie and the two dogs waited at the rear corner of the house.

"Release the hounds!" I called with a flourish.

At Melanie's command, Royally and Lilo rushed forward, taking their assigned positions beside the lawn chair. Melanie walked back to the barn. Once inside, she opened the gate to Buttercup's home. Having just consumed breakfast, the pig was having a bit of a lie-down. Melanie left her and moved back to the wide door. Once safely out of ramming range, she sang,

"My Buttercup lies over the ocean.

My Buttercup lies over the sea.

My Buttercup lies inside the bathtub.

Please bring back my Buttercup to me!"

Before Melanie got the last line out, Buttercup raced past. From there, we both continued,

"Bring back, oh, bring back, oh, bring back my Buttercup to me. To meeee."

The singing continued throughout the bathing process, though neither of us could carry a note. The adoring pig, who lay in the center of the pool until it was inflated and filled with five inches of water and bubbles, didn't care. Contented sighs followed as I scrubbed with a sponge and Melanie with the loofah brush. The only time Buttercup moved was when the water got deep enough to enter her snout. Without standing, she wriggled to the edge, resting her chin on the inflated side of the pool. After the water had been changed, the pig rinsed, and water drained, lotion was applied. The dogs cavorted in the wet grass, romping around the reclining Duchess of Porkshire, while their humans stretched out in the sun, cold drinks in hand.

"To her royal highness." Melanie raised her glass of iced tea. "May porcinsus always rule."

"Here, here," I agreed.

From behind us, we heard the sound of clapping. I sprang to my feet as if my butt were perched on a beehive. Royally's head snapped up as Sheriff Neddel walked up.

"Sheriff!" There was every chance my blush went from my hairline down to the top of the bathing suit. "How long have you been there?"

"Well, let's see." The sheriff stopped, eyeing the stiff-legged advance of the corgi. "You were singing, and this pooch was almost wetting himself to get into the pool."

His mention of Royally brought the dog's actions back to focus.

"Royally," I said. "Heel."

The dog instantly responded, but the bit of raised hair on the back of his neck didn't flatten out. Once at my side, he kept watch with a curled lip.

"Oh, look," Melanie said with a hint of sarcasm. "He's smiling at you."

"Yeah, I don't think so," said the sheriff. "I came out for a little chit-chat."

"You were just here," I said with a groan.

Prior to giving the dogs access to the pool, I had opened the air valve. The sides were now deflated enough, so the last bit of water tumbled out into the turf. Buttercup, knowing the end was near, hefted onto her feet and moved to a sunny place on the grass for a roll.

"Melanie, why don't you go along?" I asked. "I'll pick this up. Put the dogs on the screen porch until they dry out." When my daughter was safely away, I gathered the buckets, which had been upside down and draining.

"Hose?" Neddel asked.

"Compressor."

After we picked up, rolled up, or hung everything over the clothesline to dry, I felt grateful enough for the help to offer him an iced tea.

"What about her?" Neddel nodded toward Buttercup, who snored in the sun.

"She free ranges."

"Of course she does." His eyebrows had risen only slightly.

Iced tea in hand, we sat in the shade of the picnic table umbrella. Neddel was in uniform. I didn't think he would care to stretch out on the grass. He got to the reason for his visit.

"I don't know if you've noticed an increase in the amount of traffic cruising past here," he said.

"I have, mostly because there's a few who have sort of paused at the end of my drive."

"Yeah. Curiosity seekers." He took a long sip. "It's going to get worse. We're getting a lot of calls. Attention will rise when more noise starts happening on social media. Eventually, the weirdos are going to walk right up and knock on your door. I think we need to come up with a plan to nip any interference in the bud."

"I've already thought of that," I said, setting my glass aside. "Do you have a half hour?"

"At your service." He started to rise from his seat.

"Stay put. I'll be back." I told him.

Ten minutes later, I was back dressed in jeans, carrying several pieces of paper. "This way." I waved for Neddel to follow and walked toward the barn.

The thousand-square-foot building was clean and neat. Kennels on one side, Buttercup's pen in the front half of the other, then a work area. I selected a plank from Ian's wood cache bin and laid it across two sawhorses. After plugging in the circular saw, I sliced off six twelve-inch pieces. Neddel was eyeing the no trespassing signs, but that wasn't the first part of my plan. I handed the sheriff an electric drill and a box of screws.

"Do you know how to run this piece of equipment?" I cocked an eyebrow. It was a challenge.

At his snort, I continued, "Use some of those pieces of snow fencing to attach a signpost." While he worked, I threw a sledgehammer into the riding lawnmower trailer. Then I used a staple gun to affix the pages Melanie had printed out onto the signs.

FOLLOW TRAIL

TO

SITE OF RECOVERED

REMAINS

"You don't think this is going to work, do you?" Neddel asked, doubtfully.

I stacked the signs in the trailer. "What was your suggestion?"

"Keep the pig out of sight."

"Phfft," I spat.

As the riding lawnmower moved down the drive, Buttercup rose on her front feet.

"Stay," I ordered. "Stay."

The pig dropped back to the ground.

Walking beside the lawn tractor back to his car, the sheriff said, "I'm surprised the earth didn't tremble."

"She's only four hundred fifty pounds."

"Right," he muttered, getting into his cruiser to follow me down the road.

A quarter mile away, I parked at the edge of a game trail. Offering the sledgehammer to the sheriff, I held the first sign in place. We followed the trail as it angled up the mountain for about half a mile, periodically hammering another sign in place.

Neddel laughed when we had the last sign driven into the ground. "If nothing else, by the time some thrill seeker gets this far, they'll be too exhausted to keep looking."

"Well, at least the walk out will be downhill," I said. "I'll try to keep Buttercup out of sight, but the weather is getting nice. She likes to be outside."

I wanted to keep the whacky people away from my home the same way I wanted the remains to never have been on the ridge above the barn. My newly established norm since Ian's death was still fragile. Even I was still getting used to it. The cockamamie signs might work, but the wishing didn't seem to be doing a lot of good. This sort of thing would have been Ian's job. He liked to mess with the out-of-staters, sending them on fool's errands whenever possible. He had been really good at coming up with ways to fool them. I was merely an apprentice.

Neddel and I parted ways where the car and mower were parked. He reminded me again to be ready for an influx of strangers at my door, then he went toward town. I headed home. At the edge of the driveway, I found Buttercup waiting. The pig's snout was high in the air, disc glistening as it danced in the sun.

"You were looking for me, weren't you?" I asked with a sigh. She rushed right over to the idling tractor. The whole back half of her was all a-jiggle with excitement. I accepted her as she was, representing a past I would never have again and a future I wasn't sure of. I felt my loss thicken in my chest again. "This isn't going to be easy," I told her.

I let her follow me as I stapled the no trespassing signs Noah had brought to trees around the house and yard. We let out the chickens and worked with Rex. While she took a nap, I cleaned the kennel. All the while, I kept a covert eye on passing cars. The day wasn't even half done, and I was fighting the urge to chew my nails to my elbows. I had noticed the strange cars the day before and started my useless note taking. But having both Rose Ann and Neddel warn me it was going to get worse was alarming.

Chapter Seven

In the house, Melanie was making lunch. Royally and Lilo watched her every movement attentively. The application of peanut butter to toast was serious business.

"I'm assuming you and Rambo put out the signs," she said.

"No Rambo, just Porkbo," I said.

Buttercup, who had accompanied me into the house, sat down beside the dogs, the width of her hams forcing the pooches so close together they were almost sitting in one spot. She didn't care how uncomfortable the dogs were. Her attention was on the peanut butter. Melanie slathered one piece of toast heavily and then put the toast and the pig outside.

"I was thinking we might want to start locking the cars and maybe the barn?" she said.

"Yeah. I agree about locking everything other than the chicken coop. Let's face it, who's going to mess with those old biddies? And it's a cinch if they get set loose, especially in the night; they aren't going anywhere."

It wasn't until after lunch, while I was working at socializing with Rex that I really considered the possibility that thrill seekers could be more than a nuisance. I thought heavily about what both Rose Ann and Sheriff Neddel had said. At one time, there might have been people driving by, stopping to take a photograph of a lounging, four-hundred-fifty-pound pig. But now things were different. Standing out in the yard, I realized we were completely alone. Last house on the end of a dirt road. Two women and a couple of vertically challenged dogs that couldn't reach up far enough to bite you in the kneecaps. When I started looking around with the rose-colored blinders off, I suddenly didn't feel so sure of myself anymore.

I brought Rex out. It was time for his next set of lessons. We would do three or four in a day. He watched me with a nervous twitch in his eyes. I needed to relax for him to be able to learn. To progress, he had to believe we were having fun.

As a rescue dog, I didn't know what his experiences had been with other canines. I placed Royally in a collapsible metal pen. I needed Rex to realize he wasn't the only dog there. In the real world, he'd be out where there would be many others. Royally was used to this type of work. Immediately, he laid down quietly, but I was his human. He kept a close eye on me and the visitor dog. Buttercup was napping in her outside pen area. With all the people who'd been coming and going the last couple of days, I worried that, if I allowed her to wander free, there might be a pig fender bender. I would also be using up a lot of attention watching her that I should have been giving to Rex. Like most of the rejected dogs, Rex had come with his own issues. He was afraid of common household items, wouldn't sleep on a fabric bed, and more than one adult male in the group made him roll over and show his belly in fear. Doctor Rhoades had done the neutering, as well as starting the vaccine process. But Rex was good-natured. So far, he had proven easy to work with.

"Look at you," I said, using my happy voice. "Heel."

Rex was on the offside. He stopped to ponder. Giving him a gentle tug as a hint, I moved him to my left. I held the leash in my right hand, across my middle, and held my left hand in front of his nose. As soon as he sat, I opened my hand, offering a tidbit.

"Good boy."

From the corner of my eye, I saw his rump wiggle. He wanted to please. The Pitbull-boxer was a lovely shade of slate gray with a white bib and a zebra stripe across his rump. Smaller in stature than others I had received, I knew, he had been kept crated in a small, hot apartment. He was afraid of brooms, mops, and other items with long wooden handles. Around the area where we were working, I left a few such items lying in the grass. When he approached them, he stopped, tail between his legs. It was a testament to the trust he had in me that Rex moved to a position where I was between him and the enemy, instead of trying to run away. I lured him back around with a treat, then stood patiently as he inched forward, sniffing.

While I waited for him, my gaze drifted down to the road. A red Audi moved along so slowly no dust rose behind it. The driver wouldn't be able to see my car, which had been pulled around the back of the house, and Melanie had gone into town to the feed store, so her vehicle was gone as well. Our friend David had taken to trapping feral kittens in the feed barn and finally had one in the live trap. Melanie would pick it up, and we'd hold on to it until animal rescue drove over.

From where I stood, screened by the budding lilacs, I had a clear view. The driver was a man with dark hair. He wore aviator sunglasses and seemed to be studying the area behind the house. Rex had no fear of cars, but he was curious. Abandoning the broom, he moved toward the road, attracting the driver's attention. When Mr. Aviator realized I was standing there, he sped up slightly and drove away.

"Idiot," I muttered, more vexed than nervous. I drew Rex back, and we finished the circuit. Then, I returned him to his run until his next set. Fifteen minutes on, fifteen minutes off, then another fifteen on, twice in the morning and afternoon. Rex had not yet been introduced to the cats, so his visits into the house were limited and orchestrated to keep all the critters safe.

"How's he doing?" Melanie asked, getting out of her car as I released Royally.

She told me David had succeeded in catching a half-grown ginger cat. For the entire ride in the car, there had been a lot of snarling going on. Melanie put the live trap on the porch under a lightweight towel for a little time out. She was still standing there when I came inside with my arms filled with brooms and mops.

"Good, we'll try him tonight in the kitchen for a bit. Getting him to not lift his leg is the big thing right now." After pouring myself water, I casually mentioned the red Audi. "Neddel was right about the whack-jobs. You didn't notice the car when you were coming in, did you?"

"Are you sure it was an Audi?" Melanie frowned.

I tensed. "Yes. Why?" I hadn't said anything to Melanie yet about the increased traffic. To my knowledge, she wouldn't have recognized one vehicle from another.

"I saw an Audi drive by earlier while we were giving Buttercup her bath."

"Are you sure?"

"Mom, how many red Audis do you think there are around here?"

"Not many." My fingernails edged toward my mouth.

* * *

The living room and parlor on the northwestern side of the house had been converted into Melanie's office and bedroom. The large farmer's kitchen was big enough for a table and chairs, so the dining room now did service as the sitting room on the opposite side from the drive that circled back to the barn. The switchback meant if Buttercup was sneaking over at suppertime, I couldn't see her.

It had been a long day. Melanie lounged on the sofa with Lilo and a mixed variety pack of cats, while my reading chair was closer to the front window. But even with an open book in my hand, I couldn't seem to engage.

I had a clear view of the road and the first fifty feet of the driveway. Each time a vehicle approached, I tensed. If it moved steadily past, I marked the driver down as a local, somebody out trying to spot deer in the meadows beyond as dusk faded to night. If the vehicle slowed, my senses went on high alert. Royally, sensitive to my changing moods, I was unquiet, shifting back around, laying on my feet, and eventually crawling onto the footstool. He balanced there until he felt secure enough to scramble into my lap. That sent Poppy up onto the back of the chair, where she emitted tiny feline snarls until she dozed off.

By eight-thirty, I was exhausted by the stress of the day, the constant vigilance, and the amount of work it had taken to get the new ginger cat into the large quarantine cage set up on the porch. With Argyle in quarantine in the cattery, and Spitball contained in Melanie's room, the porch was our last option, except for the barn.

Lying in bed with one side of my head arguing with the other about whether I would be able to sleep wasn't getting me anywhere. Another memory of Ian rose to the surface. For Father's Day, Ian had received two animal cameras. He installed them on the backside of the property near the game trails so he could keep track of the wild critters coming down off the mountain. He spent hours sitting comfortably in front of the computer monitor, watching deer, coyotes, and even a moose come and go.

Somewhere in the darkness while I imagined cars filled with camera-toting strangers in cat's eye sunglasses pulling into the yard, I realized they didn't need to use the driveway. Vehicles could park out on the road, walk through the fields or the woods, and be on my back porch before I knew they were there. The idea of faces staring through the kitchen windows creeped me out.

"Tomorrow," I whispered to my furry bedmates, "I'll move those cameras." Royally snuggled in closer, and we both dropped off to sleep.

* * *

I woke up sweating. Time to take another blanket off the bed. Royally was lying up against me, all body heat and snores. Poppy had my ankles pinned down. I laid still. Any movement would notify Poppy I was awake. Then she would advance to the head of the bed, demand to be let under the covers, and pin me down on the opposite side from Royally. That would make two hot bodies sandwiching me in, like the chocolate cookie cake on an ice cream sandwich. Royally had crawled up on the footstool and then into my lap. There was no room for cats. And I would be the sticky melting mess in the middle.

All I could see were the planes of dark gray that were the items and angles of my room. The tilting gable roof, the cutout of the dormer windows, pictures on the wall. Nothing distinct, as in the light of day, but they weren't foreign or threatening either. A light angled across the ceiling, running down the wall like water over a waterfall. A car driving by, probably some poor lost soul realizing this wasn't the right road and turning around in our driveway. Nothing new. No car engine noise, but that didn't worry me, either.

Then the light reappeared. I realized it wasn't coming from the roadside, but from the back of the house. I got out of bed, leaving Royally and Poppy on the covers. Standing in the rear dormer, I studied the yard. Nothing. Rex wasn't barking. The barn doors were still shut.

Daft old biddy, I thought, chiding myself for being so nervous.

Then, a flicker of light shone through the trees like a star in a thorny snare. How had it fallen from the sky? High on the ridge where the going was steep, a light moved back and forth. Common sense said there couldn't be two out there. My eyes narrowed. Could a four-wheeler be up there this time of night? A quick glance at the nightstand clock told me it was 2:00 A.M. Inching closer to the window screen, I held my breath. Four-wheelers, like chainsaws, were noisy. I didn't hear a sputtering or revving gas engine. Right about the time I figured I was probably seeing the reflection off a trail marker or something, I saw the light again. Now, it moved away, following the trail. It was there; it was gone. Repeat. An occasional flash like one from a strong flashlight played peek-a-boo among the trees. It was moving fast enough to make me believe the owner had been there before.

Pulling on a pair of jeans and a sweatshirt, I crept down the stairs. Above, I heard Royally move around on the bed, but the hard thump of him hitting the floor didn't happen. He knew I sometimes went down in the night to check on Melanie. He'd wait.

In the sitting room, I opened the window and stepped out onto the wood planking of the front porch. Insect noises filled the night. A little breeze rubbed two branches together, but I didn't hear anything else. From this angle, I couldn't see the ridge. A couple of quiet steps toward the end of the porch would let me look toward Calwin Mountain. That meant crossing Melanie's window to get to the railing.

Just as I reached my daughter's window, I heard it. A car starting down the road. Exhaling, I held still, focused on where the sound had come from. The next house was the Bernhardts. Beyond that was the Davis house, where Shane lived in an apartment built over the garage.

I concentrated again. In all the years we had lived here, I had never before been able to hear a vehicle from either of those houses. This one had to be closer. Instead of continuing past Melanie's window, I moved to the edge of the porch and stood on the wide bottom plank of the front steps. Was that a spark of red? Taillights? I couldn't tell for sure and barely heard the purr as the vehicle pulled away.

After locking the window, I crept down the hall to the kitchen. On the upper level, Royally had finally decided to come down and check on things as well. With the kitchen door open so that I could see as well as hear what was happening across the yard, I sat at the table, watching through the screen, the corgi at my feet. The outside noises had changed. Now, there was an impatient rustling in the trees, and I heard Buttercup in her outside pen. She was moving around, checking out her space. If she knew I was awake and watching, she didn't call to me.

An hour passed before I closed the kitchen door. Royally and I stretched out on the sitting room sofa. Eventually, I nodded off, but my sleep was not untainted. The house was closed up, but I kept waking, sure that I could hear footsteps on the gravel, the well-tuned purr of expensive cars no farmer would drive. Every time I moved, Royally's head came up. He could feel my tension. His cold nose touched my cheek, as if he were telling me that he was there and would protect me. I fell asleep with my arm around him, grateful for his heat and presence.

Chapter Eight

I awoke in the morning to find Royally lying on his back in a most ungentlemanly pose, snoring loudly. Outside, Buttercup was calling.

"Oh, nuts! I overslept," I said aloud, sitting straight up on the sofa.

Then I realized it wasn't quite dawn. Suddenly, Rex began barking, and he sounded agitated. Both the pig and the dog had been shut inside the barn. But from the sound, Rex was out in the run. Unlike Buttercup, he couldn't open the connecting door alone.

I ran towards the back of the house, stepped into my rubber boots, and grabbed Ian's rifle. At the edge of the back stoop, I stopped. My eyes traveled along the tree line, then up to where I'd seen the strange moving light during the night. The chickens weren't making any noise, which was odd. If the problem was a wild animal—weasel, coyote, even a bear—the biddies would be raising an unholy stink.

Behind me, I heard Melanie shushing Royally. Lilo whimpered. Moving ahead slowly, I held the rifle in both hands, snugged up to my shoulder. Down the road, barely past the big double-bole maple tree, I saw the red glow of brake lights. A car started. Was this the same vehicle as earlier, or had someone else decided to come out here and creep around my property? My teeth ground together. Earlier, I had been concerned about being harassed. Now I was nothing but pissed off at the thought that the person sneaking around could be a threat.

* * *

"Listen, Sheriff," I spat into the phone. "I just finished hanging two animal cameras outside, one on the house and one on the front of the barn. They have motion alarms, and I'm going to be using them. I need you to install an animal camera down on the trail where we put those No Trespassing signs."

"I can't just go out and do that," Sheriff Neddel said. "There are rules—laws—I have to follow."

"That's bull," I said. The growl in my voice had several pairs of ears in the kitchen at attention. "We had some jerk prowling around here early this morning. He may even have come into the yard. I don't know. But he was in the barn because he let Rex out into the run."

I didn't mention that neither the dog nor the pig had let me know they were being invaded. It was odd, but a well-handled snack could have kept them quiet.

"Melanie went online and checked out the shape of the brake lights we saw. We both think it was the Audi that was around here the other day."

"How far away was this car?" Sheriff Neddel sounded unconvinced. Or maybe he was having deja vu about gossipy old ladies.

"Down past the big maple on the other side of the driveway." As soon as the words came out of my mouth, I realized how ridiculous that sounded. If he asked me where, what was I going to tell him? *Oh, yeah, out of sight, but it was right there.* I could have kicked myself, but I couldn't shut up.

"Seriously?" Neddel asked.

* * *

I slammed the flip phone shut. "Melanie, see if you can find somebody in town who has an animal camera with enough range from a quarter mile away."

While she keyed furiously on her laptop, I took my coffee outside and went out to start Rex's morning set. On the way, I opened the hatch, letting the chickens loose into their fenced enclosure. Like the other animals, the hens—four Rhode Island Reds and four Black Orpingtons—had arrived as rescues. Even though I technically only fostered the girls, they hadn't found other homes yet. They paid their rent in eggs and bug control.

Rex walked along, oblivious to the clucking calls of the ladies who felt the enclosure wasn't roomy enough and wanted to be released to free range. An hour later, midway through Rex's last set, a *Tractor Supply* delivery vehicle pulled in. The driver eyed Rex warily. The dog's golden eyes stayed on him, but more in curiosity than aggression.

Melanie and I dumped the contents of the cardboard box on the kitchen table. The animal camera looked innocuous, but the directions spelled out in four languages had been set down by a Philadelphia lawyer, in terminology that only Doctor Peabody and Sherman would be able to understand. Even Melanie's eyes were crossing.

Finally, she said, "Okay, let's try this. I'll download the app and set up the link to the computer. When I get that done, you take the camera down the road. We'll see how far you get before we lose the feed."

She handed me four heavy C batteries and started her part. I made toast. By the time I was done chowing down and Rex was secure on the overhead line, Melanie was ready for me. As I stepped outside, closing the heavy kitchen door behind me, a plaintive scree-scree-scree let me know Buttercup thought I had forgotten her.

I placed a six-foot ladder, a battery-operated drill, and an extra box of mounting screws in the trailer behind the tractor. It was a cinch I'd lose at least a few before I was done. The camera was turned on and was lying in the trailer bed. My cell phone was pinched between my shoulder and ear so Melanie could give me a running commentary as I drove down the road.

"Sky," she reported. "Sky again. Tree. Two trees. Whoa, slow down. You're getting a little out of focus. Sky. Okay, Mom. That's it. Nothing on the screen."

I was about ten yards from the path and the site sign. Slowing the tractor, I considered my best options. "Hold on," I said. Deserting the tractor, I walked back and forth in the road, checking out angles. "Basically," I said to Melanie, "I just want to see who goes up the path."

"Yeah, and maybe a license plate would be good. You'd think for the price of this thing, it would at least be in color. I'm going to call down to the

Tractor Supply store and tell Dell they need to order a better quality product."

But I wasn't thinking about her need for red and blue instead of black and white, so much as what she'd said about license plates.

"I'm going to walk around with the camera for a little way, okay? Tell me when you can see something." I held the unit against my chest and backed away from the path.

"Okay, Red Leader," she said, "you're coming in again. A little fuzzy, but I can see trees."

"If I stand here, it's blurry, right?" I looked over my shoulder. The curve of the road put a thick stand of deciduous trees between me and the house. I crossed the road, tramped through the ditch, and stood on the far bank. I could just see my porch and the corner of the house.

"Wow," Melanie said. "Way better. Angle toward the path. Little more, little...okay, hold it. That's good. I can see the path and the tractor. I can't make out individual leaves, but I can tell one trunk from another."

And from this angle way over here, no one would see the camera, I thought.

Setting up the ladder beside the oak tree wasn't hard. Staying on it while I angled, adjusted, and set screws was scary. When I was all done, I had Melanie check it out again while I searched for the setting screw, which I had dropped in the leaf litter.

"I think that's good. You won't be able to see zits on somebody's face, but you'll know they're there and maybe whether they are male or female. If they park just on the other side of the path, we will definitely get their plate number."

I headed home to sit beside Melanie and scrutinize my work on the computer screen. A car went by while I was looking at the monitor, and a little alarm bell went off. Not in my head, like I initially thought. This was an audible sound.

"What was that?" I asked.

"The app lets you know when the motion detector is activated," Melanie said.

"How long before the tape is filled up?" I asked.

"Doesn't have a tape. It's all stored in the cloud," Melanie said.

She showed me how to shut the alarm off and retrieve clips so I could look at them later. There was no telling how long I would retain all her directions in my head, but as I sat there watching the screen, I mentally flipped Neddel the bird. Throwing a football? Call a jock. Trying to get something done? Call 1-800-IM-WOMAN.

Most of the day was lost to me. Every twenty minutes, I checked out the computer. Well, maybe not quite that often. But definitely every time a car drove by.

"Noah called and asked if we wanted pizza for supper," said Melanie. "I told him only if it came with salad and maybe onion rings."

Being a good guy, Noah brought exactly what she'd asked for. It was a mess of food.

"You'll need to take some of this home," I said. "Or we'll be snacking on it for a week."

"Nope," Noah said. "Tiny apartment, even smaller refrigerator. You have chickens and a pig. I'm sure you can figure something out."

I had brought Rex into the house before supper to start acclimating him to being inside. While I was handling him, Melanie had gathered all the cats and closed them in the cattery. Only Butch, the full-time feral, and Boots, the semi-feral, remained at large. Both ate on the back porch. As Rex approached, they slunk away into the darkness. Buttercup was busy with the special enrichment ball we had ordered for her to use for exercise. The ball was large and hard enough, so she couldn't pinch it together and take a bite out of it. After placing three treats inside, I pushed the ball across the grass. Buttercup followed, pushing it herself with her snout. If she rolled it just right, one of the treats would fall out of the small hole. The porky was smart enough to tell when the treats were gone. Then, she would abandon her toy for a nap or just some rooting. Or, with the odor of cheese and garlic coming from the house, maybe she'd come to the door and try some pig-to-person begging. I latched the door and ignored her.

Rex lay beside me as we ate. Periodically, he gave me a little nuzzle to let me know he liked pizza crust as well. When we'd first sat down, he whined pitifully, so I moved him away from the table into a safari crate in the corner.

After he finally quieted down, I let him out. Once more, I had to move him into the crate before he figured out that silence was golden. On the other side of the doorway gate, Royally and Lilo watched—probably wondering how come he wasn't smart enough to be quiet from the get-go.

We cleaned up, and I put Buttercup to bed with her slice to keep her company. Leaving Melanie and Noah in the sitting room, I went upstairs. In the bedroom, I had a beautiful swing arm vanity that had belonged to my grandmother. Small, but a perfect size for the desktop computer. While it whirred to life, I hefted short-legged Royally onto the bed where he lay at the foot, watching over my shoulder. Or napping, as needed. For a few minutes, life had slowed to normal.

There was an email from the animal control officer in Berlin, an hour and a half away. Two dogs, one male and one female, had been taken into custody after they escaped their pen area and wreaked havoc through the neighborhood. The dogs were repeat offenders. They had been removed from the owner's care.

One of the dogs attacked a smaller canine. We have both in quarantine. When they are released, spayed and neutered, we will chip, provide the first level of shots, get DNA in the system, and transfer. Do you currently have room? Can we reserve space?

I responded in the affirmative, asking for a twenty-four-hour heads-up, if possible.

"Tomorrow," I told Royally as I changed into pajamas, "we'll upgrade Rex to free range on the overhead."

Though my pooch and I were snuggled down comfortably, and the dog quickly started snoring, there was an itchy place in the wide plain of my consciousness that wouldn't allow me to lie still. Getting past the long corgi, who refused to curl up to sleep like any other dog in the world, required drawing my knees up until they touched my chin. Only then was I able to squeeze out of bed.

Downstairs, I checked in first with Melanie, who was asleep under a mud mask, which looked incredibly uncomfortable. Beside her was a tiny bit of orange fur that was supposed to be in quarantine. Lilo watched me with shiny eyes. Probably hoping that I'd lug Spitball away. I peeked out at the ginger cat, then in the cattery. Each lock was secure, and though many green and yellow eyes opened to the tiniest of slits, not one feline roused enough to challenge my presence.

Nothing, I thought, ready to dope-slap myself. *See? Nothing.*

Walking by the doorway to the sitting room on my way to the staircase, I felt the wisp of a breeze caress my ankles. As I entered the room, with moonlight shining in through the tall, old-fashioned glass windows, I saw a sheer curtain billow slightly, then deflate. One of the windows on the front of the house had been left open two inches. It was an oversight that required only a dozen steps across the room and a little push that sent the lead weights in the side panel growling as the glass slid down. These lovely old four-pane windows were so tall, someone standing on the porch could easily step from the sill to the floor and pass through into the front rooms.

That had never been a worry in all the time we'd lived here, but the presence of bears, particularly at this time of year, definitely was. We never left the first-floor windows open and unlocked at night. I set the thumb press for the window latch back into position and, after a loving look over the moonbeam-drenched flower bed. With a sigh at the peaceful scene outside, I returned to my own bed. Problem solved.

I went upstairs feeling safe and sound, knowing the alarm on the animal cams would let me know if they needed my attention. I was almost asleep on my feet as I went, totally forgetting I had shut the alarm off while Buttercup had been meandering around.

Chapter Nine

Melanie was still sleeping when I arose early the next morning, but the cattery cats meowed pitifully, so I had to stop and feed them.

Standing in the middle of the backyard as the sun crept down the ledge, bringing all the colors and birds to life, was always a euphoric experience. Today, as much as any other day, I was outside and ready. I'm an early morning person, and a familiar feeling of bubbling energy was rising within me. I wanted to do something fun.

While I stood there tapping my foot, considering what exactly that should be, one of the hens ran over and pecked at my jumping shoestring. She ended up making contact with my flesh, and with a yelp, I jumped out of range. But the interruption had changed my mindset. Now, I was back to thinking about the black, disgusted yuck that had settled over me in the last few days. It was a wet blanket on a day that I wanted to feel content and enjoy being outside in my space.

"Damn it!"

Gabriela looked up. Her bright chicken eyes gauged the danger level. She hadn't eaten the shoelace, just tugged on it a bit.

"You're okay." I smiled down at the hen, who blinked and ran off to join her friends. *Silly girl*, I thought.

The trail up from behind the runs and barn would lead me to the site of the remains. Been there, done that, and not wanting to go there again real soon. If I went up the path beyond the clothesline and chicken coop, I'd be climbing up to a safe place where the area hadn't been contaminated by bad things I didn't want to see. But I turned and looked off in the direction where the road would lead toward the village. Beyond the place where Ian used to saw and split firewood was the area that had held my interest during the night. Right now, it was waving me over, as if I were sixteen, and offered me a ride in a fast car. Was I a chicken like Gabriela, or was I made of sterner stuff? If I had the guts, I'd walk past the last few logs that Ian hadn't gotten to. From there, I'd be headed up toward where I'd seen the flashing lights.

I tapped my foot a bit more. Then, after making sure I had my phone and it was fully charged, I snapped Buttercup's harness on her. The leash dangled from my rear pocket, but I wouldn't need it soon, I suspected, unless I came up on some unwary hiker, or the depositing ground for more remains. I gave Rex a nice big cookie and apologized for not taking him. As I walked towards the open place in the trees, I shook the bird feeder, sending seeds to the ground to ensure that Gabriela and her biddy buddies would stay behind as well.

I climbed the ledge, unsure of how far up the trail the flashing pinpoint of light had been. I questioned myself every time I came to a turnoff.

"Should we go there?" I asked my porcine friend.

It was getting toward mid-morning, and the day was warming up. Buttercup had slowed down and taken to muttering nasty little things under her breath. The snap in her tail was not a happy one. I couldn't decide if I was on a true path toward the narrow ledge or if I had wandered off. Even if I couldn't tell which way the night walker had gone, at least there was no getting lost up here. All I had to do was head down.

Finally, Buttercup stopped altogether. She went to the ground as if I had yanked the bones out of her. I tried coaxing, but she harrumphed at me and looked away.

Sitting on a stump beside her as she rested, I considered our hike.

"Why am I trying to find evidence someone was up here in the middle of the night?" I asked aloud. "Am I seriously thinking they left a business card for me? *Oh, hello, Doris. Yes, I was here. See you soon.*"

I got a grunt in response.

"Maybe it was some thrill seeker, somebody innocent. Or even the cops on recon, right?"

I didn't even get a grunt that time.

Then, the little nugget buried deep in the pit of my stomach surfaced. The few words I didn't want to say out loud bubbled up.

"Or—and you're not going to like this one—maybe whoever was up here was the killer, looking for some piece of evidence he's afraid the sheriff will find. Or worse than that, looking for a place to stash his next victim."

I was up on my feet and ready to go. Buttercup may not have appreciated my physically urging her up, but once we got going and she deduced we were headed home, she knew the way.

Chapter Ten

"Ah, Melanie," I said, sliding into her office.

"Mmpht?" she said, then waved at me for silence.

Part of the deal for her work-at-home job is that she's supposed to be in a place with total security. No one can walk in and overhear. It has to have a private telephone line; she has to use the computer they furnish. Yada yada yada. I stayed still until I heard her say thank you, and she gave me the tell-me-quick hand signal before she picked up the next call.

"Do you have the list of people at the cove party for Sheriff Neddel?" I asked, all in a rush.

"Hello, this is Melanie. How may I help you?"

In a moment, a single sheet of paper flew over her head.

I rescued the missive before Royally got it, ran upstairs, made a copy, and with Royally riding shotgun, headed for town. Using my copy—not the sheriff's, which I didn't bring because I didn't want to take the chance of getting it dirty before I got it to him—I checked off the young people I didn't know or had no idea how to find. There were still more names listed than I'd probably be able to find in a couple of hours.

I decided to start with girls who worked in town. But as I drove down Main Street, I looked through the plate-glass window of the bank and through the bars within. A whole gaggle of young men had formed a snorting, laughing knot in the lobby. I couldn't hear them, but guys are like male birds, bobbing, strutting, and puffing out their chests.

The bank was across the street from the sheriff's office. I didn't see any cruisers parked along the front curb, but there was probably restricted parking in the rear of the single-story brick building. Feeling pretty sure of myself, I pulled into a diagonal space right across the sidewalk from the big sign that announced there was a sheriff on the property, and this was what his tin badge looked like. Woo-hoo.

The sheriff's building was newer than most of the others lining Main Street. Fortunately, the architect had taken into consideration the town's personality, and created a design with a facade that blended in nicely. As opposed to the garish glass-and-metal lump at the end of the street that housed the medical and dental offices.

I entered the bank behind Mrs. Peabody. She's something like six feet tall and five feet around. She teaches fifth grade. Nobody, not even the parents, messed with her.

Safely camouflaged behind her flowing, flowery dress, I eyeballed the testosterone club. All mid-twenties to thirty, athletic-looking, and from the sound of them, probably unfettered. There were a couple of guys in the group I recognized and wanted to talk to. As I made my spur-of-the-moment deposit of twenty-seven dollars, I tried to figure out how to separate one from the herd. Only one of them seemed to notice my white Jeep Patriot through the window. I watched as this same male tweaked his positioning slightly so he could watch the SUV. The guy was Noah.

I was going to want to talk to him eventually, but I didn't want him sticking his nose into what I was doing canvasing around town at that moment. Besides, he was at my house on a regular basis. I could catch him there. I was close enough to the group to hear when one of the guys spoke to Noah. Still hiding behind Mrs. Peabody, I took a quick peek.

"Hey, buddy, did you hear what I just said?" Trevor Simmons jostled him.

Noah turned, smiling widely, displaying straight white teeth with nary a sharpened incisor to be seen.

"Yeah, I got it," he said. "We're going mudding Sunday. And this time I have to ride with you. Which, of course, means we're going to lose."

Back slapping and goodbyes followed before Noah left the bank.

I had no way of knowing if he had been watching the jeep earlier to see if Melanie was around. He zigzagged across the traffic. It looked like he was headed toward the sheriff's office. For a second, I wondered why. I was standing in the doorway of the bank, someone said excuse me, and Travis squeezed past on his way out. I followed him. Once on the sidewalk, I hustled to catch up.

"Hey, Travis," I said. "Can I walk with you?"

He smiled back at me. "Sure, you can. I'm just going back to work."

"That's fine. I see all you young guys are still buddies?"

"Huh?" he asked.

Okay, we're all done talking about guy stuff. Let's move on, I thought. "I saw you in the bank with Russel and Robert. Oh, and Noah."

"Yeah, we're going mudding. It's going to be awesome." His head bobbed, and he had that kind of too-much-food-and-sensory-overload look guys get on Thanksgiving and Superbowl Sunday.

"I bet it is," I said. "Listen, I don't want to take up a lot of your time. But do you remember last spring when you guys had a bonfire party down at the cove, and Melanie was there? She was visiting, and Noah took her. Later on, she got sick, and her dad came out to get her."

"Yeah," he said. "I remember that kind of." He slowed down, and I thought he was trying to pull the memory back. Then he said, "I'm sorry about Mr. Flynn. He was a good guy."

I got a little choked up, but knew I had to push past it.

"Thank you." I touched his arm as we walked. "Anyway, do you remember anybody passing around a bottle or a cooler with some kind of fruity sherbert drink in it?"

"Nope, just suds and wine," he said.

"Ah-ha." We were getting close to the garage, where he was the grease monkey closest to being in the pit. "How about that nice young forester from away?" I asked. "I'll bet you're the one who introduced him to Melanie."

Travis stopped and looked me right in the face. He's maybe only an inch taller than I am, but he seemed much bigger right then. A chill ran down my spine. I wanted to run, and I couldn't do it.

"Not me. I didn't want him there, that drug-smoking piece of trash. Back then, Jesse and I were making plans to get hitched that summer. I told her to stay away from him, and to tell her friends, too."

"Why?" I sounded a little high-pitched.

"Like I just said, drugs. He's from where they grow up all cartel, and God only knows what else. Kidnapping babies and selling them, most likely. It's good he took off. Things could have gotten bad here, you know?"

I didn't. This sounded like a grade-B movie. I couldn't tell what shocked me more, the venomous tone in Travis's voice, or the possibility that I had totally misread Juan. Travis was a good guy. I knew he was. I had known him as a child. Where had this bigoted racial bully come from? I had to wet my lips before I could speak, because now, I had more questions.

"That all sounds really bad. Who warned you about him?"

"I don't remember, but I think we all just knew it." He turned toward the open garage doors.

I couldn't help noticing that his hands were in tight fists. Small engine parts were going to be in danger.

"Say hello to Jesse for me," I called out as I backed away, smiling to try to defuse the situation. I couldn't remember if Jesse, another friend of Melanie's, was on the list.

"I will. Take care of yourself." The words were gloomy and seemed more ominous than the conversation.

He was gone, and I was sweating. I was used to the local old-timers being small-minded with their all-white, male, republican bias, but this was a young guy. A friend of Melanie's. I'd expected him to be open-minded, not coming off, like he felt across the board that anyone from below the Texas border was hauling drugs and involved in all manner of no good. I swiped my hand across my forehead, trying to remember the last time I'd seen him around where Melanie was.

Crossing the street, I went into the hardware store. With my few purchases in hand, I looked around until I saw Russel. Then I had to take a couple of deep breaths. I was walking into a situation where Melanie was going to be angry if she found out. But my conversation with Sheriff Neddel had me worried that Ian and I had glossed over something dangerous. My mom mind wanted to know.

I asked him about his folks, then sidled the conversation over to the fruit punch and Juan Noche. I got the same answers and the same angry response.

What was with these guys?

I'd try one more person that afternoon. Somebody who I knew wouldn't scare the living crap out of me. My nerves felt all jangled. I wasn't sure if it was because both of these guys had been so adamant, or if I was worried Melanie had been terribly wrong about Juan and Neddel needed to know.

In the beauty shop, Zoe was finishing up a dye job with foils on one of her customers. Her name was on my list.

"Wow, Zoe, look at you!" I smiled. "When are you going to have that little bundle of joy?"

"Oh, my gosh, Mrs. Flynn, I've got another five months. But at this rate, I'll be as big as the high school gym by the time I pop."

I sat in the empty chair, chatting with her and Missy Shaw, until Zoe tucked Missy under the dryer.

"You've got that bee-in-a-bonnet look on your face," Zoe said, cleaning her combs. "What's up?"

"Do you remember those young guys from the southwest who were here working with the town?" I asked. "There was one that used to hang around with your crowd, I think."

"Forestry, not the town." Zoe corrected me.

She had always been quick. The one in the crowd who figured out how to get around the parents before the old folks knew something was up.

"Okay. Forestry. What can you tell me about him?"

"His name was...Juan. He was very nice, polite. He rented from the Otis's. You know, one of those cabins they winterized as apartments, or whatever they called them. Why are you asking?"

"To be honest, Melanie was speaking about him a while back. Later on, I ran into a few other people who said things that are causing me to be concerned."

"Because you're worried about Melanie, right? Where her head is right now?" Zoe sat in Missy's vacated chair, crossing her legs. "I'm willing to bet your other sources were all guys."

I nodded. Melanie had mentioned more than once that Tell-a-Zoe was better than an email list.

"Well, let me tell you this: the dry seasons between skiing and the tourists arriving are the only time those twits realize they have wives and girlfriends sitting around on their hands. Then they're all about how big and strong they are. How all us little women need them. Oh, help me, help me." Zoe fluttered her hands over her head. "They hated Juan. He was different, had a cute accent, and actual manners. A gentleman. They were all jealous, because they're just ski bums. He never moved on any of us. I mean, he was always talking about his girl back home and their plans. *And* he was educated enough to hold a conversation." The timer went off, and she climbed down. "Don't let any of that blather upset you. Trust Melanie."

"Thanks, Zoe. You're right. I am worried about Melanie. You should come over for a little hen party before the big day. I'll get Melanie started on it."

Zoe gave me a hug before I went out the door.

There didn't seem to be any middle of the road. People hated Juan Noche, or they didn't. The dividing line as I saw it was jealous males versus open-minded females. No, that wasn't nice. True, but not nice.

I walked slowly back towards my car, creating the mental picture in my head. All of Melanie's female friends, standing on one side, and her guy friends on the other. In the middle was a single man. I pictured him like a rugged gaucho: Stetson, chaps, boots, standing with his hip jutted out, hands on said hips, a dangerous grin that screamed, come hither.

Okay, stop that right now. I was giving myself a hot flash.

But that's exactly what I saw as the problem. All those females were looking at this stranger, dressed in something that wasn't a ski parka, maybe with a soft drawling accent, and they were attracted like butterflies to a Dinner-plate Dahlia. I was sure there were some who blew off the mention of his girl back home and who had tried to tempt him to be more than a friend. Meanwhile, the guys who had known each other their entire lives, did everything together, and had a tendency to play follow-the-leader, felt threatened.

During summer seasons, a couple of local businesses brought in green-card labor. The year Melanie was a senior, there had been several in that group from Ukraine. Melanie brought two of the girls home with her all the time. They'd gone places together and still kept in touch. But the guys were different. There were three I could remember. I never saw them hanging around with local guys, and other than Sergei, the chef who helped out once at a church supper, I don't think I ever actually met them.

Having a big ski resort and the hiking trail system right here in the area, there were often tourists around. If they were here for four days, that was a long time. The forestry training was a six-month stint. According to Melanie, all the trainees were gone, except Mike.

I needed to talk to Mike, but I also needed to speak to an open-minded local guy to find out more. And I knew where one worked, right down the street.

Chapter Eleven

I got almost as far as the diner when Sheriff Neddel hailed me from across the street. He came trotting over, and I shook my head.

"It'll be hard for you to get the locals to obey the laws, if you keep breaking them, Sheriff Jaywalker."

He kind of blushed. I caught myself smiling, He wasn't bad looking, and he had a nice smile. Then I thought of Ian and sobered up. My husband had been dead only a year! What was I thinking? Where were my loyalties?

"I've been looking for you," he said.

"How did you know I was here?" My brows pulled together.

"Ah. Your car is parked in front of my office," he said.

I think I might have gaped. "You can tell one nondescript white Jeep Patriot from another?"

"Okay," he whispered, looking from side to side like he was about to relay some kind of major secret. I leaned forward, holding my breath. "Here's the thing. They all have different license plates."

"You're a dweep," I said, pulling back and swatting at him like he was a black fly.

"Yes, but a dweep with a badge. Do you have a few minutes to spare?"

At my affirmative answer, he suggested we pick up coffee that we could actually drink without gagging from the diner and then retire to his office. He had information he wanted to share with me.

In the comfort of Neddel's office, Royally was shredding crumbled balls of paper that the deputy on desk duty tossed to him.

"How did you get in here?" I asked my hound as he came running over, tongue lolling out.

"He was my insurance in case you tried to leave before I found you," said Neddel.

I had a scathing retort to bark out, but he wasn't done.

"You left your dog in your vehicle, ma'am. For his protection, I removed him from said auto."

"For crying out loud. It's barely fifty-five degrees right now, and all the windows are down." Even though I knew I was right, I felt more than a little guilty.

Neddel laughed. "I didn't even have to open the door. He literally jumped out the window into my arms."

My jaw dropped. I had never considered the short-legged corgi could escape.

"Thank you," I said, duly chastised. "I'll be more careful in the future."

Royally danced around in front of me. He could smell coffee, which meant the possibility of toast or pastry.

Instead, Neddel guided us into his office. Seated behind his desk, with the door shut, he lifted a small control panel, which looked like a miniature keyboard, off the shelf behind him.

"Everything that happens in this office when a victim or a perpetrator is brought in is taped." He threw his thumb toward a posted notice hanging on the wall that said so. "It's all mostly confidential, but like it says on the sign, anything can be used as evidence in the lawful prosecution of a crime."

"O-kay."

Reaching down, I scratched the top of Royally's head. Looking up, I spotted the camera lens attached to the wall. Right out in the open, above the sheriff's chair. I wondered if it was filming me at that very moment.

"Remember, I told you I'd get some gossipy old ladies and the like?" asked Neddel. "Well, I've had some other odd visitors as well."

He looked down at his watch and stood up. "Hold that thought. I have to talk to one of the deputies before shift change. I'll be right back."

Neddel was no sooner out the door than I suddenly heard someone talking and realized there was a small television off to the side. In the corner was a small, blinking sign showing a date and time.

The tape had been made earlier that day, less than two hours earlier.

I glanced toward the door. The TV-thing had just started all by itself, and I was sure I shouldn't be seeing it. I started to get to my feet, but quickly sat back down again. On the screen, Noah was smiling, once again displaying his excellent dental work. I could just see the square set of Neddel's shoulders under his uniform shirt, the lens filmed from over his shoulder. I made another short move toward the door. Then curiosity grabbed me, and I sat back down.

"Hello, Sheriff," I heard Noah say. "I'm Noah Deyak. I'd like to speak with you for a moment. I don't have an appointment, but if you have time, I would be most appreciative, sir. I don't know if you remember me? I'm a friend of Melanie and Doris Flynn."

At the sheriff's nod, Noah continued.

"Melanie told me you were asking her about some events that happened last summer and a guy who used to live here. Juan something."

"Shut the door, Noah," Neddel said. "Have a seat."

"I only have a few minutes. I ran over from work." Noah perched on the edge of the gray steel and vinyl chair. "Melanie said she told you about a bonfire party we attended last spring. She said she had some concerns because she had blank spaces in her memory. Her dad, Mr. Flynn—he died not long afterward—said it had something to do with the MS."

Neddel made a note.

"Anyway. I took Melanie to the party. She wasn't getting out much. Mrs. Flynn was concerned Melanie was closing down."

"Okay," Neddel said. "Go on."

"We had been there a while, and I went to get her a hot dog and chips. When I came back, she was talking to this foreign guy."

"Foreigner?" asked Neddel. "I heard he was from New Mexico. That would make him an out-of-stater, not a foreigner."

"Okay, I guess. I'm not sure." Noah looked around again. He seemed to have lost some of his forward momentum.

I was leaning forward, Royally pinched between my calves. What the heck was Noah doing? His actions seemed shadowy, almost covert. I never considered that I had been doing pretty much the same thing up and down Main Street.

"Other people there told me he was from further south than that. Anyway, when I came back with Melanie's food, the guy was talking to her. Have to be honest, I wasn't so sure about him. I mean, he came up here with his friends, but he was hanging around where we were, not with them. She was sitting closer to the parking lot, not down on the beach where everybody else was. I waited nearby while they were talking, messing with my cell phone. Because, you know, Melanie was kind of, I don't know, fragile right then. She'd been through a lot, and I was worried she would fall for this guy. Anyway, Melanie was telling him about winters up here and how if he was from somewhere more like a desert, it would be rough."

"They were talking about weather?" Neddel asked.

"Well, actually, they were talking about snow."

I watched Noah fidget in his chair, the same one I was sitting in. He had obviously reached a point in his narrative where he was uncomfortable with what he had to say. Or maybe he thought Neddel was bored and not paying attention.

"Anyway, this Juan guy had a cocky grin on his face. I specifically remember him saying something to the effect that snow was super cool and made everything beautiful. Sheriff, I don't think he was talking about the same snow Melanie was, if you know what I mean."

It sounded to me like Noah was afraid Juan was coming on to Melanie. But she had been clear that the forestry trainee had never done that. I realized it could have just been Noah's impression, but why was he here talking to Neddel about it? This whole thing was doubly weird because, according to Neddel, the remains hadn't been identified.

"Why didn't you cut in when you first got back there with the food?" Neddel asked.

Noah blushed. "You have to know Melanie. If she'd thought I was doing exactly that, she'd gotten all on her high horse about being able to make her own decisions. Like I said, she'd been touchy since she found out about the

MS."

"Ah-huh. Then what happened?" Neddel asked.

"That's when I did cut into the conversation. I said the others were getting up a game of volleyball and asked Melanie if she wanted to play. She said no thanks. The guy didn't move. I didn't want to leave her there with him, so I picked up her plate and drink and sort of herded her down closer to the beach."

"So, you physically moved Melanie from where she was sitting to somewhere else?"

"I didn't drag her, if that's what you mean." Noah's brows came together.

"Is it possible the guy followed her?"

"I didn't see him again."

"But you saw Melanie?"

Noah blushed. "I'm afraid I got kind of caught up in the game. After a while, I went to sit with her, and she was gone. One of the other girls told me there was some problem, and her father had come to pick her up."

"A problem with Melanie?"

"No. At least, I don't think so," said Noah.

"You didn't know she'd gotten sick?"

"Not until later. I thought she was bored. Maybe feeling sorry for herself."

If Noah had been standing in front of me right then, I would have smacked him a good one.

"Who was the girl that told you she was gone?"

Noah shook his head.

"Are you and Melanie dating?" Neddel asked.

"No, sir. Well, not anymore." Noah looked away, towards the window. "She said she needed some time."

Neddel sighed. "Okay. Do you remember who brought the punch Melanie was drinking? Or somebody lugging around a cooler?"

"You mean like punch-bowl punch?" Noah's face screwed up. "I don't remember any punch. Melanie was drinking Pepsi. She can't have alcohol anymore because of the meds. The only cooler I saw was filled with food."

Neddel leaned back, twiddling a pen. "You know, Noah. I think you might have been more perceptive than a bunch of those other guys." He reached out with the pen and lightly tapped the edge of the desk. "If I understand you correctly, you thought Juan was talking about drugs. Specifically, cocaine."

"Yeah." Noah let out a sigh. "Listen, I won't lie. When I was younger, I messed around some with weed. The feeling it left me with, like I had no control, scared the shit out of me. That was as far as I went. I don't mind a good beer buzz, but I don't want to lose my mind to drugs. I guess I'm too much of a chicken." He gave an embarrassed laugh and looked away.

"Do you think there were others at the party doing drugs?" Neddel asked.

"Mostly the guys from out of town." Noah got to his feet. "Sorry, I have to get back to work, or my boss is going to have a fit."

I could see the top of Neddel's pen as he twirled it. Then the tape ended. The screen stayed gray, occasionally flickering.

I felt numb all over. I'd trusted this kid and left the two of them alone all the time, hoping Melanie would see what a good guy he was. How stupid was I? Now I'd just heard that Melanie had been someplace dangerous, and he'd left her on her own so he could play volleyball. This was the first I had heard that there had been out-of-town guys at this party. Where had her friends been?

I wanted to believe Noah was trying to help, but his testimonial had been disjointed. First, he was watching out for my daughter, concerned she might be susceptible to a stranger. Then he was talking about drugs like she wouldn't have any idea. Didn't he know what she did for a living? By the time Noah had gotten back to the heartbroken swain part, he was as confusing to listen to as I felt right then. I didn't know what it all meant.

I was sitting there, doubting my parenting abilities, as Neddel walked in. He put the control panel back, and must have hit stop while he did so, because the television shut off.

I knew he'd set me up to hear the tape. Maybe he was waiting for me to react. What I needed was to get out, write it down, and sort through it.

"Now, where was I? Oh yeah, Melanie is making a list for me. Did you bring it with you?"

Neddel sat behind his desk, twiddling his pen, acting like we were sharing social tea. I looked across at him, trying to act like my whole life hadn't changed in the last five minutes, but behind my eyes, I was jumping around like a rabbit trapped by a snake.

I shook my head, mouth too dry for words. I wanted to get up and leave. It took a supreme effort to continue the conversation.

"Has traffic picked up out at your place? Are you getting odd phone calls, people knocking at the door? Anything that's making you nervous?"

I swallowed hard. "There are more cars, I guess, but that's it." I started to get to my feet. Then paused as I thought about the lights, but I didn't say a word. I just didn't have it in me to talk to him anymore. I wanted to go home and be where Melanie was. To lock my doors and forget all this. Nothing else felt important.

Ten minutes later, Royally and I were backing into traffic. Once I was on Calwin Mountain Road, I calmed down a little and let the car idle along while I thought about what I had seen.

"I'm sure," I told Royally, "that normally no one is supposed to see those tapes." I gave a humorless laugh. "Somebody should tell Neddel his acting skills are non-existent. I mean, it was a chintzy set-up he pulled, but the question is why did he want me to hear what Noah had to say? Because there's more than Melanie said? Or so I'd know I shouldn't trust him?"

There had been a feverish light in Noah's eyes. His feigned innocence was a sad sack act, no better than Neddel's. It almost seemed like he was pleading for Neddel to trust him. But why? My foot slammed down on the brake sending Royally flying off the seat and onto the floor. Who had given Melanie a spiked drink? How innocent was Noah? Royally whined. I pulled over to make sure he was okay. My hands were shaking. The entire experience had left me tensed up. I had never seen this Noah before. As a mature adult, I wanted to believe I didn't take everyone or everything I heard at face value. But in all the time I had been touting Noah's finer points to Melanie, I don't think I had ever considered him having some less-than-desirable traits.

We were a quarter of a mile from the house, right in front of Bernhardts. But now I was sitting in the back seat of my own car on the side of the road. I had lifted Royally off the floorboards and was hugging him close, giving him the full baby treatment. He was lapping it up, sad puppy eyes and everything. I kissed his nose. He nuzzled my chin. We were comforting each other, and believe me, he knew it long before I did. Reaching over the seat, I pulled my copy of Melanie's list out of my shoulder bag.

"Let's see, Royally, who we can check off this list."

Melanie had listed mostly just her close friends. I'd interviewed almost half. But I'd been to those kinds of parties in my own youth. I was sure there were more than eight or nine people. I was going to have to make some calls. Noah was out. He'd only gotten half a check. I wasn't ready to check him totally off. I wasn't done with him.

"I should have brought Neddel's copy of the list with me. Now, I bet he's going to drive out here for it, and I don't want to talk to him anymore."

I got back in the front seat. Royally smiled happily in the rear-view mirror. I just knew he'd be telling Buttercup how much sugar he'd gotten, while she got zip.

Chapter Twelve

I'd like to say I was wrong about Neddel coming out, but I looked out the kitchen window a few hours later, and bingo. When he pulled into the driveway, it was that low time of day when everything seemed oddly quiet, like the world was at rest. Melanie was out on the deck, resting. No pig, no chicken ran to see who the company was. I watched him get out of the car, even considered not answering the door, but then, Melanie was right out there.

"Mom, the sheriff is back," she called out.

I'm sure he heard her, but when I opened the screen door, he didn't appear offended.

"You know," he said, smiling at Melanie and Lilo lying on the lounge chair. "It's so wrapped in cotton quiet out here, I bet you can hear grass growing."

Suddenly, there was a hair-raising screech, snarl, and a growl as one feline pitted itself against another. We all flinched. Neddel stopped dead in his tracks.

"Maybe I should get back in my car. It might be safer," he said.

One last screeching wail blasted out of the living room. There was a flurry of feline fingernails racing down the hallway, skittering into the banister, a thump as one pounced off, and the noise went up the stairs. The roar subsided to a low hissing.

I turned my head to listen. It didn't sound like anyone suffered a mortal wound. Turning back, I asked, "What do you need, Sheriff Neddel?"

I didn't want to invite him into my home, so I stepped outside and sat down, enfolded in the voluminous yards of canvas that make up the slingback hammock chair. Neddel stepped onto the deck. I could tell he was still evaluating the ruckus from inside.

"What was all that about?" he asked, friendly, like he hadn't noticed the get-out-of my-yard attitude.

"One little old lady cat telling another to get off her turf," I said.

He just nodded. After a beat, he spoke. "I came out because I'd like to talk to Melanie again."

I nodded. He stood there. Melanie watched us both. Royally had followed me out, and though he hadn't made a sound, a small tuft of hair rose on the back of his neck.

I figured Neddel's silence was him telling me I didn't need to stand guard. I said I'd take Rex and Buttercup over to the orchard for a little walk.

Melanie looked a little apprehensive. He looked in her direction. I knew where I saw my child grow to adulthood, adjusting to each new day. He was seeing an attractive young woman dressed in thrift shop rejects. She was lying in the sun wearing a worn-out pair of University of Southern Maine sweatpants and a Chicago Bears sweatshirt. She also wore a big set of white and gray headphones, which gave her rounded ears like a bear cub.

"Nice accessories," said Neddel.

"Yeah, ignore that," she said before turning to me. "Where are you going, Mom?" Like she hadn't heard me.

There was a pitcher of iced tea on the table and one clean glass. I poured him a drink before plunking my butt back down. It was evident that Melanie was okay talking with the sheriff, but not so good being alone with him. She may have thought an interrogation was forthcoming. Neddel seemed to read her concern.

He looked from her, now sitting on the lounge, to me back in the hammock chair. I became intensely concerned with the status of the cuticle on my right thumb.

"I wanted to be clear to you, Ms. Flynn, and to your mother, that during the course of my investigation, your names might come up."

My eyebrows arched.

"There are times when I'm out there interviewing persons of interest. Or even people who might have insights, or those that contact the department to offer information..."

Higher arch.

"...that relates in a roundabout manner to individuals connected to the case."

I really wanted to ask him what he was yammering about. Fortunately, Melanie had the same question, and she spit it out.

"So," she said, studying an ant crossing the deck, "somewhere along the line, somebody offered you information about, oh, let's see...me. And you want to know if it's true or not? Am I understanding what you are asking in whatever convoluted cop language you are using? And are you considering me a suspect in Juan's murder?"

Her reference to being a suspect had me swallowing a lump of bile, that had risen suddenly.

"You're pretty close on the first part," Neddel said with a sigh. "But currently, I'm not considering you a suspect. However, what I have is the opinion of several people regarding your position at the last known sighting of Juan Noche."

My head snapped up. I thought I'd just sit there like a bump in the chair and not engage in the conversation. With what Neddel had just said, that was going to be difficult. It sounded like a positive identification of the remains had been made. I had been out of the loop for the last day or so, and if this news had come across the airways, I'd missed it.

"Are you referring to my friendship with Juan, or alluding to something from the cove party that probably didn't actually happen? Or perhaps some donkey-minded idiot told you how I was suffering right now." Melanie paused. In one fluid motion, she pushed herself upright off the lounge chair. "Are you referring to my mental health?" Her voice had risen two octaves. "That's it, isn't it? Some person, who professed to be my good friend, told you they were concerned about my, and by extension, my mother's, mental health because of the traumatic incidents occurring in this household over the last year, which couldn't possibly be anything anyone else would *ever* experience. Let me tell you what I do for a living."

Uh-oh. My daughter was on a roll now. When others, a lot of them medical personnel, challenged her abilities and where her life was going, she'd gotten on this soapbox. We would be sitting together, and they would address me about her, like she wasn't there. She was quick to let them know; she knew what was going on, and she had a plan.

"I went to college to be a pharmacy tech. I'm not a pharmacist, though I might have gone that route, eventually. My job for a while in a pharmacy setting was to assist my boss, the one who made the big bucks. The closest I got to drugs was passing the paper bag over the counter. Now, I'm not even in the same building. I liked my job. I worked in a good place, had plenty of benefits, my own apartment. It was all hunky-dory until the day a big, green explosion happened in my brain."

There was an edge to Melanie's words. I was ready to intervene if some kind of meltdown occurred. This was the first time she'd ever reacted to her story with such anger. I knew she was coming on pretty strong, but I held my seat.

"For ten years, I thought I had Lyme's disease. You know, from a tick bite. Then I had this major episode. I spent eight days in the emergency room until a doctor with a brain suggested a spinal tap. That's how they find multiple sclerosis, by identifying the little damaged pieces of nerve sheath floating in your spinal fluid. Finally, we had a true prognosis. It wasn't a great one, but after ten years of searching in the dark, I could move ahead. I came home for a few days, then I went back to my own place and back to work."

I had to give Neddel credit. He didn't flinch as Melanie spit out the words.

"My department head, Mrs. Avery, is a wonderful woman. Kind and compassionate. I spent an hour and a half with her explaining what I knew, and it was, at that point, still very random. There were some suggestions my neurologist offered to help me adjust. Mrs. Avery was all into helping me do that. I thought I might actually be able to go on as I had. Then, my dad passed away. As if my mother didn't have enough to deal with, I had another episode. Stress and MS don't cohabitate well.

"My mother came to stay with me. A week grew into ten days. All the time she was there, somebody else, our friends here, stepped in and helped keep the farm together. It was tearing my mother up. The loss of Dad, my new physical limitations, the knowledge she'd have to give up her lifestyle, and ultimately *all* the animals to take care of me."

Even though I had been watching Melanie as she spoke, I had to look away. It was too painful. I had never told her these things, but she's perceptive, this girl of mine.

Melanie continued, "While I was in my apartment recovering, going to physical therapy so I could speak clearly, walk, do small motor stuff, and even get exercise for my eyes, my boss, Mrs. Avery, came to visit me several times. Mom was going to come home, farm out the critters, and close the house. I couldn't let her do that, knowing I wasn't even sure how I could work more than a couple of hours a day. I told Mrs. Avery, with my mother sitting right there, that I was moving back here."

Neddel looked at me. I couldn't meet his eyes. When Melanie had told Mrs. Avery she was leaving her job and moving in with me, I had been blindsided. I think we had both known her getting by might be an issue, but if it came to me staying where she was so she could continue, at least for a while, I was willing to do it. She never asked. She just told that lovely woman she had made the decision to leave.

"Mrs. Avery told me to stop talking," said Melanie. "Then she said she wanted to talk to me like my friend, not as the representative of the company I worked for."

Melanie was wandering around now, not really pacing, but not standing still for longer than a second, either.

"So, she explained to me there were a lot of side issues in the business world I had no knowledge of, and unless I had a lawyer, I might never know. She told me the company couldn't fire me. This wasn't a pre-existing condition I had kept hidden from them. It never showed up on my pre-hire physical. She had brought information that talked about insurance support that was available to me, as well as my rights under the Family Medical Leave Act and the Employees with Disabilities Act.

"Her generosity meant that when I met with HR, I was ready to ask them to change the type of job I did so that I could still work. HR stepped up and offered me a position where I could work from home. And as long as I met the company's requirements, I could work less than a straight eight-hour day."

Neddel looked confused.

Melanie huffed in frustration. "In other words, I could work four hours, take a two-hour break, work another four."

He nodded.

"Mrs. Avery championed for me to be able to have this job. My file is filled with letters from customers thanking me for my help, congratulating the company on having hired such a knowledgeable and compassionate individual. I was an asset. Now, instead of assisting a pharmacist at the counter or prepping a prescription, I work from home, dealing with customers over the phone, doing insurance settlement research. There's an 800 number. They call, explain their problem, and usually under three minutes, I find them a resolution."

"Seriously?" asked Neddel.

"Sure. Wrong form, misspelled name, error entering client number, wrong dosage, generic available, there's a long list of what an insurance won't cover, and why. There are times it's more complicated, but you get the gist. We were able to meet all the legalities for a home office. If I have to drive down to the city, I stay with a friend and come home the next day.

"The ability for me to still work, even if I had to give up my apartment, was an enormous boost to my mental health. As time goes on, I may have to step back further, but for right now, I am whole and well. As far as my mother is concerned, yes, she has also been through a lot. But if there's one thing she is, it's strong. Mentally and physically. She also knows to ask for help if she needs it. My grandmother's favorite saying was, Take it with a grain of salt. It means, accept what people say to you, then draw your own conclusions instead of blindly accepting theirs. That's a problem for a lot of people around here and probably all over the world. Do you have any other questions?"

"Only one," Neddel said. "The unofficial report is the remains are those of Juan Noche. We're waiting for dental records. This isn't information we're putting out there. Yet, I'm hearing his name being thrown around. The folks I've talked to at the forestry and from his group have key-holed his last activity as being the party at the cove. I need to know everyone who was there, no matter what their status is."

Melanie bit her lip. "My list is short. I just don't remember, and I never really got down to where everyone else was."

"So, you stayed up near where the cars were parked?" Neddel asked.

"No." Melanie paused. "My memory is so murky. I just don't know."

"Okay."

"Is there something else?" she asked.

"No, you pretty well covered it," said Neddel.

"Before I go back to work, I have a question for you," Melanie said. "How far can we trust you not to destroy our lives while you're trying to round up Juan's killer?"

Neddel put his empty glass aside. "Let me tell you about *my* job. A lot of the knowledge or information I gather to work with is in confidence. But be aware that every man has his limits. Anyone who tells you they would never do an illegal thing is either lying through their teeth or has such a big head their feet don't touch the ground. I am sworn to my duty, and I've yet to cross that line. On the other hand, if I caught my mother speeding, I would probably only write her a warning. Unless she was going to bingo."

"Thank you," said Melanie, exiting gracefully.

"Well, that wasn't what I expected," I said.

Neddel moved toward the steps.

"There's another thing," he said. "While we're talking about job responsibilities. One of mine is to keep the population safe while I try to find out why something went wrong. Or find the person or persons that caused the rift, the type of thing where one person says everything is good, and another tells me I just sat down with the devil." He looked directly at me. "Like I said, I hear things. I will know when someone is poking around where they shouldn't be. I'm going to tell you straight out. Step back. I wouldn't want either you or Melanie to be in danger. A few casual questions are one thing.

90

Rattling the cage is something else. Just remember, I'm always trying to figure out the truth. Usually, I ask people if I need clarification. Sometimes I get a crock of bull, so maybe later, I ask the same thing from a different direction. No matter the answer, I keep at it until I have the truth."

"Okay," I said. "I'm thinking you have a burning question in your gut you want to ask me."

"It's about the pig." The tips of his ears turned red. "I don't understand the in the house thing."

I was rather stunned. It wasn't what I had expected at all. I got up walking down onto the back lawn. He followed. Across the yard, Buttercup was stretched out in the sun on a grassy spot. Rex, free-ranging today on the overhead runner chain, was lying with his head on her shoulder. Even the hens seemed to want to get in on the cuddle. They were crowding their fence at the spot closest to the pig and dog.

"Ever have a dog?" I asked. "One you got as a puppy? One who thought the sun rose and set within you?"

"Yes, of course."

"Most dog breeds live ten to twelve years. Corgis eight to eleven. We had a mutt that went sixteen. Melanie almost cried herself to death when Pete died. Hampshire pigs can live as long as twelve years. Buttercup came to us as a healthy, twenty-pound piglet. She was just too big and too much for the city people who had bought her. They had seen something on TV about potbellied pygmy pigs and believed some salesman's story. I don't know what they were expecting."

I sat on the step. Neddel sat beside me. So close I could feel the heat from his shoulder on mine, and I wasn't offended.

"When I brought her home, Melanie was all over her. Treating her like a baby, like a new little sister or something. Gave her bubble baths, played with her, taught her to come when she was called, all that. But everything she did was guarded. Like she expected the piglet to be gone at any moment."

"Like die?" Neddel asked.

"Yeah. Or maybe, like Rex, she'd go to a different forever home." All the time I spoke, I watched Buttercup. I knew she could hear me talking just by the way her ears tilted. She had no idea she was the subject of our conversation, but she knew I was right there, and she was keeping track.

"Anyway, Melanie was all grown up, already in college, and ready for the next big step. Yet, as far as Buttercup was concerned, Mel was still my little girl. And to Melanie, Buttercup was more than a normal pet."

"How so?"

"Melanie made Ian modify Buttercup's home pen and open it to the outside so the pig could come and go at will. She did all this online research on pig feeding. My kitchen was covered with printouts. But the big thing was that, at night, Buttercup had to come in the house to sleep."

Neddel moved a little on the step, probably to work that info into his brain. Finally, he asked, "Where was Melanie when Pete died?"

"It was a hot and oppressive night in the fall. Melanie had stayed at the college that night instead of coming home so she and a friend could go to a concert. Pete was sleeping on the screened-in porch. He could have come through into the house if he'd wanted. But he stayed there." I gave a little choked laugh. "I told Ian I thought Pete was waiting for Melanie. And it would be a long night."

I had to stop talking. The memory still broke my heart.

"Ian found him the next morning. By the time Melanie got home, Ian had built a coffin and dug a grave. Out there." I nodded with my head. "Those are Pete's lilacs."

I stood up and walked away, feeling like an old fool. My eyes were full of tears. I didn't need this almost stranger seeing them. Neddel walked along, a step behind me.

"So, Melanie thought, if Buttercup slept in the house, she'd be safe," he said finally.

"Yes. They were great buddies. When Melanie got her job and moved, she was so excited. She kept telling Buttercup that she'd come back every weekend. Of course, that didn't happen. It was okay, though. Buttercup was still young. Her affection transferred over to me, and like Melanie, I let her sleep in the house. She doesn't roam free everywhere. She knows the kitchen is as far as she should go, though sometimes, if the gate is down, she'll wander down the hall.

"So, you see, the reason a four-hundred-and-fifty-pound pig thinks she's a lapdog is because that's what we taught her."

Opening the car door, Neddel looked over the roof toward the snoozing pig. "I had this one dog when I was a kid. A twelve-inch beagle. My grandmother gave him to me for Easter. My mother was not impressed. His name was Bagel, the Easter Beagle. For a time, I wouldn't take a bath if he couldn't get in the tub. Drove my parents nuts."

I watched the cruiser drive down the road. Tired of napping, Buttercup and Rex wandered over.

I rubbed both heads at the same time. "I think," I said slowly, "the sheriff and I just had a moment."

* * *

It was a surprise to see Shane's vehicle pull into the driveway, even though he lived just up the road over his parents' garage. I would have thought he'd be following Burt Kennett from corpse to cadaver and back.

I was just coming out of the house, with Melanie behind me in the doorway. Buttercup left her spot in the sun to go down and greet him. When she realized I was there, too, the tail wagging really got started.

"Mom sent rhubarb sauce." He grinned. "It's early, but it looks like a banner patch this year."

"And you're staying for ice cream?" I asked with a smile.

"Gotta go. Doctor Kennett called. Fatality in the notch. I need to meet him at the morgue."

I waved goodbye. He'd said that so cheerfully.

The Davis family lived closer to town than we did. Shane was the last of four children and the only one still home. He was the only young adult besides Melanie anywhere nearby. They had ridden the school bus together, went to each other's birthday parties. As Melanie had grown, her popularity had increased, but Shane had stayed just as he had always been. He was a kid she hung around with, more bookworm than others, but always polite. I don't know how many times he'd sat at our supper table. The last few years of high school, we saw him less. He worked after school, saving toward tuition. College had been in his plan. When they were all done getting educated, Shane got a job locally, but Melanie stayed in the city. Shane had never been a guy turned boyfriend, like Noah. Instead, this tall, still a little gawky young man was the brother Melanie had never had.

* * *

"He's got a cool job, but it's also creepy," Melanie said when I mentioned Shane had been called to an accident scene. "Did you give the sheriff his list?"

"He's, ah, coming back out for it," I said. "Passing it over kind of slid under the ropes, what with everything else we'd been talking about."

"Mom!" Melanie said, exasperated to the nth.

I had left Sheriff Neddel's copy under a magnet on the side of the fridge next to the wall-mounted landline phone when I'd gone out on my little information-gathering venture. He'd asked while I was in town and again while he was standing on the deck, and still, when he'd driven off, the paper was lodged under the turnip-shaped magnet.

I suspected that between Melanie's dressing down and Buttercup's biography, the thought had gotten lost in the stratosphere.

Plucking the note down. I sat at the table, mentally checking the names again.

Melanie was scooping ice cream into a bowl when I heard a little splat, followed by the scuttling of pig feet.

"Oops," said Melanie, looking down at the vanishing blob of frozen vanilla custard with a smile.

I didn't need to look to see who was cleaning up after my oh-so-clumsy daughter. I went back to perusing the list.

"Mel, you didn't put Shane on this list," I said.

"Shane?" She looked confused.

"Yeah, the guy that just left? Brought the rhubarb sauce you're dishing onto your ice cream?"

"Oh, Mom, that's so funny. Can you imagine Shane at one of the bonfires? You know those guys are all way too jock-strappy for the likes of him." She left the room licking her spoon, with a parade of critters following.

"Jock-strappy?" Now, there was a word I had never heard before. It was, however, a perfect description.

I spent a few more minutes eyeballing the names, then looked at the clock. I had an idea and enough daylight before I had to put supper together to get it done. Snapping open my flip phone, I opened the list of contacts, stopping at the first name that was followed by a -Mel.

"Hi," I said cheerfully to the answering voice. "This is Mrs. Flynn. I'm thinking we should get together for a little potluck?"

Chapter Thirteen

With Mel and her animal groupies snacking and spoiling their supper, I went out and fired up the riding mower. My other choice was to walk, and I was feeling a little fatigued.

With the mowing deck as high off the gravel road as I could get it, I shifted into drive and laid the hammer down. I might have been moving at a fast 5.5 miles an hour. The wind was in my hair, my spirits were rejoicing, and I was flush with pride at the ingenuity of the American Woman on the Road. Now I knew how Jacob Frizzell must have felt the day the state police busted him. Of course, he had an older mower, with no headlights, and had a buzz on. He also had the mowing deck down and was throwing gravel everywhere. Ten o'clock at night on a Fourth of July weekend, and he was roaring southward in the northbound lane. I'm sure he was busting a groove right up until the DWI threat stopped him cold. Basically, I had the same feeling of empowerment. No one got hurt, and he got an air-conditioned guest room with three squares for sixty days. Like Jacob, I was on a mission. If I were a betting person, I'd say the only drawback was that neither one of us knew what our missions were.

When I reached the point where Neddel and I had hammered the first to-the-site directional sign into the ground, I lifted my right foot off the gas and swung into the turn. I might have been going a little too fast, as there were a couple of hairy nanoseconds where I shifted my weight seriously to the side, then counterbalanced. Then maybe counterbalanced the counterbalance. I'm not sure, because my life was flashing in front of my face as the tractor rocked from side to side. By the time I rumbled over the culvert, though, I was back in control. So, not to worry.

Forty feet into the woods, the trail started to climb. I was seriously losing speed. I think I could have crawled faster on all fours. At the next marker, the trail pointed left, but I went right. After that, I zig-zagged up and down every trail I came to until the gas gauge was lip-smacking close to the red. Nothing I saw jumped out and offered me a clue. Frustrated with having found nothing, I turned around for the last time and headed home.

Melanie was lying on the sofa with a bowl of popcorn balanced on her stomach and two dogs trying to crawl over her bent knees to reach the buttery treat. All the while, as she fended them off, she chortled at the goings-on of the crew on Space Balls. A family classic. I left them all there and started putting together the evening cat chow. I put Rex back in the kennel after his day out on the run and poured Buttercup's supper in the trough. You can't imagine my surprise when she didn't rush right out of the home pen to eat.

"Ach. That little bugger is in the house begging for popcorn with the rest of the moochers," I told Rex as I buttoned up the chicken coop. I called out, "Pig, pig."

Sometimes, my porky little friend could be so obstinate. I went through the kitchen and into the sitting room. Lilo and Royally were working up the courage to jump down off the sofa. Even Melanie, who had paused the movie, was getting up.

"What's for supper?" she asked.

"Where's Buttercup?" I asked.

I got a blank look and a dropped jaw for an answer. Finally, Melanie said, "With you?"

My heart dropped into my bowels. The two of us went out and looked all over the yard. Buttercup was nowhere to be found. The only explanation was that when Melanie had refused to share the popcorn, Buttercup had followed the lawn tractor and was somewhere on the side of Calwin Mountain. My four-hundred-fifty-pound lap pig, wandering around alone.

"What do we do?" Melanie was verging on hysterical. In four years, we had never once lost this pig.

I grabbed a gas can and poured fuel into the tractor, spilling some of it on my own feet. "Get Dad's megaphone. Start calling her. Try not to sound upset. You know how she is. Offer her food, peanut butter. I'll head back down to the trail. If she shows up, call me, okay?"

Melanie sniffled.

"It will be okay." I tried to sound calm and encouraging, but my stomach had fallen to the ground and was digging to China. "We'll find her. Keep using the megaphone. Let the Bernhardt's and the Davies know she's missing." I was already rolling down the drive while I was still talking.

By the time I reached the trailhead, the forest was starting to look dark and forlorn. We have coyotes, bears, and the occasional coy dog. One might not be a problem, but a pack or a sow bear with cubs would be a cause for alarm. Pulling the headlights on, I started singing my walk along with my song.

"*Doris had a little swine, little swine.*
Doris had a little swine.
As cute as cute could be."

I didn't get a lot of verses out before I was so choked up, I couldn't sing. I listened for woofs, squeaks, and the rustle of Buttercup rooting in the leaves. None of those noises came to me. Nor could I hear Melanie with her megaphone, maybe because of the tractor noise.

I don't know how long I was up there, but it felt like hours. It was so dark. I knew I had to get out, or I'd be spending the night among the flora and fauna as well. There was no stopping my tears. I had failed my big girl. My inattention had put her in danger. I headed down the mountain so blinded by grief I was snagging on saplings.

At the last turnoff, I almost went the wrong way. My phone vibrated in my back pocket. Rolling to a stop, I stood up on the mowing deck and pulled the cell phone free of the denim.

"Please," I whispered. "Let her be found."

"MOM!" Melanie screamed into the phone. "Mom! She's here. Mom, can you hear me?"

I just nodded, to overcome with emotion to speak.

"FOR CRYING OUT LOUD! MOM!"

"Okay, Melanie. I hear you. I'm on my way home." I paused, almost unwilling to ask the next question. "Is she okay? I mean, she's not gouged or clawed or anything?"

"No," said Melanie. "She just walked out of the woods and started looking for her supper."

My daughter tried to laugh, but it sounded like a sob of relief.

* * *

By the time I got back, Buttercup was done eating and tucked into her straw bed. Melanie and I stood in the barn with the fluorescent lights snapping and crackling above us, just watching her. It wasn't like she had never gotten out during the night before, but she had never left the yard to wander into the woods alone.

"I'm sorry, Ian," I whispered. He had done so much to keep Buttercup and all of our foster animals safe. All I had to do was put dinner on the table and babysit, and I hadn't even done well at that. I felt like I'd failed him.

"What?" Melanie asked.

"Let's shut off the lights and lock up," I said.

When the barn doors were secure, I walked back over to the path where Melanie had said Buttercup emerged from the forest land. I was just walking off my nervous energy and ended up headed that way. My brain was filled with immense gratitude that Buttercup had found her way home and hadn't suffered any injury.

A few yards from where the path disappeared into the bushes, I found a fairly large piece of cloth. Thinking it was a grain sack or even an item off the clothesline Buttercup had pulled down and I couldn't identify, I picked it up for disposal. Holding it up, even in the fading light, I realized right away that I was holding a pair of trousers. They were a muddy taupe color and made of gabardine. But on my way over to the burn heap, I stopped cold. These were uniform pants, like the guys from the forestry service wore. If they had burst into flames, I couldn't have dropped them faster.

Running back to the house, I asked Melanie if Buttercup had been dragging them.

"I didn't see any pants," she said. "When I first saw her, she was playing around like she always does. You know, kind of dancing. I called her, offering a snack, and she came running."

"If she brought those out of the woods with her, she might have found more," I said.

"Are you going to pick them up?" Melanie stopped, loaf of bread in hand.

When the realization that the remains were probably Juan Noche had settled on her, she had gone to her room and closed the door. From where I stood, silent in the hall, I had heard her weeping. She hadn't shared her grief with me, and now she was watching me closely, wanting to ask, but probably afraid of what I would answer. Once again, the specter of Buttercup's discovery among the ferns was rising.

"Yes. No. Wait. No, I don't want to touch them. I'll call Rose Ann and tell her. I think if this is directly related to the remains, she should be called in. Maybe she can drive over." I kept tap dancing back and forth while I worked it out. At my feet, Royally jitterbugged with me. The more wound up I got, the more nervous he was.

Rose Ann's phone went to voice mail. I left a message. We had a big tin washtub hanging on the front of the barn. I used that to cover the pants on the ground so none of the animals could touch them. I hauled a couple of man-rocks over and stacked them on top. That would keep any critter smaller than Buttercup away.

"If I don't hear from Rose Ann by the morning," I told Melanie, who was nervously chewing her cuticles, "I'll call Sheriff Neddel."

Every doctor Melanie had seen had stated she needed to avoid stress. I should have kept my mouth shut, I thought. Like high heels on an ice patch, my thoughts skittered around while I tried to figure out how to neutralize all the excitement that had been dumped in our laps in the last three hours. But while I stood in the kitchen, multi-tasking with that and trying to decide what to slap together for supper, Melanie was messing around with her laptop at the table.

"Holy cat crap," she said. "Look at this, Mom."

She had turned on the app to check out the animal cameras. This was the camera labeled ONE, the unit installed on the front of the barn that filmed down the side of the house and most of the front yard. The film was running in the darkness, with only the infrared light. Because it was a clear night and the moon was over the river, we could see the shadow—or, more accurately, the silhouette—of a person standing near the big maple. Then he moved away. The time and date stamp told us this was the night when I had walked through the house and locked the sitting-room window.

"This is bad, Mom," Melanie breathed out.

There was a hot spot in the middle of my gut. "Okay. We need to come up with a plan."

Melanie and I spent the next hour trying to attach an alarm to this older camera that would alert our cell phones.

"Why wouldn't either Rex or Buttercup let us know there was someone out there?" Melanie asked.

The frightening answer that I would not utter aloud was that the person was probably not a stranger to them.

We had tea and grilled cheese and called it an early night. Well, we both went to bed early, anyway. It took a while, then I got up and took a nice, long, hot shower, hoping it would help me to sleep. When I came out of the bathroom, Melanie and Lilo were waiting in my bed, right beside Royally.

Chapter Fourteen

Having a four-hundred-fifty-pound forager in residence made it a little iffy to figure how much produce I would be able to harvest from my garden spot. Even hiding the cultivated area across the street in the orchard hadn't worked because, besides Buttercup, there were deer, woodchucks, rabbits, and Mother Nature to figure in. But Ian and I had been tenacious. If it was going to take six-foot tall fencing, we'd find a way, preferably without having to mortgage the property to do so. We initiated a countywide dump-foraging event for chain-link fence. Ian had a wide network of friends. We sent all of them begging emails, with requests for shares, and also engaged in basic check-around-your-neighborhood conversations in town. We even took out a classified ad in the local paper.

That was how we'd ended up with an eighteen-by-forty-foot enclosure on the other side of the driveway. The eyesore of mismatched fencing and cedar post construction was no deterrent to my desire to raise tomatoes, zucchini, peas, and lettuce, among other things. Inside the house, flats of tender young plants I had started during the late winter months were asking—no pleading—to be let outside into the sun.

Leaving the gate to the garden patch open, steel rake and hoe in hand, I entered that hallowed place. The pig and chickens followed. Buttercup was going to stick right with me on this venture into a place, she could root with abandon. Today she got a limited access pass, allowing her to assist as she saw fit. It kept her close without me having to worry that after the previous days free ranging out of the yard and into the woods, she might wander away again at will.

A friend had brought her rototiller over the previous week and done the hard ground-breaking. I would smooth the lumps, haul out the clods of unwanted greenery that had invaded since last season, and, with any luck, tuck my growing vegetable stock into beds by the morrow. Buttercup and the biddies were there for moral support and any browsing or insect collection that might need to be done.

Just before the car broke cover at the edge of the yard, I heard the sound of its engine. Shading my eyes, I looked hopefully for Rose Ann, but Noah's blue Audi purred into sight. Parking nearby, he stepped up to the fencing, staying on the outer side where mud and chicken splatter wouldn't mar the shine of his shoes. The sight of him reminded me of Neddel's tape, and I felt something stronger than annoyance rising. I didn't want to talk to him or have him in the yard. I was doing inner battle because I didn't want to send him away either.

We exchanged casual greetings as I continued hacking clods. I got a cloying feeling, like wearing a wet bathing suit, that told me without turning that he was still standing right there, watching as I hacked and chopped. Sweat soaked the back of my shirt, and my breath came out in unladylike grunts.

Don't look up, I thought. *Don't make eye contact. Do not look at that washtub.*

"So, you were walking with the pig—just walking, and she found the body?"

His question caught me unawares, jarring me away from the pastel-colored place of peace my mind had been romping in earlier. There was the tiniest, little-bitty catch under the bottom edge of my wing bone, like a poison dart from a pygmy blowpipe. A lightning-fast, pointy, sharp bit of nothing that would fester, infect, and forever ruin my day.

That wasn't very kind, I chastised myself. Then my right brain whined. *Who cares? Make him go away. I don't want to think about all that bad stuff right now.*

"Yes. Actually, I was walking Rex. Buttercup was following behind. I guess the smell attracted her." *There you are. All the gruesome details you've already heard. Now go away.*

Not to be.

"But the body was, like, old, right?" Noah asked.

Why is he asking all this now? Is he fishing for something he thinks I know, but he doesn't? "According to the medicolegal crime investigator, the remains had been there from almost a year ago."

I switched from the hoe to the steel rake. Buttercup inched closer. When used with restraint, the backside of the rake offered a way for her to get a satisfying scratch. She was willing to let me practice.

"If it was up on the mountain, how could the pig smell it?" Noah persisted. "You know, from miles away."

He stood with his fingers hooked in the fencing, head turned toward the ridge leading up to Calwin Mountain. The small creepy in the center of my back started growing like refrigerator mold. I wanted to tell him the pig had a name.

"It wasn't miles away," I said. "To be honest, I would have thought she could have smelt it long before we went up there. The MCI said the lye kept the stink down."

He turned to me, eyes wide like those pictures and figurines sold as precious child portraits. "Lye? You mean, like acid?"

I wanted to close the gate with me on one side and him on the other.

"No, the type of lye you put down to sweeten the ground. Not a corrosive industrial grade."

Noah faced the ridge again.

What is he looking for? I wondered. Then I shook a little in my shoes. *He wants to see what I can see from here. If I might be able to tell if something hinky was happening on the ridge.*

My previous estimation of his character slipped another quarter of a notch. He was really creeping me out now.

Buttercup started bumping into me, demanding the rake's attention. I moved away from her, wondering if I could slip through the gate and get past Noah. I visualized myself locking doors and calling the cops, sprinkling holy water, or stringing garlic. I had to almost physically hold my head to keep it from turning toward the washtub.

I moved. Noah moved very slightly. Was that intentional? I got all the way to the gate, ready to kick off the cumbersome barn boots and run like hell.

"Hey, Mom?" Melanie stood on the edge of the deck, holding a pitcher high. "I've got lemonade and tuna rolls."

I looked back. Noah offered a happy little boy smile, obviously waiting for an invitation. I returned his grin with difficulty. Though some of the creepy had evaporated, that little anchor piece of pygmy poison held on.

We all sat at the picnic table. The tuna was wrapped in romaine instead of bread. For a little while, our meal was hassle-free because Buttercup was still snuffling around in the garden plot. There was a little flutter in Melanie's hands that indicated she was nervous. Perhaps she knew something I didn't. Had Noah said something to her that upped her radar?

"I thought you were going mudding today, Noah?" I asked around tuna and hunks of celery.

"Yeah," he said. "The guys are going. I texted Melanie asking if she wanted to go, but she said no."

This was it, I thought. The thing that had Melanie nervous. She knew I had a problem with people who didn't seem to remember or maybe think about what was safe for her. Offers were made that she turned down, knowing it wasn't good, but they always made her feel less than she was. I wasn't always able to hide my irritation.

The fluttering increased as Melanie cut in. "I told Noah I was headed down to Rochester today. I had a couple of errands and was going to go to Market Basket. He, ah, volunteered to go with me." She gave a weak smile.

I chewed on my tuna roll-up, watching Noah from under my lashes. He had to have known Melanie wouldn't go for something like four-wheeling through the mud and woods. It was physical and dirty. Before, she had always been willing to try anything, but now her ego was sensitive and easily bruised. Her father's death on the cusp of the MS diagnosis had yanked away her free spirit. But right now, my now-reclusive daughter seemed to have a second agenda going. The two of us had talked about doing the big shopping, but our plans were still up in the air.

Scooping up the lunch litter, Melanie said, "If he wants to go with me, so be it. But don't expect us for supper because I'm going to make him take me to Olive Garden."

I wondered if this ploy was due to the possibility Rose Ann would show up and the trousers hidden under the washtub. Melanie had one concern. I had another. This wouldn't be the time to tell her about the tape.

"Are you sure your friends are going to be okay if you back out at the last moment?" I asked Noah.

He shrugged and sucked down the last of his lemonade.

By this time, Buttercup had ambled over. Noah hefted the orange Coleman cooler Melanie had prepared in the kitchen, complete with ice packs, and lugged it down to his car. Melanie had her arms filled with fabric grocery bags, her purse, and the inevitable sipping thermos. More than anything else at that moment, I wanted to drag her inside the house, close the door, and share what I knew. I had this burning acid feeling where my stomach should have been and caught myself holding my breath. I didn't want her to go with Noah. But what if all this crap swirling around in my head and gut was my own imagination? How could I explain that?

"And you think I can't be sneaky? Enjoy your afternoon *all alone*," she said, blue eyes twinkling. Then she kissed my cheek and ran to catch up with Noah.

I waved them off on my way back to the garden plot.

"Well, I guess now we know what she was up to," I told Buttercup. "She's faster on the uptake than I've ever given her credit for."

* * *

By the time Rose Ann's car pulled into the drive, the shadows had shifted low on the west. I was halfway done with the second raking of the garden plot.

"Did you give up on me?" she asked, getting out of her big SUV with the state seal announcing she was the medicolegal investigator.

"No." I straightened up, back creaking. "I did, however, give up counting the number of curiosity seekers who cruised by."

Rose Ann grimaced.

"As long as they stay out on the road, it's okay. Let me dump this wheelbarrow of clippings in the chicken yard, and we can have a cold drink,"

I said.

"Where's Buttercup?" Rose Ann asked when I joined her at the table five minutes later. She had retrieved the pitcher and glasses from the kitchen.

"She opted for a nap in the home pen." I cranked out the shade umbrella before lowering my weary butt onto the bench. "The black flies are out and ravenous today. They won't bother her in there."

"It's been a long day," Rose Ann said. "Three sites starting at four this morning. Tell me what you've got before my brain shuts down and my ears stop working."

I told her about the pair of gaberdine pants I had hidden under the bucket. Her smile edged away as I spoke.

"I don't think Buttercup found the pants where we found the remains because she came out of the woods in a different place." I took a long swig of lemonade. "If I were a betting woman, I would say that the pig found a place where Juan Noche's personal effects were dumped. I'm going to call Mrs. Otis, or maybe stop over, and see if Juan packed all his stuff when he moved out."

"Didn't he have a car?" Rose Ann asked.

"Pickup truck, but nobody has seen it around here. I don't know if anyone has talked to his family. I'm assuming they have, but there's really no reason for somebody to call me up and say, oh, by the way…"

"Yes, there's that. But when you found these pants, you had a solid idea where they came from. But you didn't call the sheriff because…?" Rose Ann asked.

"Because *you* said people weren't giving your position with the medical examiner's office proper due." I stood up, still trying to eradicate the kinks. "No one besides myself and Melanie knows about those pants. Nobody. My next call is to Sheriff Neddel. But if he and his posse show up, they'll do a step-by-step search of the ridge. Those volunteers aren't going to know how to be careful. Let's face it, whoever murdered Juan went to the trouble to let the general population know he had left town. It wouldn't have taken long for the Otis family to mention at the post office or church that the guy had left behind all of his stuff, including his vehicle."

"Okay, Doris," Rose Ann said softly. "There are a couple of points here. First and foremost, you should have called Sheriff Neddel immediately. My part of the investigation involves the scene, the remains. That's my job. To look at what is found after an unaccompanied death, that is, by a medical professional, and determine if it might have been unnatural. Okay? Got that?"

I nodded. I couldn't help feeling shamed. When I started to turn away, she touched my arm, pulling me back.

"What you, or rather Buttercup, found sounds like evidence. Even if it's something that might come across my examination table later, Neddel has to be involved."

"I'm sorry," I whispered.

She gave me a small smile. "You know all about dogs like Rex, pigs, even I'm sure every furry that might show up. I know about this. We can share information, okay?"

"Yeah. I'm glad Melanie and Noah are gone. I don't need them witnessing me pulling a whopper," I said, but I was thinking, *Especially Noah.*

Rose Ann nodded and followed me down the steps. At her SUV, she pulled out a couple of paper masks, disposable gloves, and a big evidence bag. Just about then, an auspicious black and white head with ears like an antenna, up and in the alert position, stuck out the barn door. Immediately, a long, fairly lean body followed. Buttercup was coming out to greet our guest.

Rose Ann and I headed toward the overturned washtub at one angle, the pig at another, but we all ended up in the same place.

"Stay," I ordered Buttercup. We didn't need her flickering snout in what I wanted to show Rose Ann. After throwing off the rocks, I flipped the washtub, positioning it between the clothing lying on the ground and the pig.

Rose Ann had also carried over a strong flashlight and a camera. She shined the light over the fabric remnants, even though the shadows hadn't quite reached us yet. Then she took pictures. When she had the first set done, she asked, "Did you touch these?"

"Yes. I didn't realize what they were and grabbed one leg to keep them away from Buttercup," I said, pointing out the spot while still watching Buttercup in case she wanted to intervene. "As soon as I touched them, I knew the fabric was gaberdine. The light bulb in my brain went off a moment later, so I dropped them. I knew if I moved them, there would be a chance I'd lose any trace evidence still clinging to the fabric. Covering them with the washtub and rocks was mostly to keep the weather and chickens off."

"Yeah, a couple of rocks wouldn't have stopped Buttercup," Rose Ann said.

She gingerly turned the fabric over to take more photos. When she did, the fabric flapped slightly, and Buttercup showed an increase in interest in what was going on.

"If you don't need me," I said, "I'll take Buttercup into the barn for supper. That will get her out of the way."

Rose Ann nodded. I wasn't sure she really heard me, but using the bucket and my knees, I worked my porcine friend into her home pen on the far side of the barn and securely locked the doors. Rex was in his outside run watching the medicolegal investigator, so I left his dinner and went back to the kitchen to start dishing up cat chow.

With the tray filled with cat dinner bowls, I rang the bell and walked into the cattery. Rose Ann, who had finished outside and packed all her equipment and evidence bags in her vehicle, followed me. She stopped to gaze at the wall of housing crates. Across the room was the maternity unit with Pitch, and in the other corner, a separate crate with an old guy, Argyle. His area was sheathed with Plexiglas.

"So, this is just another side of your complicated personality," she said, looking around the room.

I laughed. "It used to be the woodshed."

"Why is this guy all alone?" she asked, making a sad face at Argyle.

"That's Argyle. He's new and still in quarantine. He'll be coming out tomorrow because there's a ginger cat being housed on the porch, who needs to come in. These other ladies are just fosters. The sad thing is, most of them are elderly, some have medical issues. No one wants them, but here, at least they have a place to sleep that's warm, with their meds and plenty to eat."

"But they stay in the crates all the time, right?"

"Absolutely not. Except for Pitch and Argyle, they roam free in shifts throughout the day. I button them up at mealtimes to make sure the right cats eat the right diet mix. Oh, and at night, too, so there's no arguing to wake me up."

"Phenomenal." Rose Ann extended her fingers toward Pitch and got a hiss and a growl for her trouble.

"Don't put your fingers in there," I warned. "Pitch is a soon-to-be-mama and feral. I keep her inside so I can have access to her kittens when they arrive. When they get to be about four weeks old, we'll separate them and have Pitch spayed. A rehabber will work to domesticate the kittens. Then I'll let her out in the yard. I already have an older male feral and a three-year-old semi-feral in residence in the barn."

"Semi?"

"Boots was probably a house cat at some point. The people didn't want her anymore or couldn't keep her. She was released near a farm outside of town. The woman there was all worried Boots would starve or freeze. Animal control live-trapped her. She eats on the deck and comes when she's called. If I leave the screen door open, she'll come in and walk around the kitchen, but the closest I can get is about two feet away."

"Is she a tuxedo cat? I think I saw her earlier," said Rose Ann. "She was right at the top of the steps, rubbing on the rail and talking, making soft paws. But she wouldn't come up to me."

"Yup, that's her. The orange ring-tailed tigers belong to me. Pumpkin and Poppy are sisters. Rusty, the twenty-three-pound bruiser, was a drop-off at the end of the driveway when he was a kitten."

Around the room, multi-colored eyes watched, ears forward, listening. Rose Ann was new to them, and the cats wanted to be ready if there was going to be danger.

"What would you like to have for supper?" I asked. "I put a couple of bakers in the oven when I came inside. Besides that, I have chicken, steak, broccoli? I eat it all, so it's your choice."

"I'll go with the steak," Rose Ann said.

While the grill heated, Rose Ann laid the evidence bag on the picnic table. She didn't open it but flipped the big plastic bag over, pointing out places on the fabric as she spoke.

"I think you're right about this being a forestry service uniform. I don't understand all these slashing rips. No blood residue or staining. And I guess I have questions about this being left in the woods. If it was, it was somewhere offering some protection."

"Okay." I turned the steaks over so they could grill on the other side. "First, the slashing is probably from Buttercup finding the clothing and playing with it. I have to watch her around the clothesline. Sheets in the wind have a particular allure for her. I'm thinking when you test for body fluid residue, you'll find an excess amount of pig drool."

"I should take a Buttercup sample," she said with a laugh, spreading out the plates and silverware.

"That's too funny. But I'll get you one. Or if you'd like to try you could collect your own. Rare or medium on the steaks?"

"Medium." She poured iced tea. In the house, the microwave dinged. The broccoli was done.

"When Buttercup came down off the ridge and back into the yard, she came in from a trail that didn't connect with the site where the remains were," I said, transferring the steaks from the grill to plates. "Like most big animals, if she's given a chance, she'll take the path of least resistance. Which means, when offered a cleared path as opposed to tangled brush, she'd go where a human would."

I brought out the potatoes and broccoli. We slathered butter and sour cream and dug in.

"So, you believe Buttercup wandered into someplace different?"

I nodded. "She followed me, and I was on the tractor. I went into the woods about a quarter of a mile down the road. She probably did as well. That means the area that should be searched first is on the south side of the barn."

Rose Ann looked upwards. The ridge was taking on shadows. "That's still a lot of area."

"We can trim it down more," I said. "While I was out dubbing around, I strictly followed paths that veered off to the right. If she was scent-tracking me, she would have as well. Most of that area is abutted about halfway up by a twenty-foot ledge. She wouldn't be able to scale that, so that cuts the top off the ridge and leads us away from Calwin Mountain proper."

"But if your theory is right," Rose Ann said, "and the murderer—because it definitely was a homicide—dumped the victim's personal effects off on the trail, he wouldn't have left all of that stuff in plain sight. Why find a second place to get rid of stuff? Why not just burn it?"

"I would have gone with the burning, myself," I said with a grimace. "Perhaps killing Juan was a spur-of-the-moment thing. So, the murderer gets rid of the body. In the cold light of dawn, he considers somebody will miss this young man. He gathers Juan's possessions and heads back onto the ridge."

"Maybe he's not from here and has no idea where he left the body," Rose Ann finished.

"Or something changed unexpectedly since he was there last, and he can't get back to the site the same way."

Royally poked me, begging for a bite of steak. When I offered him one, Lilo started doing her pretty-girl dance. Rose Ann was still looking at the ridge.

"What do you think the chances are Buttercup would go back to that same spot?" she asked.

"On a good day? Maybe fifty-fifty. If she got close enough to remember, she had already been there."

We both looked toward the barn.

Chapter Fifteen

"Guess who brought strawberries and whipped cream?" Melanie hung out the passenger window of the blue Audi, waving us over.

"Don't let her see you're interested," I whispered to Rose Ann. We had just locked the evidence bag containing the pants inside her SUV. "It's a trap to get us to help haul the groceries in."

Rose Ann had turned and was already swerving towards the blue Audi, laughing as she went.

Because the large grocery stores were an hour and a half away, we only did the big shopping once a month. The smaller markets nearby could be expensive. Then, too, I absolutely hated to shop. I didn't care if it was for groceries, clothing, or comparing rates for insurance. It drove me nuts. Melanie could wander among the aisles, reading every tag or label for hours. A testimony to that was the glazed look in Noah's eyes as he unloaded bag after bag from the back seat. Even with four of us hauling, we made multiple trips.

"We should have taken two coolers," he said, grunting with the effort of carrying the one they had taken into the kitchen.

We, the womenfolk, were soon totally immersed in a grocery sorting party while he slumped in a wooden chair, cold drink in hand.

"Who knew there were so many big box stores in such a small area?" he moaned.

"You were only gone about eight hours." I pointed out. *Mediterranean mix, interesting. Melanie usually goes with Romaine.*

"Longest eight hours of my life," he lamented.

Melanie was putting away perishables, but she didn't seem to be making a lot of headway. She'd look, look again, pick something up, and move on to something else without completing the first task. I was watching, evaluating, and caught Rose Ann peeking from beneath her lashes. Melanie's behavior raised the concern she was overtired or had suffered another multiple sclerosis event.

"Are you tired, honey?" I asked, moving closer. "How about if you sit down with your tea? I can finish this."

Noah didn't pick up on what was going on, but Rose Ann also moved closer. Melanie fluttered her fingers at me, looking pained. There was something else going on in her mind. Her distraction stemmed from that.

"I'm good," she whispered, returning to stocking the fridge. With her head still in the vegetable crisper level, she said loudly, "Noah, tell Mom what your grandmother did for you and your cousin."

"Hmm?" said Noah. He sounded like he had been dozing off.

I thought it was time for him to go home to get some shuteye. I was ready to push him out the door, but Melanie's raised hand stopped me from suggesting he leave.

"It's so cool. Tell her," Melanie prompted, speaking loud enough to jar him to consciousness.

"Yeah, my grandmother. Well, she's, ah, old, like in her seventies, you know?" The intense look on his face let me know he wasn't trying to give me a little jab because of my age. "I never knew her really well until I came back here. She and my father hadn't spoken in years. The only family she has left are me and my cousin in Boston. She had to sell her house and move into a senior place. There was a big sit-down meeting with her lawyer. The guy told her about inheritance tax, legal fees, and all that, so she decided she'd beat the system. She didn't want to leave what she had to Dad. She went to this car dealership and paid cash for two brand-new cars. One for me and one for my cousin."

"That's awesome, Noah," I said. I knew he had a new car. It was a cute story, but so what?

"And?" Melanie leaned her head against the freezer, as if the next move would be to beat her brains into the kitchen appliance.

Noah continued his story, meandering along, yawning between every three words. "Grandma never asked us what we wanted. She just bought those cars. She got us both the exact same thing so we wouldn't fight."

"Isn't that funny?" Melanie asked.

It sounded like the end of the conversation. Then Noah said, "Yup, exact same thing, except she gave my cousin the red one."

Melanie's eyes met mine over the refrigerator door. The only sound was the squeaking of Noah's chair as it scraped the linoleum.

"Man, I am so wiped out. Sorry ladies, but I gotta go."

He wasn't the only one who was exhausted. A few minutes later, Melanie also retired. Rose Ann and I sat in the sitting room, wrapped in the warm, furry bodies of felines and canines. I told her about the lights on the ridge and the red Audi that kept cruising past.

"Does Noah's cousin live here too?" Rose Ann asked, sipping from a single-serving bottle of Zinfandel Blush she had brought.

With a similar bottle and a bowlful of strawberries to share, I said, "No, like he said, she lives in Boston. But she works for some Greenpeace group, and travels with them. Before she went to lay down, Melanie said while she's gone, Noah's cousin stores her car at Noah's instead of renting garage space in the city."

"What are the chances?" Rose Ann asked.

I shook my head.

The television was on, but the volume was muted. Beyond the front window, cracked open to let the sweet-scented air in, one last peeper frog offered a serenade to end his season.

"We need to notify Neddel," said Rose Ann.

Nodding, I took my cell phone and went into the kitchen. Neddel's business card with his private phone number hung on the front of the fridge. I tapped the number into my phone. When the message screen appeared, I wrote: *Items found on ridge, possible connection to Noche. Going up to check in morning.* My finger hovered over the send arrow. I needed to send that message. I knew I did, really, really, really. Yet, somehow, I didn't want to tell that pretentious, but still good-looking, so-and-so anything.

"Done?" Rose Ann called out.

"Yes." Leaving the message waiting to be sent, I clicked the cell phone off and went back to the sitting room. I'd give myself a few minutes to figure out why I was having issues, and then I'd send it. Maybe.

"So, tomorrow is Sunday. I have the day off. What time do you think Neddel will show up? Are we headed up the ridge as part of his volunteers?" Rose Ann asked.

"Yeah, we're going right after coffee."

If we left a little before Neddel arrived, oh, well. If the text didn't bounce back to him from cyberspace for a while, how was I to know? We settled down to watch the news. I felt a little guilty and might have been sweating just a tad. Royally, who was laying across my lap, seemed to know something was up. He couldn't take his eyes off my face.

Chapter Sixteen

It felt like morning came before I'd even laid down. Once past the breakfast feeding for the animals, I worked in the kitchen, making sandwiches and packing snacks for us humans to take. Rose Ann pulled items she might need from the back of her vehicle, making a stack on the ground to be loaded in the mower trailer. Melanie, who had also been drafted, sat at the table, forehead down on the familiar wooden surface, a to-go mug of chai tea steaming beside her.

"Why?" she moaned.

Laying my hand on her shoulder, I spoke. "You know what? You don't have to go, honey. Rose Ann and I can take care of this."

"You're kidding, right?" She lifted her head. "Juan was my friend. It's only right that I help. I'm a little tired, but as Dad would say, I can man up. Then there's the fact this is the most exciting thing that's ever happened in this berg. All that, and you want me to sit it out? No way."

Shaking my head at the confusing tilt-a-whirl of her moods, I went back to filling my backpack. "Sandwich, power snacks, two waters, drinking dish for Buttercup."

"You're taking Buttercup? Into the woods? After what happened two days ago?" Melanie, who was dragging her own pack out of the pantry closet, spun around, giving me an incredulous look.

"I'm hoping she'll go back to the same place, or at least give me a clue when we get near it. Camera, charged cell phone, Ziploc bag of peanut butter snacks. I'd better put those in my pocket."

The three of us rendezvoused in the yard.

"Okay, Red Leader," said Melanie. "What's the plan?"

"You take the tractor and trailer with Rose Ann's gear. Rose Ann gets to take Charlie One."

Melanie guffawed. Rose Ann looked concerned.

"Go in down by the animal camera. Rose Ann, there's an old-fashioned upright mailbox hanging on a tree. Inside are the trail maps Ian made. Take one, then keep to the right as you go up. Spread out, and don't go any higher than the ridge. We're looking for something off the path, but not too far. Buttercup could go in without leaving a lot of signs, but if she started playing with those trousers, she would have torn the ground up some. Stay alert. Watch for bears."

Melanie loaded gear into the trailer. I motioned for a rather concerned-looking Rose Ann to follow me.

"It's broad daylight. Wouldn't the bears be back in their dens by now?" she asked, rubbing her fingers together.

"Hungry mamas, demanding babies? Maybe not," I said.

In the back of the barn, I pulled out an old, battered dirt bike rusted to dull orange. This was Charlie One, or so Ian had called it. A first-generation innovation, Charlie One looked like a stripped-down scooter. Nothing like a modern dirt bike. When I laid my hands on it, I could hear Ian laughing.

I wheeled it out to the front on its tiny eight-inch tires and went back for the portable charger.

"Let me explain how this works before I start it."

"You're sure it's going to start?" Rose Ann looked doubtful.

"No. But the gas tank is full. If it blows to kingdom come, we've already gotten our money out of it."

She stepped back.

The lesson was short. The final warning was clear. "Do not shut Charlie One off. If it stalls, leave it in the middle of the path and we'll go back with the trailer to pick it up, okay?"

Rose Ann nodded, but she still didn't look really impressed.

I attached the cables and gave it one quick jolt.

Nothing.

I gave it another hit of juice and got a weak cough. A third jolt sent a roaring vibration through the metal frame that threatened to shake the pieces apart. A cloud of oily blue exhaust rose, bringing tears to my eyes.

"There we go." Turning with a smile, I found Rose Ann with her mouth hanging open. "What?" I asked.

"I don't know," she said. "When you charged it, I rather expected sparks to fly out for twenty feet. Then the whole contraption to lift off the ground, with maybe a neon glow to cover all that rust."

"Yeah, I know. Cool, isn't it?" I knew my wide grin was watts brighter than her tentative smile.

Throwing a leg over, Rose Ann rode-walked down to the mower. Melanie was ready and waiting. Their progress out of the yard was so slow, I wanted to call them back.

"Maybe I should have asked Rose Ann if she wanted a helmet," I mused.

Rex was giving out a low whining moan, letting me know he wanted to help. In the house, Royally and Lilo were flat-out barking. I felt bad, but I couldn't take them.

Melanie and Rose Ann had made it beyond the big maple. With a shrug, I reached for Buttercup's halter. She and I entered the forest where she had emerged with the pants. We went by the spot the trousers had lain on the ground, and she stopped to take a snuffle. I took that as a good sign. Her leash hung out of my pocket. There didn't seem to be a need to use it. As I walked along, she followed, singing her grunty little piggy song. She'd snuffle here and there. When she did, I'd turn back and check things out. Mostly, I found deer droppings and terrified chipmunks trying to make a hysterical escape.

We weren't moving very fast as I watched for places she might have rooted or dug up the old bracken. For most of the week, the sun had been shining, and it was fairly dry. A few odd spider webs held shining dew droplets to offer unwary insects. Even if I had come into the woods, Buttercup had walked out, I wouldn't have found many tracks.

At a fork in the path, I waited for Buttercup's lead. Every tree was doing its bit as a speaker for the surrounding cacophony of birdsong. Inhaling deeply,

I drew in the sweet scent of moose bush blossoms and unfurling green. The loamy odor of the forest floor as it absorbed leaf litter and scat from the previous season made me think of new hope, babies, and the overall wonder of the surrounding space.

We kept moving along. At each juncture, Buttercup took a turn, right or left. I marked our way with surveying tape. If today's mission didn't pan out, I'd try a different route later on.

Finally, we came to a place where the slope headed into a shallow vale. The tree cover was still thin and spread across the apron of brown leaves and moss were dozens of snow-white Trilliums, the biggest patch I had ever seen in my life. I took out my camera to snap photos.

"I'll have to bring Melanie up here before all these blossoms fade. She'll love them," I said to Buttercup.

I turned back to the path where the pig had just been standing. She was gone. Again, I had lost her. A trill of panic ran up my spine.

Running ahead a few steps, I looked down into the vale. Maybe the scent of the Trillium had lured her to do some rooting. She wasn't there. But she couldn't have gone to the right. There was a tight stand of birch saplings with the ledge right behind them, and it was a cinch she hadn't backtracked. I ran further on, starting to really panic.

"No," I told myself, forcing calm. "She had to have left the path near the Trillium grove."

I went back to the edge of the vale, bent over with my nose almost close enough to do some rooting of my own. Inch by inch, I scrutinized the leaf litter. If she had gone over the side, she would have disturbed something. There would be a mussed-up place where one of her hooves would have dragged, flipping over the dried brown to expose the moister bottom. I knew these would be the signs that Buttercup had passed. I willed the moss to flip over and tell me something. Sweat was running down my sides from my armpits.

My back was crying out and my knees answered with their own whines. Straightening, I drew my cell phone out of the back pocket of my jeans, intent on sending out a SOS for pig searchers.

I was three taps in, but then had to delete two because my shaking fingers couldn't land in the right place. Frustration would soon give way to tears. Shoulders slumped, chin on chest, and eyes closed, I exhaled.

Shake it off, I thought. *Relax and try again.*

The calls of small birds and an occasional low woof were the only sounds that broke the quiet of the forest.

Woof? My head snapped up so fast I almost gave myself whiplash. Two choices on the woof, bear or pig. No snorting, just a woof. Then another. I turned my back on the Trilliums. Four feet away, the birches shuddered, and a glistening disc appeared. With a more solid grunt and a shove, Buttercup's strong shoulders parted the saplings, and she walked out. I sat back on my heels, feeling faint with relief.

Tired from her exertions, she lay down on the path. I knelt in front of her, scratching the sensitive place between her eyes as I studied the birches. At almost three inches on the stump, they were growing close enough together to make parting them a problem. I got out Buttercup's bowl and bottle of water while I considered why she would have gone through the saplings.

"Stay," I said, offering a snack as an incentive.

Buttercup didn't appear inclined to move. Putting her on the three-foot leash would have hampered my ability to move around, so I left her there, crunching happily.

Trying to push the saplings apart was useless. Peeking between the tops, I saw the uneven rock face of the ledge. Near the bottom, I couldn't see beyond the curling white bark. I thrust my hand in a few different places, taking pictures with my cell phone, but when I pulled it back, all the screen showed was more rock.

By this time, Buttercup was stretched out and snoring. I walked up and down the wall of birches, looking for a place of egress. Maybe ten feet away, I came to a place where the saplings gave over to thin pines. Pressing through the pines revealed a space of about eighteen inches between tree and ledge. And a sneaker.

I quickly backed out, hopped up with what I'd found, and flushed with excitement. I needed to call the others.

Melanie had set up a connection on my cell phone for me to contact both her and Rose Ann.

I'm on the blue trail, near the ledges. Find me. I keyed into the phone. Then I pressed the arrow to send the message I had started to text Sheriff Neddel the night before. As soon as it went through, I sent another. *We are up on the ridge. Come out here now. No lights, no sirens, come alone. Text when you arrive.*

"I hope he understands we don't want anybody else, like Burt Kennett, involved right now," I said to Buttercup. I sat beside her on the path. After a short time, her ears fluttered, and she gave a little snort to let me know someone was approaching.

* * *

"Are we going to wait for the sheriff?" Melanie asked after I showed her and Rose Ann the photo of the white Adidas sneaker.

"Looks big enough to be a man's," Rose Ann mused.

"I sent Neddel a couple of messages," I said, not mentioning one was the original. "Heaven only knows how long it will take him to get here."

Rose Ann had her nose in the evergreens. I expected her to have the sneaker in her hand when she pulled back, but she was empty-handed. Even if I was impatient, she was still professional.

"I'd like to take some photos, but there's no room." She studied the evergreens. "Can we get a chainsaw and cut some of these trees? Once the sheriff arrives, we'll probably have to cut some of this out."

"Actually, I don't think so," I said. "This is a National Forest, and these are healthy trees. We may need to get some kind of permit."

"Seriously?" She did not look friendly.

I don't make the rules, but I'd rather not do jail time. From the look on her face, though, I gathered she was used to eventually getting her way.

"Then, too, a chainsaw would create a lot of sawdust and chaff. That would be messy," I said.

That had her thinking. And frowning.

"Maybe," suggested Melanie, "you should have the sheriff bring somebody from the forestry department. You know, like Keith Ramp?"

I wanted to shove my fingers down my throat until my elbow disappeared and gag. I can't stand Keith. He's good at his job, but he's evangelistic about the sanctity of the woodlands and the wonder of all they have to offer when he is dealing with the public.

My distaste must have shown on my face. Or maybe it was the smirk Melanie was trying to hide behind her hand.

"What's the issue?" Rose Ann asked, left eyebrow headed for the ionosphere.

"Difference in opinion as to the manner in which informational training on state forest rules and regulations should be disseminated to the masses," I said.

Now, both of Rose Ann's eyebrows went up. "What?"

"He acts like he's better than most other people. When he gets on his soapbox, it's hard to get him down," said Melanie.

"So, are you saying he's like a hundred years old, never set foot out of the valley, wedded to his job?" Rose Ann asked.

Melanie and I both nodded, but dutifully I sent Neddel another text suggesting he bring a forestry ranger with him because of the location.

"Do we have a Plan B?" the medicolegal death investigator asked.

"I'm not sure." I chewed on my upper lip. "But I'd like to point out that, even though we found the sneaker over there, Buttercup came out from between the birches here. She never showed any interest in the shoe at all."

"And usually, if she can get her mouth on footwear, it's all over for your soles," said Melanie.

"Like a hound dog puppy," I added.

We three stood for a minute in silence, facing the birches.

"Somebody will have to squeeze in back there and see what else is lying around," said Rose Ann.

She and I turned toward Melanie, the smallest of us all.

"You have to be kidding," my daughter said, taking a step backward. Unfortunately, the tractor was right there, stopping her retreat. "Aargh. I should have stayed in bed."

Rose Ann pulled open one of her big, black duffel bags and outfitted Melanie in hazmat from head to toe, then handed her a big flashlight and a warning. "Watch where you step. Take photos as needed. Don't touch anything. Just talk to us, and we'll make a decision. Okay?"

Melanie didn't answer. Her lips were a tight line.

"Melanie?" I asked. "Have you got all that?" I was starting to feel like this wasn't a good idea. If my daughter got in there and had an episode, it could be bad. "Hold on, let's think about this again."

"I'm not talking to you," she said. Then, like a little elfin fairy, she disappeared behind the evergreens.

Buttercup, snoozing near the tractor, didn't appear concerned.

We could see Melanie's light blue hazmat coveralls between the tree trunks. She turned on the flashlight and inched along between the birches and the ledge. We could see the glow, but not what it illuminated. Rose Ann and I kept up with her on our side. We heard her grunts and occasional soft curses about spiders as she moved.

"Easy," I said. "Easy."

"Oh, be quiet," she said crossly. "Okay. I'm close enough so I can see what looks like a green cloth bag."

"Not a plastic trash bag?" asked Rose Ann.

"No, it looks like something that maybe came from the Army-Navy store. Maybe canvas? And there's stuff spilled out all over. There's like a little recess down here."

"A cave?"

"Hmm. I don't know. I'm trying to see inside..."

I saw the blue suit shrink as she bent or squatted closer to the ground. Suddenly, she screamed.

"OUT! OUT! GET ME OUT OF HERE! MOM!" There was no denying the terror in her voice.

"MELANIE!" I grabbed at the birches, pulling and twisting, trying to rip them out of the way. Rose Ann also grabbed for whatever handhold she could get.

My daughter screamed again, and I got bulldozed out of the way. Buttercup had come to life with Melanie's first distressed outcry.

"SCREE! SCREE! SCREE!" Buttercup's high-pitched squeals bounced back off the ledge. Unseen birds took to the air, crying out in fear.

Melanie wasn't her alpha, but she was a litter mate. Buttercup was coming to the rescue. Thrusting her snout in a tiny crack between two saplings, the pig grunted and pushed, but there was no easing between the living wood posts this time. She was going in fast and hard. My fear for Melanie overrode any thought that this young, strong pig could do more than I could. I was still grabbing at birches, my breath coming in sobs.

I heard a sapling crack. Buttercup was in, up to her shoulders. I could see Melanie now. She had risen back to her feet and was plastered against the rocky ledge, one arm covering her face. Buttercup was still pushing saplings apart. I was standing spread-eagle over her.

Reaching in over the pig's back, I grabbed the front of Melanie's hazmat suit right below her chin and yanked. Another set of hands reached in with mine. Together, we pulled Melanie out right over Buttercup, and all three of us humans tumbled to the ground. With Melanie behind her, no longer screaming, Buttercup backed out, darn near stepping on all of us.

I had my arms around Melanie, rocking back and forth while she sobbed. Rose Ann checked her for injuries or snake bites while Buttercup nudged her disc in my armpit, trying to find a place for comfort. Eventually, the pig got her cold, wet disc against my naked back. I think I jumped about six inches.

Melanie was taking deep breaths. "No snakes."

"Holy cow," said Rose Ann. "I thought I was going to have the big one."

"What happened?" I didn't want to let go of Melanie, even though she was trying to pull away.

"No snakes," she repeated. "Another body." She held her phone up. The video app was still recording, but when we backed it up and replayed it, we could clearly see the death grin of another lost soul.

Chapter Seventeen

My cell phone rang, causing all of us humans to jump apart from each other and away from the birches. Buttercup watched us over her shoulder as she snuck along, edging toward home. She had experienced enough excitement for one day. I reached out, grabbing Buttercup's harness. She towed me along as she went.

"I'm parked in your yard," Neddel said. He didn't sound very friendly. "Where exactly are you?"

"I'm sending Melanie out with the tractor," I said, letting go of Buttercup. "Go in the barn. You're going to need a chainsaw, an ax, a handsaw, and anything else that looks pertinent for cutting saplings out of the way. You can bring them up with the tractor. We think there's another body."

"Ask him if we have to wait for Officer Ramp," Rose Ann whispered. "Oh, and maybe have him grab a couple more of the big evidence bags out of my car."

Melanie had also had enough excitement for one day. She was more than willing to follow Buttercup and head down to turn the tractor controls over to Neddel.

"Make sure he gasses up before he leaves," I called out as her back disappeared.

Hard to tell because of all the fluttering leaves, but my daughter might have flipped me off. She was still fully hazmatted.

My cell phone dinged. Incoming text. *Nothing yet from Ramp.*

While we waited for Sheriff Neddel to come up over the trail, I crept down among the Trillium, admiring their fleeting glory. Rose Ann spent the time

126

measuring, taking photos, and prepping her equipment. Melanie did not text me that she and Buttercup had made it down safely, but Neddel said she'd stepped off the tractor, ignoring his questions while declaring the need for a shower and nap immediately to follow.

The putt-putt-cough-gasp-wheeze of my elderly Cub Cadet announced the sheriff's arrival. He brought more water with him and some energy drink he and Rose Ann seemed good with, but which sent my eyeballs whirling in my head.

"It's a good thing the pig went in the sty by herself," he said. "I closed the gate to make sure she would stay there before I left."

"We don't call it a sty. Buttercup has a home pen and an outside pen."

Neddel rolled his eyes. I was dead serious, but it was hard to hold the scowl in place with Rose Ann leaning on my back, giggling. If I hadn't already known the heat and the walk would be the perfect prelude for an extended porcine nap, I would have felt bad that my chubby buddy had been secured behind bars.

Neddel started spitting out some rhetoric about how he should have been notified immediately. Like thirty-six hours prior, as in, when the pig came out of the woods. And definitely before Rose Ann, Melanie, Buttercup, and I had taken on the job of searching for the murderer's stash. There was some mention of evidence and chain of control.

The day had gotten hotter. My clothing was sticking to me all over, as was a lot of forest debris.

"We didn't know we were going to find evidence," I said.

"But you knew you had part of a uniform." Neddel scowled.

"Actually, I didn't know for sure until Doctor Lombard confirmed it."

Okay, that might have been stretching the truth. I don't usually take the coward's way out, but right now, I wasn't interested in having him walk up one side of me, dance around on my head with his attitude, and slide down the other side.

Before the sheriff could say another word, Rose Ann jumped in. "I don't know about you people, but I get paid by the hour. So, either you get down to business or get off the pot."

Neddel gave Rose Ann a dirty look. I wondered, in this type of circumstance, who outranked whom.

Our toe-to-toe confab broke up, and Rose Ann and I moved out of the sheriff's way. He reached for the saw.

"Wait a minute," I said. "What about Ramp?"

Neddel gave me a look equivalent to the one he'd dropped on Rose Ann moments before. Then, using the mini utility saw, he cut out the three pines in front of the sneaker.

Rose Ann and I exchanged a look while we waited for him to finish. Silence seemed to be our best answer for a few minutes. She took over photographing, bagging, and tagging.

"I took samples all the way around," she said. "I think the person who stashed this stuff got in and out using the same route Melanie did. Whoever it was couldn't be very big. Unless they got hung up or scratched going in or out, we aren't going to get much we can use to track them down. The sneaker probably got dropped out of the satchel unseen."

I agreed. Sheriff Neddel gave us both The Look again. I don't think he liked us doing his job. When he turned away, Rose Ann stuck out her tongue in response to his scathing frown.

From there, we moved down to where Buttercup had split the birches, trying to get to Melanie.

"What happened here?" he asked. "Did you try to break the trees by hand?"

"No, that's where Buttercup went in to rescue Melanie."

Neddel looked at Rose Ann and me as if together we had six heads. "What?" he asked.

We had to take another few minutes to explain. When I stopped talking, Neddel was frowning again.

"We have it on video if you need it for evidence," Rose Ann put in.

Neddel didn't say anything else about Melanie. Instead, he walked back and forth in front of the birches.

"I don't think we need to take down the whole row of trees," he said. "We can start with a few unless we see signs of evidence."

He took out the split birches, then a few more. I was watching down the trail, sure Keith Ramp was going to appear in a cloud of disapproval.

"Is that enough?" he asked when he was through. The space was about fifteen inches wide.

"Yeah," I said. "For a ten-year-old."

He took out another six saplings, and Rose Ann waved him aside. There was enough light for her to take pictures now. Before we went any further, we sat on our heels, discussing what her snoop camera had shown.

"First thing," said Rose Ann, "I know it scared Melanie, but the other skull isn't some new thing, or even a body left here. It appears to be in a glass box."

"Don't people in South America have some custom where they keep the skulls of their ancestors to honor them?" Neddel asked.

"You mean like the Day of the Dead?" I asked.

"Sort of. The honoring ancestors part. But I'm talking about human skulls, all decorated and displayed in fancy boxes. I saw a PBS special once showing them being carried all over a town, getting blessings and treats."

"You've made contact with Noche's family, right?" Rose Ann asked Neddel.

"Yes. I spoke with his father and his girlfriend."

I kept my lips pressed together and stayed still. If they were going to discuss aspects of the case, I wanted to hear all that was said.

"You should check with them, see if he had a traveling buddy before we start searching the mountain for the rest of the skeleton," Rose Ann said. "The rest of the stuff here looks like personal effects. Clothing. I think I see one of those wallets on a chain back there. Maybe shaving gear."

Neddel agreed with my theory that the bad guy hadn't remembered exactly where he had left the remains on his first trip out. "Even if the killer was familiar with the area, in the dark, he could have gotten confused. Then add the emotional instability of having just committed a grievous crime. It's hard to tell where his thoughts might have been."

Rose Ann was pulling stuff out, laying the items on a sterile tarp while I photographed. Each piece went into its own evidence bag. The glass in the skull box was all cracked. The skull was diffused behind the spider-webby-looing fissures. Rose Ann pulled the door open, and we both laughed with embarrassment. The skull was made of some waxy substance. A curio.

"Well, that was anticlimactic," she said. "Why would he carry a fake head with him?"

My shoulders jutted up to my earlobes. "Who knows? Maybe his grammie gave it to him, and he couldn't leave it behind."

"Maybe," said Neddel. "It's like the volleyball in the movie *Airplane.*"

I think my mouth fell open. He had just said something non-official, or snarky. Before I could ask where he'd come up with that, a black fly flew in, and I was choking and coughing, trying to spit it out.

Neddel marked the bags and stacked them in the trailer. At one point, Rose Ann lay on her belly in the rock depression. All we could see were her lower legs.

"It's not really a cave. More like a natural depression, I think." Rose Ann's voice came back to us muffled.

"How would someone have found this place?" Neddel asked. "Like you said, there's a chance the killer couldn't find where he left the body, yet he knew this cavern was here? It doesn't make any sense. How would he have found that hole behind the trees?"

"It's not really that strange," I said. "Twenty-five or thirty years ago, the property owner clears cut the entire holding. The land itself wasn't worth much. No one would ever be able to develop the area. After the owner wrung every last dime out of the timber, he donated the land to the state. He got a big tax write-off and unloaded undesirable land in the same swipe of a pen."

"I guess that means," Neddel said slowly, "whoever used this hidey-hole is a local. And they have been here since before these birches grew up. I bet there's a mess of these small caves."

Rose Ann came scrabbling out of the hole again. "I think this is the last of it." She had a small metal box in her hands with a spring latch on one side. When the latch was released, the whole top opened on the hinge on the far side.

"I've seen these before," I said, reaching out a gloved finger.

"It's a military ammo cartridge box," said Neddel. "They were actually pretty common forty or fifty years ago. I'll bet there are a lot of them in attics, basements, and garages all over the United States."

I nodded. There were two in my barn. Ian kept his guns in the house but stored the ammunition away from where we slept.

Rose Ann tipped the box on its side and gently shook out the contents. There wasn't much. A ball of string, the stub of a pencil, a woodland guide to tree species, and a couple of small fabric pieces. I picked one up, moving so the sun shone on it.

"Our bad guy used to be a boy scout," I said, and handed the medicolegal death investigator the Wilderness Survival merit badge.

Chapter Eighteen

About the time we got back to the yard with Charlie One and the evidence in the trailer, Keith Ramp was pulling in. He had a four-wheeler that looked like it was on steroids loaded in the back of his pickup.

"Step back," he cautioned. "Unloading this equipment can be dangerous if you don't know what you're doing." There was a lot of clanking and adjusting as he put the ramps in place to back off. He wore a helmet, knee and elbow pads, and biker driving gloves.

"Give me a break," Rose Ann said. She might have discreetly taken a picture with her phone.

She and I unloaded the trailer and got her bag from the house before Keith was done messing around. Neddel stood off to the side, watching the older man. When he was finally ready to head up the ridge and had made sure his precious pickup was locked, Keith turned to Neddel.

"I'm afraid you'll have to walk, son," he said. "It's not safe to carry passengers."

"Oh, I'm not going with you," said Neddel. "I have work to do in town. I was just waiting until you were ready. Here's a map. I'm sure an experienced woodsman such as yourself will see the fresh cutting when you get to the spot. We were careful to leave all the trees we cut in a nice, neat stack." With a vague salute, he strode to his cruiser, pulled the list of names left for him out from under his windshield wiper, and drove down Calwin Mountain Road.

Rose Ann and I ducked behind her car to cover the giggling. We watched

Keith pull away toward the entrance to the path, elbows akimbo. His speed made the lawnmower look like a race car.

* * *

"How's it going with checking out the people on Melanie's list?" I asked Neddel later that afternoon.

I didn't add that Melanie had found it still hanging on the side of the refrigerator and had left it where he'd make sure to find it. We sat in the diner, having a cup of coffee and sharing an English Muffin. It wasn't date food, just me trying to be polite and casually asking if he'd like a piece. Bingo, there went half my snack. I still wasn't ready to tell him I had my own copy of the list, even though I didn't seem to be making a lot of headway in my covert attempts to learn anything about the people on it.

"I suppose it's going okay," he said. Pulling the folded paper from his shirt pocket, he purposely opened the sheet. One flip, then another, and he finally laid it on the table, smoothing it with his strong, blunt-tipped fingers. No ring, no shadow of a ring, and no watch that might have had a "To My Beloved" inscription.

The typed list faced me. To the left of each name was a handwritten symbol. "The X indicates I have made initial contact with that individual," Neddel said. "As you can see, there are two I still haven't found. A double X means either I interviewed them via Zoom, or a member of the police where they are currently living did. If the X-marked individual is local, and I face-to-face interviewed them, there's a check."

"Ah-ha, but your notes aren't here," I pointed out.

"Well, I really couldn't share that information with you, now, could I?" He gave me a sad smile.

True. Melanie had included her own name at the top of the list. That first entry was marked on the left with an X and a checkmark. About six names had a check on the right-hand side as well. Each belonged to a young man. I knew every one of them.

"What do these marks mean?" I asked, pointing.

Sheriff Neddel sat back against the vinyl booth. I felt the passing of his foot millimeters from mine when he stretched his legs out. He tapped both of his forefingers against the tabletop and stared at his half-full mug so intently the waitress hurried over to top it off. I don't think he even noticed.

Finally, the argument he seemed to be holding within his own head was resolved. "These are individuals I need to speak to further."

"Because you don't think they told you the truth?" I asked.

"To be honest, I think they all told me the truth, more or less. My radar rose because I don't think they told me everything they knew. Or I discovered something in their past that might have skewed their version of the truth."

"Ah-huh." I placed my finger on one of the names noted. "This is Noah. He's at my home several times a week. I'd like you to tell me why he's in question."

Neddel had let me see the tape from when Noah was in his office. Now he was showing me his list of names and explaining his marking system, telling me point blank he wasn't done investigating Noah. The hair was rising on the back of my neck. I was sure Neddel was warning me to be aware.

"I can't do that," Neddel said.

"But you showed me this list, so if you're not going to tell me what you know, or what you want to know, I can only assume you need something from me to clear your questions."

I'm not easily intimidated, so while he blew out his cheeks and watched me from below his bunched-together brows, I sipped coffee. A scowling man was nothing compared to a pissed-off, four-hundred-fifty-pound pig.

With a deep sigh, Neddel said, "I am looking for a venue where I could have a conversation with *each* of these individuals that would be like good cop meets speed dating."

"You're a candy ass," I said, opening my cell phone. "Hi, Melanie? Yeah, why don't you call Noah? Tell him I'm making taco supreme for supper if he thinks he can handle the heat." I broke the connection and pocketed the phone. "Okay, sheriff, supper will be on the table at six. Do not wear your uniform. Now I'm going to have to go to the grocery store. I'll make sure you get the bill.

134

"Oh, and that odd rattle in your pickup truck? You should drop in, down at Stan's garage on a Saturday afternoon. The guy who will be there alone, manning the gas pumps and filling windshield fluid tanks, is Travis. Son of a gun, his name is on your list as well. Another guy you want to have more discussion with. Huh, there's a Qawinky-dinky."

* * *

The rest of my afternoon was lost in chopping and spicing. Taco Supreme dinner includes tacos, tortillas, Mexicali salad, nachos, and follows up with pistachio ice cream. A guaranteed recipe for heartburn. To make sure there were no interruptions when Neddel got his chance with Noah, I got all the animals fed and put to bed early. After I explained what Sheriff Neddel was striving for, Melanie and I went over our code words in the event a graceful exit was in our cards.

"So, let me get this straight. This is not a double date?" Melanie asked.

My jaw dropped to bedrock. "There is no way this is even a single date," I said stiffly.

"I'm just saying, Mom. Somebody, like maybe Noah, might ask how come you invited the *sheriff* to supper." Her eyebrows danced like Groucho Marx.

"Then you can tell *somebody* it's my way of saying thank you for his trying to help get the mess on the ridge straightened out." I ripped the Romaine apart so vigorously bits flew through the air. "Unlike some guys, I'm not buying him a fifth or taking him out for a beer somewhere."

"All right, then." There was a pause while Melanie puttered around straightening silverware. "Still, I'm not sure I'm good with this, Mom. Neddel isn't exactly, you know, friendly. Him asking you to do this feels like he's putting you on the spot. Do you know what I mean?"

"There's a lot about this that bothers me as well," I said, retrieving the runaway lettuce and dropping it into the chicken bucket. Once again, it was on the tip of my tongue to tell her about the tape with Noah and maybe Neddel's list. But then, I'd have to tell her how I was feeling as well. "If you're having reservations, perhaps you should sit this meal out."

135

"Yeah, right, like you could carry this off without me."

She flounced away to freshen her makeup. I didn't have time to consider her words, because there was a rap on the door. Expecting Noah, I saw instead Shane's smiling face.

"Shane," I said weakly. "What are you doing here?"

"Triple chocolate chunk brownies," he said, holding the plate up.

He came through the door before I could stop him, circling around me to the table. As soon as he saw the works, I could tell he knew what I was putting on the table for supper. Yanking his cell phone out of the back pocket of his jeans, he gave a fist pump, and direct dialed.

"Hey, Mom," he said, almost immediately. "Don't wait supper for me. I'm eating with Melanie and Mrs. Flynn." He looked at me questioningly. "It's okay, right?"

I floundered. Behind Shane, Noah was coming in the back door. Outside, a flash of sunlight on chrome announced another car pulling into the driveway. And suddenly, there was Melanie, all smiles. I was trapped between the proverbial rock and a hard place.

"Phfft, of course, it is, Shane. What, you don't think there will be enough food? For me, this meal is a quasi-Thanksgiving." My words might have sounded all confident, but whether this get-together would work out the way I had planned was definitely in question.

For the next several minutes, I was busy with last-minute prepping. There were dogs whining from the hall and me slapping male fingers away while I moved bowls and platters from counter to table. It took a little song and dance number, but eventually, everyone was seated appropriately. Neddel, in jeans and a short-sleeved plaid shirt, was on my left at the end of the table. On the other side, to Neddel's left, was Noah. I had placed Shane at the other end, which seemed to suit him fine because he was around the corner from Melanie, who sat next to me. Shane seemed pleased as pie, but Noah looked a little concerned. I think, because Melanie and Shane were talking and laughing together.

We had just gotten started when I realized Neddel's attempts to open a conversation with Noah were hampered by his quarry's attention being drawn away to my daughter.

When Melanie reached for the chopped onions, Noah grasped her fingers. "Whoa, look at this fancy manicure job. Raspberry Sparkle?" he asked.

"Magenta Glitter," she replied, tugging her fingers free.

Not to be outdone, Shane made a grab at her other hand but was thwarted by a bowl of shredded Monterey Jack cheese I thought he might want. "Melanie," I whispered as I leaned past her, "change seats with me."

With one quick look, my very perceptive daughter got it. Every male set of eyes watched in confusion when we dosey-doed our butts and plates. I laughed and waved toward the door.

"This is where I usually sit, so I can keep an eye on the barn. Force of habit, sorry to interrupt."

"Would you rather sit here, Mrs. Flynn?" asked Shane, already half-risen from his seat, plate in hand.

"No, that's sweet, Shane, but I'm good." When I reached for the bowl of lettuce, he finally sat back down, his smiling glow morphed slightly into a tiny frown. Now Noah looked to be the one more pleased. I got a sly wink from Neddel as I plied Shane with more food every time he opened his mouth.

Neddel opened the conversation with a laugh at his over-full plate. "I definitely believe working up here has raised my appetite. Must be the fresh air."

"Or the miles we are from anything else," Melanie said. "Right, Noah?"

Before Noah could say a word, Shane jumped in. "Getting anywhere or finishing everything you need to in a day is all about better time management. If everything is five minutes away, you don't notice all the time you waste going back and forth. Around here, because of the distance and tourist traffic, you could spend the whole day and only get a couple of things accomplished. You have to think your day through before you begin. Plan ahead, follow a route."

I cringed, unsure how to stop him from intervening. "How come he showed up tonight?" I whispered to Melanie behind my napkin.

"That might be my fault." She looked down at her plate, shoulders scrunching up. "He sent a text about the brownies. I said they would go good with pistachio ice cream. He made the leap to tacos supreme, I guess."

"Why would he text you in the middle of the day?" I asked.

Now she looked right at me, in a not-friendly way. Even though her lips barely moved, I heard the words hissing out. "His texting has gotten to be an everyday thing. I was trying to work." Her eye movements signaled added emphasis to her displeasure.

"Is something wrong?" Shane asked, looking from Melanie, to me, and back to Melanie again.

I didn't dare look at him. Instead, I reached for the lemonade. "No, sweetie, I was wondering if I should have put out iced tea."

"Where I grew up, in high school, we had plenty of extra-curriculars to do," said Neddel. "Activity clubs, sports, stuff like that. But we didn't have 4-H or Boy Scouts. I'm sure you had all that out here."

"Yeah." Noah nodded, folding a tight tortilla wrap. "I didn't get into 4-H. My folks wouldn't let me have a field mouse, let alone a farm animal. I was in Boy Scouts for a while. The reverend was our troop leader. It was practically mandatory."

"Then you had the pledge and the merit badges, all that stuff? Maybe a pup tent?" asked Neddel.

Shane jumped in over Noah. "Well, not the tents," he said. "We both belonged to the same troop. There was only one in town. Cub Scouts from five-thirty to six-thirty, then Boy Scouts for an hour. We did get to go to jamboree once a year."

He went on and on until Melanie shut him up by asking if he was ready for more Mexicali.

"How high did you go in the Scout ranks, Noah?" Neddel asked.

Again, Shane cut him off. This time, Melanie was ready. "Noah, tell Mr. Neddel about the birdhouses you boys made one year for the church to sell."

Shane made a squeak, like he had something to say. She shot him a look that made him clamp his lips shut. When he did, Melanie gave him a little smile that said, *good boy*. Like I did with Rex.

For the rest of the meal, Neddel and Noah talked casually about sports, colleges. Melanie stayed under the radar as far as the two young men were concerned. I focused on keeping Shane occupied. It wasn't easy until I stumbled on the subject of Melanie's upcoming birthday. Suddenly, Shane was very attentive, wanting to know what my plans were.

We had our own whispered conversation going on. In the wings of our back-and-forth, I heard Noah mention something about his father. I totally lost my train of thought, as Shane and I were orchestrating a surprise party.

"Yeah, my dad was a woodsman. You know, a lumberjack. He worked all over the mountains around here," Noah said. "My mom worked part-time with the Red Cross. If they were having a blood draw, or some kind of in-service day with some company, she would go. There was a couple who lived in Eaton that did the same thing. They used to pick her up."

"Weren't you kind of little, to be left home alone?" Neddel asked.

I held my breath, waiting for him to say he had a relative, or his mom had a friend who watched him. Someone Neddel could talk to.

"I didn't get left home by myself." Noah laughed ruefully. "I think my folks were afraid I'd burn the house down, or maybe wander next door and make a friend. I'd have to go to work with my dad. While he cut trees, I'd wander around on the mountain."

"This mountain?" I croaked without thinking.

Noah nodded, but before he had time to think about my interruption, Neddel spoke up.

"And never got lost?"

Noah shrugged. "Nay, all I had to do was follow the chainsaw buzz back to where I was supposed to be. I got pretty good at getting around."

My few moments of distraction were all it took for Shane to get around me and back to hogging Noah's talk time. I looked at Neddel. He told me in a glance it was okay. He was all done with Noah for a while.

"I used to hang out on the mountain, too," Shane said. "Way back, most of the trees were kind of puny. Me and my cousins used to tramp all over the place. You remember them, right, Mel? Gary and Derek?"

"Yes." Melanie smiled at him. "I haven't seen them in forever. I guess they don't come around anymore, huh?"

"Sure, they do." Shane stuffed another taco shell. "They come up a lot to ski and hike. I mean, they're only, like, four hours away."

It had been a great evening for tacos and ice cream. The crispy chicken fillets I had fried up to wrap in the soft tortillas with chopped onions and guacamole were a huge success. I'm sure I wasn't the only one who needed to unbutton my jeans, and there was a lot of food coma happening around the table. The radio played a little soft jazz by Anne P. The urge to lie on the floor and snore threatened to overwhelm me. I drew a deep breath...and almost choked.

"What is that stink?" Noah demanded, fanning the air in front of his face.

If a smell could have a descriptor, this one would be oily, green, and roiling. And I had a pretty good idea where the noxious reek was coming from.

Looking down, I found Royally lying at my feet. He wasn't lying all sprawled out like he normally did, but more like a sphinx with his feet under him and his head up, and focused towards the door. Nothing moved except his eyes. They kept rolling back to me, then darting away.

"What is that smell, boy?" I asked him. "Is that you? Are you a stinky little doggie?"

Neither the head nor the ears flicked in my direction. Only the rolling eyes again, which didn't linger, but immediately looked at anything else before sliding back. Guilt, shame, and a begging for forgiveness. And maybe a little glory at his power to level the masses to gasping, stuttering organisms.

"Noah," Melanie accused, "did you feed Royally potato chips?"

"He asked," Noah answered, now vigorously fanning as the odor rose again.

"Okay, Mr. Man," I said to Royally. "Time for you to take a break, out on the veranda."

"I don't think I could eat a bite after that," Noah said.

Shane, Melanie, and Neddel had no such compunction. While we settled into the last round of tacos, Melanie said, with an evil glint in her eye, "If you think that's bad, we've got one even worse. Tell the guys about the Great Guacamole Gaffe, Mom."

I really should have said no, but I loved that story.

"Way back when we first started fostering Buttercup, the people at the animal shelter were concerned about how we were going to find a home for her. Ian suggested we take her somewhere where people with pigs in their future would see her as a pet, not as lunch. So, we entered her at the fair. It was only fifteen miles away, so we figured we could take her for a day or two. Once we decided to go, Melanie did some research and found a list of events for animals of a porcine constitution. After the first year, it became a regular thing. We even entered other fairs in the area. All the same people travel a planned circuit. Every year, in one event or another, Buttercup took the gold. Or, in her case, the blue. Ribbon.

"We had a good time, met some cool people who also had pigs or were involved with the 4-H. It was good for us, because other pig owners shared information that we needed to keep Buttercup healthy. Anyway, we were surprised to learn one season that we had unintentionally made an enemy. To this day, I don't know what Dudley Prentice's problem was, but he spent a lot of time mean-mouthing our contestant.

"Buttercup was about two-hundred-seventy-five pounds and quite full of herself. At the pig display, handlers use big pieces of plywood with handholds cut out of the top like shields to move the pigs from one place to another. Not all pigs are friendly, and when multiple boars get to where they can scent each other, things can turn nasty. We didn't need the handlers to shuffle Buttercup around. I'd put her in her harness and attach the leash to walk her out."

I paused, looking across the yard toward the barn, thinking how proud Ian had been.

"As soon as she entered the ring, as they say, the crowd went wild. For what turned out to be Buttercup's last-ever event, Mr. Prentice was one of the handlers. The rest of the guys knew the drill. They just stood back and let Princess Pig do her thing. Mr. Prentice was sour on that for some reason, maybe because the pig wranglers weren't needed. He came out into the arena using the plywood to push Buttercup around, kind of smacking her with it. She didn't like it. He'd get near her, and she'd jump up like a Kung-Fu queen to face him.

"One of the judges got on the microphone and laughingly told Mr. Prentice to back off. While the two men had a spirited discussion, Buttercup ducked around the plywood and came up behind Prentice. She goosed him good in front of a bleacher full of people. And she won the blue ribbon.

"Later that afternoon, we were in the barn visiting with people we knew when the event their pig was signed up for was called. We all went to watch. Now, if you aren't from around a place that has a county fair, you may not realize some families come and camp out with their stock for the whole week. People in campers, pay big money for spots, but farmers get to stay free with their stock. As long as they are discreet, no foul."

Melanie giggled. All the guys looked at her, but she waved them back to me.

"This time, the people in the next area had coolers filled with food, and we had been snacking on nachos. There was a big bowl of guac. I don't know how it happened, but someone must have left it out. One way or the other, Buttercup got custody of the guac while we were gone and ate the whole thing."

The guys laughed, but I wasn't done.

"In a short time, her belly swelled up like a fifty-five-gallon oil drum. Through the rest of the afternoon, she lay in the straw, making this little sad woofing noise, like moaning and groaning. There's a vet on premises and he made a house call. He gave me a Pepto Bismol tablet the size of my thumb and told me to get it down her throat and then offer her warm water. After that, we should try to get her up and walking. It took both Ian and Melanie to hold her down and keep her mouth open so I could push that tablet down far enough so she couldn't spit it out. She wouldn't drink the water and didn't seem to be getting better very fast, so we decided to take her home.

"Whenever we transported Buttercup to the fair, we borrowed a horse trailer for her to ride in instead of using a pig crate. Ian pulled the truck and trailer up to the door at the end of the barn and dropped the tailgate of the trailer. All she had to do was walk into it. Melanie and I got Buttercup up onto her feet. She'd take two or three steps and stop. It was frightening to watch. Her back was all humped up until she was bent like a horseshoe, her nose was dragging in the dirt, and she continued to moan something awful.

"We weren't the only people who were worried about her. A lot of the pig people tried to help. Most of them had more experience than us with the species, so I can't tell you how appreciative I felt. Anyway, we managed to get her about halfway to the barn doors when she stopped walking. That was it. She was all done. Her back got higher; her sides were rock-hard. I heard a gurgling from her guts. Melanie was on her knees in the dust in front of Buttercup, trying to get her to move, and I was rubbing her belly from the side. My friend Martha was on the other side doing the same thing.

"Mr. Prentice walks up. Buttercup had stopped right in front of his pen area, blocking the gate. That lousy excuse for a human being opened his mouth and spewed all these vile threats about her being contagious and whatnot. He just kept talking, getting louder and uglier. Her stomach rumbled again. I felt all the muscles in her back tense up, and her eyes rolled back. Martha and I were looking at each other, trying to figure out what to do. I just knew Buttercup was going to keel over dead on the spot."

I paused for effect, then continued.

"Suddenly, this solid stream of slimy, green pig poop shoots out of her like it was fired from a cannon and flies three feet straight back to where Mr. Prentice is standing. He had poop from his groin down to his feet. The whole barn went dead silent. Buttercup gave a little shake, and then she trotted off toward Ian, who was waiting at the trailer. All the time she's moving, we can hear her farting. *Fllattt. Fllatt. Fllatt.*"

Melanie leaned on the table, laughing. "Mom grabbed my arm, and we ran. When we got home, we had to rinse out the trailer and give Buttercup a bath. She got a total of three wash downs in two days before she was all better."

"Holy cow." Neddel was laughing, too. "What happened?"

"We never fed her avocados again," I said.

143

Chapter Nineteen

The sun was up, and my early morning chores were done. I had been awake most of the night, tossing and turning, itching to know more than I did. I was all set to drive into town and park in front of the sheriff's office until Neddel showed up.

Perhaps unreasonably, I had expected him to call me in the evening after supper and tell me what he had gleaned from the conversation with Noah. I'd been right there through the actual yada yada, but Sheriff Neddel was fairly new to me, and what was going on inside his brain was a mystery. If he'd had questions regarding Noah's story that were serious enough that he had to recruit my assistance in getting an answer, I felt I'd earned the right to know what the outcome was.

Walking into the police station didn't feel like my best play. Perhaps if I parked in his private spot, that might get his attention. I'd demand to know what he had uncovered. I had a right, didn't I?

I Don't think so; I thought as I made coffee and reconsidered my plan. Being the property owner didn't get you much more than having media, identify you to all the wackos wandering around loose.

I picked up a tray of seedlings to take out to the garden spot, then put it back down. I dragged out the vacuum cleaner. Neither the still-sleeping Melanie nor the cats would care for that.

Instead of dancing around in the yard, I headed to the feed shed. Ian and I had bought the solid metal body of a small refrigerator van that had once been used to haul seafood from the coast. The truck had been totaled in an accident, but the body had been offered to us practically free if we'd haul it off. It was perfect for our needs keeping varmints out of the animal feed. It wasn't quite tall enough for me to stand up in, and there was no room to swing a cat, but neither Buttercup nor any wild critter could get inside and help themselves to rations.

There was a definite lack of full feed bags filling the space when I swung the door open. Easy fix.

I backed the Jeep Patriot into position in front of the small open utility trailer and hooked up. It was a quick trip to the feed store. It always amazes me that when you tell people you live outside of town, they think you must be miles out in the boonies. Calwin Mountain Road is a small dirt turnoff of Route 16, right in the middle of town. On one corner is the 99 Restaurant. AC Tire is on the other corner, and straight ahead, if you don't make the turn onto Route 16, is Panera, my new all-time favorite place. I am literally one mile away from a cup-of-soup-and-half-sandwich fix.

At the corner, I waved a greeting to the happy green and cream façade and banged a left. Two traffic lights to the south, I pulled into the feed store.

I was surprised to find the parking lot packed. Then I saw the big sign announcing it was Flower and Plant Day. The soft sides were up on the tractor-trailer, and employees handed down hanging pots and flats even as racks of more tiny green shoots were being offloaded from the rear with the hydraulic lift.

Not to be deterred, I went inside and found David. He's the general manager and handles my billing for animal chow through the trust Dr. Rhoades set up.

"I can come back," I said, handing over my order. "I'll just leave the trailer. Whenever you have time to get to my order, will be good."

"Awesome," he said with a sigh. He pointed out where to leave the trailer, and I backed it in.

At loose ends, I could have gone home and accomplished maybe nothing. Instead, I drove back up Route 16, right past Calwin Mountain Road, and all the way to the next village. Right off Main Street is an old farmhouse with a sign out front: OTIS CABINS. NO VACANCY.

I cruised by, turned around, went back to Main Street, and turned again.

Across the street and one house before Otis's, is one of those little free libraries. They're built like birdhouses, but way bigger, and painted in bright colors. The doors are glass, so you can see inside. They are put up by private citizens, and the idea is to take a book, leave a book, and share what you've got.

I parked in front and opened the glass door. While I perused the offerings, I also looked over the Otis property. Beyond the house was a driveway that turned off to the left for their garage and to the right to make a soft half-circle where the cabins were. There were six cabins, each one with a sign over the door with a name instead of a number. The cabins were named after Snow White's dwarfs. I knew originally there had been seven, but I remembered a newspaper article mentioning that Dopey had burned down. I took a few photos with my phone before sending Melanie a text. *Which cabin did Juan live in?*

Don't know, she messaged back. *Never went there. He did say one time it was small, but a happy place.*

Deductive reasoning led me to believe that was Juan's tongue-in-cheek reference to his cabin being named HAPPY, which was the third one from the far end. There was a space between each cabin wide enough to park two cars, but most of the vehicles were right out front. There were family items on the tiny porches and the grassy spots that served as lawns. The kids' toys and lawn furniture offered evidence that most of the inhabitants weren't tourists. This was where they lived.

I tried to decide exactly what information I had been hoping to obtain. I could see that, if a vehicle had driven in to the space in front of Happy, no one from the Otis house would be close enough to actually see who had pulled in. How long would it have taken to pack Juan's possessions? If the killer had driven Juan's truck, taken a few boxes and a duffel bag out, and driven away, no one would give him a second glance. And if he'd wanted to be really safe, he could have done it all under cover of darkness.

While I stood there, Mr. Otis pulled out in his pickup. I followed. At the Irving gas station, the pickup pulled in and up to the pumps. I pulled into place on the other side.

"Hey, Mr. Otis." I smiled. "How's it going?"

"Good." He smiled back.

"Are you full up for the season?" I asked as I pulled my credit card out and lifted the nozzle.

"Oh, no tourists anymore. Now, we rent the cabins out like condos. Way less hassle."

"I bet," I said, selecting the grade and shoving the nozzle into the tank access. "Must be nice having that forestry guy living there. Like having a cop on the premises."

Mr. Otis didn't say anything about hearing that Juan had died, or about talking to the cops either. But then, his head didn't turn in my direction again.

He cleared his throat before speaking. "Noche? He left almost a year ago. We got up one morning, and he was just gone. Poof. If he hadn't left his television, you wouldn't have known anybody had been there. You never know, I guess, with them foreigners."

With that, he flipped the lever, shutting off the flow of gas to his truck, and without so much as a wave, drove off.

"Moron," I said to myself as his truck rolled down Route 16. "New Mexico has been a state since 1912, or thereabouts."

With my two and a quarter gallons of gas topping off my tank, I sat at the stop sign until a car pulled up behind me. At the feed store, my trailer was still empty. I continued south for another twenty miles. At the last Dunkin Donuts before Marilyn Helder's house, I stopped and picked up two lattes. Marilyn was a good friend, and the tenth-and-eleventh-grade English teacher. She's sharp-minded enough, so I knew to be right up front with her.

"I come bearing great gifts to the keeper of the celestial knowledge," I said when she opened the door.

"So, you want me to give you an A in what?" Marilyn waved me inside. Her little house is about eight-hundred-fifty square feet. She and her husband share the space with a lovely Sheltie rescue and a deaf green-gray tiger cat. She likes to say that all three of them are rescues she stumbled across.

"How's my star pupil?" she asked.

"She's good. However, there is this guy."

"Seriously?" Her eyebrow went up. "Isn't she old enough to figure it out?"

"The issue isn't what we know. It's more like what we are trying to surmise. Which is why I am here, to seek information from your crystal ball."

"What's his name?"

"Noah Deyak. You would have had him in the same class as Melanie."

"Hmm. Noah and Melanie, huh?" Marilyn went to the tall, narrow bookcase and selected two yearbooks. Opening the first one, she flipped through to the class picture and discarded the yearbook. In the second, she found Noah seated in the back row of the class staged on the bleachers. We searched for his name or photograph affiliated with any of the clubs or organizations, but all we had was that one minuscule shot. "Going to need a magnifying glass for this one," she said, retrieving said glass from where it hung on the side of the bookcase. "So, this guy shows up in the sophomore class, but he must have left before the pictures were taken for the junior class the next year. Do you want me to search back further?"

I shook my head and let her ruminate on the face, which showed slightly out of proportion in the glass before asking if she could recall anything about Noah.

"I don't really remember too much," she admitted. "Quiet kid. Heard he was a fighter, but I didn't think he was a bully. Had the look of a kid whose family was undergoing hard times."

"Who said he was a fighter?" I asked.

"I don't remember. I know I wasn't one of his class advisors, or I would have marked the yearbook. It may have come to me as faculty scuttlebutt. You know, the kind of thing where we get warned to keep our eyes open. He seemed pretty harmless."

"How do you know that?" I asked.

"Gut feeling from years of teenage exposure, I guess."

I refrained from telling her this time I thought her guts were off. We gabbed for a bit longer before I left. I hadn't learned much, but maybe I'd gotten an affirmation of what I believed Sheriff Neddel had been trying to work out over tacos supreme.

There was one more stop I wanted to make before I headed home. On the Kancamagus Highway, the first building after the traffic light was the forestry headquarters and tourist information building. A young lady looking freshly scrubbed and wearing a khaki-colored uniform was filling the brochure display.

She offered to help, and I told her I was checking to see if a young man who had been in training with the forestry service the year before had returned.

"His name is Juan Noche," I said.

She nodded. "I knew Juan. He was here for about five months but left unexpectedly at the beginning of summer. It left us a little short, which was good for me because I got to be out on the job more than usual."

From the way she was speaking, I could tell that when Neddel had been here to speak to the higher rank, and I was sure he must have, they had not yet disseminated the information to the rest of the staff.

"Well, I hope you enjoyed your time in the field," I said. "I'm sorry Juan isn't around anymore. He was a good guy." I waited to see what her take was.

She studied the brochure wall. Her smile was gone. "Yes," she said quietly, "he was."

Somebody had told her, I could tell. *Maybe she was ordered not to get drawn into a conversation about Juan,* I thought.

"We get a lot of recruits who are rough and tough cowboys," she said. "You know, gonna get the bad guys, save the baby moose. You can't relax around them because they immediately start thinking about you as an incapable female." She looked up with a rueful smile. "Then you have to take 'em out. It takes up a lot of energy."

I smiled back at her. "I am sure you are perfectly capable of the job and knocking those guys down a couple of inches. Thank you for speaking with me."

"Come back anytime," she called out as the screen door closed behind me.

My trailer was ready to go when I got back to the feed store, with six big sacks in the back that were going to make me sweat getting them unloaded.

"This is the one time I would have loved to find either Noah or Shane here," I said to myself as I pulled into my deserted yard. Even Buttercup wasn't interested in greeting me. About half the flock followed me to the steps. They were all complaining about something. I looked up just in time to see Melanie coming up to the door on the inside. Normally, she's all about the hair and make-up, even if she's not going any further than her desk. But this was wildly different.

"What happened to your hair?" I asked.

"What?" she asked, running both hands through it.

There, was the explanation for that question. I wasn't going to mention her shaky make-up application. Her speech wasn't confused, which led me to believe her appearance wasn't related to either the MS or maybe a migraine. But something had put her off.

"Zoe called to warn us the paper ran the story about the remains again. Only this time, they gave out our address and mentioned your name."

"Really?" I asked. That didn't sound good, but explained Melanie's appearance.

"Then the phone really started ringing off the hook. Wait until you hear the messages. Everything from the *oh, my god, what can we do to help you*, to the pant, pant, drool." Melanie backed into the house. "Look out, here comes another car."

I looked over my shoulder. A car with New York plates pulled in, almost to where I was standing. A young woman leaned out the window, took three or four photos, and then backed out.

From behind the screen, Melanie was still talking. "At first, I didn't pay any attention, but when I realized there was a constant cloud of dust, I pulled up the animal camera on my computer. It's ridiculous. And the red Audi has been out here again."

"Can you find the Audi on the tape and maybe get the plates?"

The shadow of Melanie behind the screen door disappeared. I went out to the barn and, in a couple of trips, lugged two sawhorses and some planks down to the end of the drive, where I built a barricade. After that, I was working with Rex when a more smoothed-down version of Melanie came

150

outside.

"I think I might have singled out the Audi," she said. "But from the angle of the camera, all I see is the car roof. No way to even see the driver because he didn't get out of the car, never mind the plate."

Buttercup and the biddies followed me into the garden spot, where I finished raking. Until I actually was pressing seedlings into the ground, they couldn't do any damage. But after lunch, when I was out there in my big straw hat, kneeling in the dirt surrounded by vegetable flats, they sat on the other side of the chain-link fence, giving me a big piece of their tiny brains.

It was some hot out there, but the forecast was for rain the next day. This was the perfect time to get plants in. Even Melanie, who didn't do well in the heat, took a half day off to bang in stakes and run string lines.

I hoed rows for the stuff that went in as seeds, like lettuce, radishes, and carrots. All afternoon, I heard cars drifting past. I ignored them, my notebook and pencil pushed aside by the need to get the garden in. The space was small enough that by suppertime, I pretty much had everything out. Discarded plastic flats were strewn outside the fence where I had tossed them. Buttercup had destroyed a couple, playing with them until she got too warm.

"Hey, can I play in the dirt?"

"Hey, Rose Ann!" I sat back on my heels, soaked with sweat, but feeling good about getting the planting almost done. Behind me, tied out on the overhead run, Rex was barking. The noise had started a while earlier, but after doing a visual check of the yard a couple of times, I figured he just wanted to be free to run with the pig, who had given up lying in the hot sun and moved to a cooler spot.

Rose Ann came in through the gate. Two hens, one red and one black, made a run at it, but she was faster.

"I had to come up this way for a court hearing tomorrow," she said. "Thought I'd check and see what was happening at Hotel Flynn before I tried Holiday Inn."

"Lucky for you, we had a recent cancellation," I said with a laugh. "Let me move the driveway barriers so you can pull your car in. Shush, Rex!"

He stopped for a minute, then began his intermittent barking again. I figured some chipmunk with a death wish was probably teasing him.

"Stay where you are. I can get them." She slid back out, making nah-nah noises at the hens who still wanted to get inside the garden fencing and the yummy green shoots.

By the time her car was in, her bag lugged into the house, and her clothing changed into something more casual, I was almost done.

"What's left?" she asked.

"I guess just bringing the hanging vegetables in." Using the legs from old jeans and tomato cage wire, I had made my own upside-down vegetable pots. The seedlings were stuffed through a hole in the center of the round piece stitched into the bottom of each leg. The top was filled with dirt and the wire kept the shape. Six feet above my garden spot, like ornamental loggias, crossbeams held heavyweight hooks ready for the tomatoes, summer squash, zucchini, and cucumbers that would grow hanging downward like bunches of grapes, waiting for the harvest. When I'd first started them, they had been on the deck, but Buttercup had taken notice. To keep the fledgling plants safe from Buttercup and the chickens, I hung them in one of the empty dog runs. They had grown fast and with their greenery already growing down close to ground level, were already a handful to relocate.

Once again, chickens ran at our heels. This time, they tried to snag the ends of the plants.

"These are pretty cool," said Rose Ann.

Fortunately, she was tall enough to carry one of the hangers without dragging it on the ground.

"Yeah, it's my own innovation, because I'm too cheap to buy the commercial ones."

We had all but the last four moved, when Rex started barking again. He sounded more agitated this time.

"For crying out loud, big guy," I said. "It's okay. No one is coming in the yard."

He stopped barking to look at us.

"I hear people talking," I whispered.

Rose Ann motioned toward the woods, then beckoned me to follow.

"Wait." I put Rex's harness and leash on him, and we headed up the trail just outside the kennel area. The one that led up the ridge to the remains site.

Rex pulled strongly on the leash. I kept drawing him back, but within seconds he would advance again. We hadn't gone far when we came to a place where four people, maybe thirty years of age, were pawing at the leaf litter. I pressed Rex down into the sit position. Rose Ann held up her phone, taking a video.

"Just look around," one of the women said. "You know how the cops are. They were sure to miss something."

"This is the right place, isn't it? Where the body was found?" the other woman asked.

The man jumped in. "You see that yellow marker? The cops left it so they could find their way back here."

"Actually," I said, loud and clear, "where you are is in a deer scrape from last season. All that stuff you're shoving into bags is poison ivy covered with animal urine."

The four whipped around. Rex selected that moment to stand and step forward. The group took off running. I watched them go with a certain amount of smugness.

"What now?" Rose Ann asked.

"Well, this isn't my property. It belongs to the state. The only thing we can hope is they don't get lost up there."

We headed back down the ridge, both of us giggling. Rex came along nicely, but his ears were up. One time, he stopped and looked back, then with a snort that said the trespassers were gone, he trotted ahead, ready to tell Buttercup that he had gone on an adventure, and she hadn't.

Once the rest of the hanging plants were out, I headed up for a shower, knowing I'd lose four pounds of dirt and sweat. Melanie had checked the animal camera down the road and verified that a vehicle was parked right in front of the sign directing people up the mountain.

"Hmm," I said. "Well, they weren't as big dummies as I thought they'd be."

"How's that?" Rose Ann asked.

"I put out two sets of signs. One was designed to lead people away from the site. The other was no trespassing signs. They didn't follow the trail away. Instead, they went toward the no trespassing signs and eventually ended up close to where Buttercup found Juan's remains."

"Want to know why?" Melanie tapped furiously on the keyboard. "It's not for the reason that you think. Look at this."

Both Rose Ann and I crowded close to the monitor. On Facebook, under a heading that said HUMAN REMAINS FOUND ON CALWIN MOUNTAIN, there was a photograph of the sign Neddel and I had posted at the end of the path.

We read down further. The person who had created the posting passed out a lot of facts. Like murdered, forestry employee, New Mexico, and last but not least, detailed instructions on how to get to the actual site.

"How is it somebody has all this information?" I mused. "Even my name." I turned to Melanie. "Can you scrub that?"

"Nope. See this spinning number chart? It's a counter. This site has already had over twenty thousand hits." She turned to look at me. "You are one popular mama, Mama."

"Well, that's just great."

"This isn't good. Either somebody is leaking information, or the killer is flaunting what he knows." There was no mistaking Rose Ann's anger. "For you, the great part is that people aren't showing up in even bigger droves."

She took out her cell phone and started keying furiously.

"Yup, that's me. Always the bridesmaid, never the bride." I walked over to the window and gazed down the road. "How can we fix this?"

"We can make it less appetizing," said Melanie.

"How's that?" I asked.

"Post messages on the website and on the actual trail. Like, I got poison ivy on my privates walking the trail. Or, long hike, spent the night in the woods listening to bears' growl." Melanie laughed.

"Oh, how about, who knew porcupines will chase you, or how do I get skunk stink out of my hair?" said Rose Ann. She still had her phone to her ear.

"Hello?" she said, walking toward the outside. "This is Rose Ann Lombard..."

She flashed a grin as she disappeared. Melanie shut down her computer, and we headed into the kitchen.

"If this set of yahoos aren't gone by dark, we probably should notify the sheriff," I said. "God knows, they could get lost. There's got to be some way to keep people out."

"It's public property, Mom," Melanie said.

I knew that. Having lived in this area for a long while, I also knew what would happen if tourists got lost in the National Forest. It took big money to get out there and rescue them, and a lot of times they didn't pay a dime toward the bill. Not to mention having them come back out in my backyard was a distressing thought.

"We should leave them paper and markers. Let them be the first bunch to leave irate messages." Melanie said.

"I've put out the word that the case has been scooped," Rose Ann said, coming back through the door, Buttercup behind her.

"You called Neddel?" I asked.

"Well, I called the forestry service state office and told the operator to patch the message through to all local and state-related personnel. It's faster."

Melanie pulled out the pitiful remains of the taco supreme from the fridge while I threw burgers and a foil-wrapped mixed-veggie steamer on the grill. Buttercup, Royally, and Lilo were dogging my steps.

"That sounds delicious," Rose Ann said after I'd explained how I slapped the steamer package together by chopping leftover vegetables, adding spices and oil, and roasting it all on the grill.

After I got the critters fed and Buttercup back outside, we sat inside because, with rain in the forecast, there was a significant cloud haze. The black flies were arriving by the busload, and the mosquitoes were selling tickets. The offering for this evening's repast was a mixed array of food. It looked like we'd be there for a while.

"Fortunately, there's not a lot of any one thing here." I laughed.

At the end of the table, Rose Ann stared at the screen door, unmoving, as she held a hamburger at the edge of her mouth. I swiveled to see what had given her that stunned look. On the other side of the screen, some kind of Frankenstein monster hovered. The body was a tall white tube, the head rectangular with one large eye. The low light shining from behind created a diffused edging around the creature, making its size immeasurable. A chill ran up my body and my fingers crawled toward Melanie, who sat with her back to the door.

"Mrs. Flynn?" the alien said.

"Shane?" I squeaked.

"I'm sorry. I didn't know you had company. I just wanted to talk with you for a few minutes."

I opened the door to let him inside. With the cloudy screen gone, his outfit was easy to identify.

"Are you putting beehives in across the street in the old orchard?" I asked.

"Dad is. I'm only helping. It's early in the season, but we already have some hives we had to split." He pulled off the beekeeper's hat and ran a hand over his sweaty, spiky hair. "I can come back later."

"No, that's all right," I said. The trickle of cold fear sweat in the center of my back had evaporated.

Shane chewed his lip, looking at Rose Ann and Melanie. I figured he wasn't here to mooch a meal.

"Would you like to talk in the sitting room?" I asked. At his nod, I led the way.

The poor young guy was clearly agitated. "Listen," I said, laying my hand on his arm. "If whatever you have to say is bad, think about a Band-Aid. One quick, hard pull. Okay?"

He nodded, looking almost anywhere but at me.

"I know Melanie is starting to get a little sore at me." Shane's feet shuffled. "You know, because I've been calling a lot and whatnot? But Mrs. Flynn, I can't help it. I'm worried about her."

"Why?" I thought he was about to give a declaration of love for my daughter or ask for her hand. But Shane had a different thing going on.

"I know I'm only the kid that lives up the street. Unfortunately, I'm the kid who lives up the street and who works for the coroner. I spend a lot of time with Doctor Kennett, and he spends a lot of time gossiping with cops, other doctors, and the ambulance guys. You may not realize it, but a lot of people are actively working with the remains you found, or just on the case."

I was surprised to hear that. I mean, I knew Burt Kennett, and by association, Shane, and Sheriff Neddel, but what Shane was saying sounded like a large circle of people and not all of them local.

"Why? Who are these people?"

"The state police are in on it. Officer Ramp has been asking a lot of questions. We're still getting results back from all the testing the sheriff had us do. And there are, ah, others, as well."

"Why is this?" I asked. "We know who the remains are. Juan Noche, right?"

"Yeah, but cause of death is still up in the air."

He hadn't mentioned Rose Ann, but I knew she was a big part of the investigation. If Burt Kennet was gossiping, was she in the loop? I thought about what Rose Ann had said about medical examiners who were too old to be doing the job. I didn't say anything.

"It's clear at this time it was no accident, but a homicide," said Shane.

"And?"

He sighed. "Even I know you've been asking around. I'm worried you're going to put yourself or Melanie in danger."

He seemed to be on the verge of something else. I was annoyed. For some reason. I had believed my few words with the people who had been at the cove party would evaporate from their brains in thirty seconds, and the memory would be forever lost. Shane looked cowed, and I realized I was frowning. Wiping that from my face, I spoke softer.

"What else is in your craw, Shane? Spit it out."

"The sheriff has been doing a lot of poking around about Noah Deyak. Some of his deputies are talking about it. How the sheriff is flying to Dannemora to talk to Noah's father. He's incarcerated at Clinton Correctional Facility. That's the prison in New York."

"Prison?"

"Yeah, see, that's exactly what I'm talking about," Shane spoke in a hushed tone. "Noah's not telling you that he's been in jail as well. You know, because he had to leave high school here after he beat that guy in Maine so bad. Or that his dad is doing time for armed robbery. He's going to be there a while, from what Doctor Kennett says."

"What are you talking about, Shane? This has to be just gossip." I was so surprised, I sat down on the edge of the sofa. Shane had to be wrong. If Neddel knew this, he would have told me. Shane sat beside me.

"Did Noah tell you his mother has been missing since he and his dad moved away from here? That no one can find her? Or that Noah was the last one to see her alive? He's not a good guy, Mrs. Flynn. But he comes and goes around here like he owns the place, and he's making Melanie dependent upon him. He stayed right here in your house while you were down helping Melanie after Mr. Flynn died."

I knew that. I had told him he could. It would be better for the cats to have someone in the house. *Oh, my god*, I thought. *I allowed him to be where he could riffle through everything!*

Shane tugged at my fingers, pulling my attention back. "I'm, well...afraid for you."

I held my hand up to stop Shane's rush of words. My heart had risen into my throat, and drawing a breath was painful.

"Stop," I said. "Please stop."

I was having a problem processing everything he'd just told me. I hadn't known. What about Melanie? No, I was sure if she had heard any of this, she would have said something. I needed to speak with her. But Rose Ann was here.

How, I wondered, *am I going to do this?*

He reached out for my arm, but I pulled away.

"I need to think, Shane. I need time to consider what you're saying. You should go help your dad now. I'll call you later, after I've had time to process all this."

"Melanie..." he began.

"I'll watch out for Melanie," I said. "You go along. Give me some time."

Shane left through the front door, and I walked slowly back to the kitchen. Both Melanie and Rose Ann were waiting. I glanced at the remaining food spread across the table, but I wasn't thinking about taco salad or burgers and buns. My mind was all wrapped around what Shane had just said. About Burt Kennett and his cronies, and then about Noah and his parents.

I wanted to talk to Rose Ann and Melanie about what I'd heard from Shane. Just not both, at the same time. My instant logic was that different parts of Shane's warning were appropriate only to Melanie or Rose Ann.

"What's going on, Mom?" asked Melanie.

"Oh, you know Shane," I said, swallowing the knot in my throat. "He's all worried about us. Mostly, it's Burt Kennett's fault, I think. I told him to relax. Now, if we don't eat the rest of this, we'll be having it again tomorrow."

"No way," my daughter said, with a laugh. "I'm going to divvy up the remainders for the pig and the dogs."

"Better than a garbage disposal," Rose Ann said, reaching for another burger.

I looked at mine, unsure if I would be able to eat at all.

* * *

After supper, I went into the cattery and took Argyle out of the quarantine crate. Melanie was in the living room, and because Argyle had been a pet before he came to us, I felt safe leaving him in there to stretch his legs for a while. I needed time to think, to figure out exactly what my questions for Rose Ann were, and then how I was going to approach Melanie. To keep my hands busy, I started cleaning the quarantine crate for the next tenant. When I went back into the kitchen, Rose Ann was working on her laptop.

"What can I do?" she asked.

"Can you help me carry the crate inside from the porch? I want to move the ginger cat into quarantine, where she can get used to being around us."

While we wrestled the crate inside and got both that one and the quarantine crate lined up door to door, then pushed together, I popped the question.

"You were really upset at Burt Kennett the first time you showed up here."

I swung the door open on the quarantine crate. The other one had a drop door. "Did you guys get over that? You know, are you, like, communicating about the case?"

Rose Ann gave a hard little laugh.

"I'm thinking someone told him I was more than a little pissed. I called, but he didn't return my call. There was information I needed, and it showed up as an email that day and a hard copy through the mail a few days later." She swept her hair back from her face with her hand. "He doesn't want to talk to me. Poor baby."

"Phfft," I said. "You've got that right."

What she had just told me meant that Burt was gossiping with others. But who?

"How is this going to work for the cat?" Rose Ann asked and then slyly added. "Does your question have anything to do with Shane's visit?"

I dropped a blanket over the quarantine crate. "With this box covered, I'm going to tip the ginger cat inside. Hopefully, she'll go through to the dark. Once she's moved, I'll let her get acclimated for a bit before I uncover the crate. Shane made a remark about Burt and other people talking. That might be the leak. I was trying to think of a polite way to ask you if Burt pumped you for information."

"The next time, just ask me," Rose Ann said. "I think the ginger cat needs a name. How about Ruffles? See how she has long white fur around her face? Kind of like ruffly lace."

"Ruffles it is." I penned the name on a card and used a clothespin to attach it to the crate.

"You know," Rose Ann said as she headed to the door. "I think Shane is sweet on Melanie."

"According to her, they're just good friends. But maybe you're right. For him, it might have changed. She said he's been clingy lately, possessive even. Today, he sounded afraid."

"Of what?" Rose Ann asked. "Oh, I know. He's worried that Noah and Melanie are going to be romantic, and he'll be left behind."

"Maybe," I said, not wanting to tell her about my fears concerning Noah.

I'd need to sit down with Melanie first.

It was time to put Argyle to bed and shut out the lights. Too bad I couldn't shut down my thoughts as easily.

Chapter Twenty

The meteorologist on Channel 8 had predicted a day of continual soft rain, perfect for tender young plants. He had been spot-on. I woke to the patter of rain on the leaves of the oaks outside my window, not the pounding of torrential downpours. I lay there for several minutes, listening for the far-off drum roll of thunder that would predict a devastating deluge on the way. A force of water right now would drown my newly planted garden spot.

Please, I prayed. *Have pity on those tiny green infants.*

I could hear my Catholic mother chiding me about the proper use of prayer and the frivolity of those souls who didn't take God's power seriously. For not the first time in my life, I apologized to that long-dead woman and to God, too. The lesson that always followed her lecture was the one regarding actions instead of words.

While I dressed, I listed all the good deeds I would accomplish that day while not allowing myself to be diverted. I was half buried inside a cat housing crate, cleaning out a bad reaction to very stinky shrimp and crabmeat canned cat food, when I heard Melanie yelling down the hallway. I had hoped to get done before she got up for the day, and my gag reflex failed, but it was not to be.

"Car out in the driveway. Can you get that?"

Sure, I thought with a sigh. *I'm not doing anything else, anyway.*

A very pretty claret red Rogue pulled up to the bottom of the handicap ramp. The woman stepping out of the driver's seat was about forty, nicely dressed. Obviously, no one had warned her there might be assorted animals roaming free here, because she stopped dead in her tracks when the corgi and the pug ran around the front of her vehicle. If Buttercup had come running through the wet mud, the poor lady would have probably had a breakdown.

"Hi," she said tentatively. "Mrs. Flynn? I'm Kathy Wilcox. Did the people from Pine Terrace call you about Tiny?"

I had taken a second to rinse off my hands and flicked the towel at the dogs. They ignored me, continuing to sniff and mutter.

"No, I didn't get a call," I said. "How can I help you?"

"This is my mother, Harriet, and Tiny," Kathy said.

In the passenger seat was an elderly woman with a big smile. She held a pink and purple cat carrier on her lap. Harriet was so frail-looking. I was surprised the cat carrier hadn't busted a leg bone as they bumped up the road. Kathy explained that her mother was moving that day into Pine Terrace, which was a long-term senior housing complex, just around the corner on Route 16. Tiny was Harriet's nine-year-old Siamese who wouldn't be able to move with her and who Kathy, with three large dogs, couldn't take home.

My radar dinged.

"Mrs. Odgen at Pine Terrace told me that you have emotional support animals and take in cats.

"Well, that's a generous overview, but yes, I have a cattery. And I do bring animals down to Pine Terrace twice a week." I was trying to figure out how to explain that just driving into my yard wasn't how this worked.

"So, you'll take my Tiny?" Harriet's voice was as weak as her body.

I opened my mouth to say no, and this voice behind me said, "Absolutely. Would you like to come in for a cup of tea and meet some of the other feline ladies?"

I don't know who was more surprised, myself or Kathy. Melanie opened the car door, took custody of the yowling critter, and helped Harriet out.

"Hold on," said Kathy, suddenly galvanized into action. "Let me get your walker, Mom."

We sat in the kitchen sipping tea and munching down Oreos. Harriet got a tour of the entire first floor of my house. She was introduced to every cat and both dogs, but when she expressed an interest in meeting Buttercup, I drew the line. Buttercup seems to know children are fragile people. I don't know what she would think of this wizened little old lady.

"I'll tell you what. You probably have lots to do today, and Buttercup is still napping. How about the next time she comes down to Pine Terrace, we make sure you meet each other?"

Kathy looked incredibly relieved. While her mother said an affectionate goodbye to Tiny, I raced out and threw a fistful of Oreos among the straw. Hoping as I ran back Buttercup would be so busy searching, she wouldn't stand up on the fence to see the company.

Once Kathy had her mother back in the car and they drove away, Melanie returned to her office. That left me to find Tiny, who once released from Harriet's grasp, had shot off looking for a place to hide. We had rules about quarantine, but they had been rendered moot the second the kitchen door was opened and the yowling had entered. In seconds, every fur ball not locked in a housing crate ran over to get a look.

Harriet had left me with an envelope containing Tiny's medical records, which was a good thing because my information form was left unfilled on the table as Tiny stared back at me, cross-eyed and terrified. We were officially full up at the Kitty Motel.

"Oh, you poor baby," I said, cuddling the trembling body to my chest. "I think you're going to have to spend tonight in my room. But I tell you what: we'll make Melanie drive down and get the rest of the information from your mom once we get you settled.

At my feet, Royally dropped to the floor and lay quietly. He knew fear when he saw it.

* * *

I sat on the side of Melanie's bed, still cuddling Tiny. Lilo was hanging over the arm of the desk chair, trying to get a sniff.

"Are you working yet?" I asked.

"Nope. Shopping. Upcoming baby shower."

"Okay. I need a few minutes of your time."

"What now?" Melanie groaned dramatically, throwing her arm across her eyes.

"Couple of things. Shane..."

"Who was here yesterday, whining," Melanie said.

"...appears to have taken the next step up from buddy."

"What are you talking about?" She finally turned to face me, frowning.

"I think he's looking at you with new eyes. Like, more, I don't know, or in less than a brotherly way." I licked my lips. I wasn't enjoying this.

"Eyeh! No way." Melanie pulled away as far as the high-backed, ergonomically correct seat would let her go.

"Yeah, there's that," I agreed. "And there's the bit about him taking umbrage at the amount of time Noah is spending with you."

"Tell me you're kidding," Melanie said.

"No, and I'm not sure how to say this." I studied the chocolate tipped ears of Tiny and came up with nothing. "Okay, here's the deal. Shane had some negative things to say about Noah."

"Like about how Noah's father used to knock him around, and Noah would come to school all bruised up and angry." Though she spoke cooly, I could hear Melanie's rising temper. "He'd get in fights. His family wouldn't support him. His mother took off. His dad dragged him away from here. Any of that stuff?" Melanie demanded.

"Actually, no." I was at a loss for words.

Melanie looked back at the computer screen. "It's time for me to go to work. Before you accept what Shane has to say as the god's honest truth, you should sit down with Noah. It's his story, his choice of who he shares it with."

I went down the hallway, thoughts swirling like a tornado. Had I handled the issue? Solved any problems? Or had I created a new one? Tiny and I left. Royally followed us. I have a pouch that closes in such a way a cat's head can stick out, but the cat won't fit through the opening. I put Tiny in that, slung her across my chest, and let her ride there until she fell asleep.

Chapter Twenty-One

There was a cast over the sun, but the day was bright enough not to warrant lights on in the house. Instead of a heavy rain jacket that would leave me sweating beneath, I opted for barn boots and a wide-brimmed hat to keep my head dry. Unfortunately, I had to go back and add bug spray because, though the light rain would feed my new garden and wash the last of the pollen from the trees, it was not enough to deter the black flies and mosquitoes. They were an annoyance buzzing around my face, but the spray kept them from alighting everywhere while they searched for warm human flesh that hadn't been tainted by noxious anti-bite chemicals. I'd left Tiny with Melanie, who was napping, but carried a large ceramic cup out with me. I needed a caffeine boost. Tiny's first night had been rough. Her wailing calls had kept us all up until the wee hours of the morning. Now, succumbed to exhaustion, she cuddled up with Melanie and Lilo.

They were doing better than I. It seemed each gulp of coffee was infused with protein due to the number of black flies, dive-bombing the black brew before considering the need to swim.

With Melanie asleep, I started working in the barn. Buttercup had wandered out into the yard. I knew she was probably under the deck. Even though she knew she wasn't supposed to go there, it was a shelter from the rain and biting flies. The radio offered a straight, no-interruption rendering of the best of old Hank Williams tunes until noon. I sang along with songs I recognized and shimmied to the rest. Boots and Butch, whose primary residence was right where I was working, moved from bale to bale as I cleaned up the windblown straw and hay. The gate was open, but when

Buttercup returned, making disgusted noises about the cold, damp space beneath the wooden platform, she was more interested in reworking the fresh hay and sawdust I'd dumped in her home pen than she was in being under my feet. Her housework would keep her busy for a while, then she'd either take a nap or, if bored, wander outside again.

I wiped down pig tack, broomed cobwebs out of the corners, and swept up sawdust that had scattered in the weeks prior. Coming back from the orchard across the road after dumping the trailer, I spent a few minutes looking at the house through the eyes of a stranger. It looked so peaceful, like the home of a graceful older woman comfortable in her own skin and in no hurry to do anything. The image was laughable. We had endured so much drama since Buttercup's find on the mountain. As I worked, I went over what I'd learned. A few short breaks while I wrote a note or question down, and I kept at it.

While I was hauling soiled straw across the road, a car buzzed by. The occupants, who I assumed were curious about the type of people that would find a long-dead body near their home, were focused on the house and didn't see me. I got off the tractor and stood by the side of the road. Calwin Mountain Road is a dead end. The car had to turn around and come back. As it drew near, I took a step forward and set off the flash on my cell phone. The driver's head whipped around to where I stood. I smiled and waved. The driver had a look of fear on his face as the car jerked toward the ditch. The driver did a quick correction, then the vehicle jumped from twenty to forty in a single bound. As I stood there laughing, the cell phone rang. I almost dropped it.

"Hello?" I sounded shaky. Before I could clear my throat and try again, Neddel spoke.

"Mrs. Flynn? Are you all right?"

I laughed. "Sorry, the phone startled me."

"Will you be coming into town today?"

"I'm not sure. Do you need something?"

"No," said Neddel, "I have some information to share. I wanted to make sure I would be available if you were around."

My happy little glow at scaring the beejebus out of the gawker dimmed. "Is it life-altering?" Sitting down for a chat with Sheriff Neddel might get some of my questions answered, but he was just as likely to irritate me.

This time, he was the one who laughed. "No. Don't make a special trip. If I don't see you today, we'll catch up later."

I got back on the tractor and puttered into my yard, backing the trailer into its spot next to Buttercup's outside pen. The conversation with Neddel had vanished from my mind.

Left alone in the barn with only the cats for company, Buttercup had looked for a more entertaining activity. Because I had left the gate to her home pen open, she had come out and moved to a wallowing place on the far side of the chicken coop. Early on, when she had shown a propensity to dig holes, Ian staked out an area at the very furthest reach of the garden hose. He'd go out and wet it down, and Buttercup would follow, her tail whipping from side to side and a happy little grunt-grunt escaping. It had started as a small mud puddle that, with her help, grew until we brought in big rocks and created a barrier lining both the inner sides and the top. The step down had developed into a ramp, and to keep the hole from going too deep, every other year, we had a yard of sand dumped into the middle. Spreading it around was Buttercup's job, and she did it well. With the rain, the sand and soil were wet and gushy. She rolled, squealed, flopped, and played other little pig games. She would be banned from the kitchen today.

Instead, I brought Rex inside the house for a little socializing and conditioning. He was good with the other dogs, and the house cats found a place to watch and stay out of reach. Tiny was placed in a house crate with food, water, and a hot water bottle. On the other side of the screen door that kept the cattery separate from the kitchen, I heard a few forlorn meows until Rex went over and stuck his nose against the mesh so he could see what was going on in there. Even though he didn't growl at them, or make any other aggressive move, the old lady cats decided this was a good day for a nap in their condos.

My original plan when I rolled out of bed had been to get some much-needed and distasteful housecleaning done. The day was half done, and I was looking for another alternative. After my conversation with Melanie, I'd spent a while considering polite openers with Noah. It seemed nothing I came up with fell under the heading of polite, non-invasive interrogation. I remembered Neddel's call. Just thinking about going down to the police station and sitting across the desk from him while the recording tape ran made me nauseous.

"I should go back out and make sure the garden isn't flooding," I told Rex. "I may need to do a little extra trenching."

He looked at me like he knew I was planning an escape.

"Okay," I sighed. "We'd better start in the bathrooms, because I don't know how long I'll last."

An hour and a half later, we moved into the living room. Rex found a comfortable place and settled in until whatever human need, I was trying to fulfill was accomplished. I could hear his brain working. *What's a little dust? Who cares if there are nose prints on the windows? Even if they are at more than one level.* He was good until I started the vacuum cleaner, then he exited. When I finished, I found Melanie in the kitchen.

"Are you just now getting up? It's the middle of the afternoon," I said, trying to look stern. She was an adult. How much could I say?

"Phfft. I got up hours ago. You were outside, and I had a few hours of work waiting, so I've been doing that."

There was a rumble against the wooden kitchen door, but the deadbolt held. "Don't open the door, piggie is filthy," I said, but toast in hand, my daughter was already headed back to her own space.

A moment later, she came rushing up the hall. "Mom, Shane is coming. Tell him I'm not here."

Shane! Somebody else I didn't want to talk to that afternoon.

"Right. Your car is in the driveway."

"Then tell him I'm having a bad day. Just don't let him in, okay?"

"What's going on? Did you two have a fight?" *Or maybe*, I thought, *she didn't like what he had to say about Noah.*

I didn't either actually, well no, that's not right. What I didn't like was that one of the few people I considered totally harmless had crossed the line and

169

done his best to upset my world more than it had been. I needed recovery time, but I wasn't getting it.

Before she could answer, there was a knock at the door. Melanie disappeared into the bathroom.

"Tell him." She hissed.

I unlocked the wood door and opened it enough for me to squeeze out.

"Has someone been out here harassing you?" Shane asked. "I mean, it's good you have the door locked, but you look kind of frazzled."

I looked over his shoulder. To be honest, I was having a problem looking him in the eye and lying. I went with a half-truth. "Buttercup gave herself a mud bath, and I'm cleaning. I don't want her inside right now. What can I do for you?"

"Is Melanie here?"

I motioned with my hand for him to speak softer. "Shh, honey, she's having a migraine. Can I take a message?"

"No, I don't have to be at work until four. I thought I'd just visit for a while."

He knew she should be working. I pointed out that, once she was feeling better, she'd have to get back to it.

"It's not like she's never let me just sit there before." He laughed, moving ahead a tad.

I held my ground. "Not today. If she wakes up to find you sitting there, she'll scream until the cows come home. See you later, honey. I'll tell her you stopped in." I moved back inside, leaving Shane on the back porch. Moments later, I heard his car start and pull out of the drive.

"Okay, Melanie, he's gone. Come out and tell me what's going on."

She came out dressed in her requisite work-at-home sweats and tee but as usual, her makeup and hair were all done, like she was going to an office somewhere. Maybe she was just ready for a Zoom meeting, if ever required.

She brewed a Keurig chai tea. Having had my fill of housework, I sat at the table and waited.

"I'm sorry, Mom," she said, sitting down with the steaming mug in front of her. "I know how you hate to push people aside like that, but I have to tell you, ever since you and Buttercup stumbled on those remains, Shane has been incredibly annoying."

"I thought we talked about this," I said.

She shrugged, looking down at Rex. He looked back, a little frown on his brow. "Well, you know…Shane and I have always been friends for as long as I can remember. There was no division between girl and boy, he and I. We were just friends. A normal, easy relationship, like breathing. When things…happened last year, he got a little more protective, maybe. I'm not sure if that's the right word. I thought it would pass, like when he broke his leg in fourth grade. I did everything for him until he got better, you know?"

I nodded. Their friendship had always been on an even keel. When it dipped to one side, it righted itself in time.

"I told you before, he's gotten to be a pest. Lately, it just seems to be getting even worse."

"Why do you think that is?" I asked.

My fingers curled tight around my coffee mug. If Melanie had more, she hadn't told me. I needed to know. Rex turned his golden eyes toward me. Lilo was standing on tiptoe, waiting for Mel to pick her up, and unusually quiet. As was, I realized, Tiny.

"I don't really know. But I have the same theory you came up with, that in his mind, our relationship is becoming more of a male/female thing."

I liked Shane. However, I had to admit, there was no way I could visualize the two of them dating. When Rose Ann had brought it up, I'd felt, I don't know, repulsed.

"Yeah, and it's creepy. It would be like kissing your brother."

Melanie didn't have a brother. I had three. There was no way that I'd kiss any of them.

"Right. And, oh, while I'm thinking of it, when did you let him sit in while you were working?"

Melanie pulled back, frowning. "I have never let him sit in. He gossips like a grandma. He'd be telling everyone he ran into what I was doing for who. A lot of that information is confidential. People give me their private data. A couple of times, he's asked if he could, begged even. Every time he does, I go all over it again, why he can't. He knows better than that. Can you imagine if Mrs. Avery heard that I was letting people hang out in my office while I was working? I had to sign a contract that my space was private. I'd be all done in a heartbeat." She shook her head, dismissing the notion.

"I don't want to send him away, Mom. I don't want to not be his friend anymore. It's just that every conversation we have lately evolves into ridicule, or worse, about my other friends. Things Shane doesn't like. What he believes I should know. I'm sure it's not all true. There are a lot of people he doesn't care for. Like Noah. Shane is my friend, but he is getting really intense. I don't know what time he gets up, but that's when he starts texting. If I don't answer by nine, he'll call. I don't know if you've noticed, but he's here every day. It's like he has radar. If Noah arrives, Shane will follow. You saw him when Sheriff Neddel was here. Shane wanted Noah totally out of the conversation. I didn't invite Shane to come over for supper, did you? Or did he just stay?"

I felt uncomfortable. Shane had just walked in and I had accepted his appearance, like it was nothing.

"Well, he's comfortable being here," I said, then realized it sounded like I was making excuses for him. "I thought you and he had the same friends."

"So did I." Melanie sipped her tea, then started ticking off friends. "He's been telling me stuff like Russel is an idiot. Zoe is a whore. Travis can't be trusted, and from what Shane's saying about Noah, he believes he's guilty of murder."

"Melanie!" I gasped.

I was gulping for air. I had seen the tape. Allowed Sheriff Neddel, who I barely knew, to make me part of his fact-finding scheme, and heard Shane, a young man I totally trusted, say terrible things about Noah. And yet, I was still appalled to hear those words come out of my daughter's mouth. Edging to the end of my seat, I opened my mouth, ready to tell Melanie all of that, but she wasn't done.

"I'm sorry, Mom. I don't like it either. It's just...I can't tell anymore if the stuff Shane is saying about Noah is gossip, or if he heard things from his boss, Doctor Kennett, that the sheriff isn't telling us. And get this—he told me he's thinking of parking across the road down by the big maple and stopping traffic from coming up here. It's a public road! What we did, with the signs and all, is harmless. Shane is talking about a face-to-face confrontation. He's acting all nuts!"

"He can't stop people from driving by here," I said. "Not one of those lookie-loos has done anything threatening. I may not like them cruising back and forth, but there's no law against it."

Lilo had gotten into Melanie's lap. Rex had his chin on her knee. Even Royally was lying at her feet. They were concerned and so was I.

"Okay, one last thing here. Has Noah ever said anything about where he went, like what town, when he and his dad moved away?" I asked.

"Not much." Melanie got up to rinse her cup. "They left here and went down to Peabody. I thought he would say they moved around a bunch, but Noah said no. His dad got a construction job near where they lived. Then, he kept getting caught drinking on the job. The company fired him. He just went out and got a job with a different company. It's a big area with a lot of growth happening around the outskirts, so once they found the dump they lived in, Noah's old man didn't bother to move. But in his senior year, Noah decided he wanted to go to college. His high school advisor helped him figure it all out, and when Noah came to school one day all beaten up, Sam—his advisor—found him a host family to live with."

This is like afternoon drama television, I thought. *Impossible leaps from lily pad to lily pad.*

I was sure that Noah hadn't just figured it out and gone to college. But then, I also believed his job at the bank required a BA.

"How did Noah afford college?" I asked slowly.

"Loans, I bet. He did say he had worked all through the summers while taking core classes. That way, during the school year, he could still have time to work. He earned an internship during his last two quarters."

Where would Noah have gotten an internship? I wondered. Then suddenly, I thought about Juan. He'd been an intern, right? I needed to talk to his friend, Mike.

The timer went off in Melanie's office, reminding her it was time to go back to work. She started to go, then turned back to me.

"Another weird thing happened. I didn't notice at the time, but later I wondered about it. Sheriff Neddel was talking about Juan Noche being down at the cove. Shane keeps saying I should never have been sitting there alone with Juan that night because he was dangerous. How would Shane know that if he wasn't at the party?"

"Somebody had to have mentioned it, I guess," I answered.

"Just another case of the gossip mill working overtime." With a shrug, Melanie left.

Was Rose Ann and my daughter, right? Had Shane fallen in love with her, and now he was jealous of Noah? I wiped down the already clean kitchen counter, mulling over the whole young male thing in my head. And how had Juan fit into this? Melanie said they were just friends, but sometimes she could be intense. Had some other male read that friendship, as something else? Jealousy would certainly explain why quiet-as-a-church mouse Shane was bad-mouthing Noah. And, by extension, people who would support Noah because they had elected to be his friends instead of Shane's.

"I am so glad," I told Rex, "I didn't have half a dozen daughters."

The door rattled again. By the unhappy grunt, I could tell Buttercup wanted to come inside and maybe have a cookie. I went out and put treats in her roll-around ball, hoping that would keep her occupied until suppertime. One look at the mud caked on her flanks made me sorry I had changed her hay earlier that day. My black and white Hampshire was a mucky brown from head to hoof. My only hope was that, while she chased the treat ball, the rain would rinse some of the mud off. A two-hour deluge might get rid of all of it.

Bathing Buttercup alone while fending off Royally and Lilo was exhausting. The pig stayed in one place while the pampering was happening, but the dogs dashed in and out, running from place to place demanding attention. The excitement lasted until the final drop of water dribbled off the tarp into the sod. Buttercup moved from where the wet plastic was sticking to her hide to a spot on the cushy lawn. I brushed strands of grass off my knees that had embedded themselves while I had been scrubbing the pig. I complained about the humidity left over from the previous day's storm. Nobody was listening.

"Come on, you guys," I whined. "How about a little support here? You could just agree a little. Maybe give me an *Oh, we're sorry, Mom?*"

But every single critter, except the snoozing pig, had disappeared. My shoulders bowed. The allure of picking the equipment up before starting another task disappeared like mist. I'm not sure how my knees held up long enough to carry me over to where Buttercup had stretched out. I sank to the ground beside her, leaning against her back. She felt like a soft, sun-warmed cushion. Across the yard, I could see the barn and the trail leading up behind it. A quick photographic memory lit up the backside of my brain. I could see the lush green ferns, Buttercup's black and white spine covered with bristly white hairs, and my hands reaching out to part the leaves, allowing the grisly smile of bone and teeth to appear.

I physically shook it off, allowing the comforting worth of my porky buddy to lull me back to peace.

"So bizarre," I said with a yawn. "Something as horrible as that happening right up there behind the barn, like he just walked up the path and keeled over."

But he didn't, I thought.

I was too far gone for my mind to stay on that thought. My eyes fluttered. I yawned again before snuggling down further against the warm pig, the rise and fall of her breathing rocking me towards my own nap in the sun. I shifted, trying to force myself to stay awake. Shafts of light shined into the barn. Boots was lying with her feet all curled up beneath her, enjoying the warmth just as I was. The whole scene could have been a picture puzzle. I smiled, twisting slightly when Buttercup wiggled. My eyes lit on my trusty old Cub Cadet.

"I should give it a name like we did with Charlie One. Something like the Shanemobile. After all, he uses it more than I do." I gave a soft laugh and pictured Shane coming across the back lawn on the mower.

The keys are in it.

I know.

I bolted upright, my hand covering my mouth as I remembered that conversation with Shane the first day I'd met Rose Ann Lombard. My eyes locked on the faded yellow and orange tractor as if I expected it to grow horns and a pointed tail.

"Who else knew about the keys?" I whispered.

The answer was everybody. Anybody who had been hanging around here in the seventeen years we'd had the tractor would know the corroded key couldn't be pulled out of the ignition. Any of Ian's friends who'd helped on any of thousands of projects. All of my friends, or the kids who had come over to hang around with Melanie and enjoyed the thrill of rumbling around on the piece of shaking, knocking equipment.

"For crying out loud, if somebody just walked into the yard and looked, they'd see the damn key." A sobbing laugh escaped my lips. "And if they needed gas, the two-gallon can is right there by the barn door."

I got to my feet and moved slowly toward the house, doing the math as I went. Rose Ann had said the remains had been there since mid-summer the previous year. That meant Noche could have died during the weeks I was busy far away, taking care of Melanie after that second big MS episode. Then there'd been the packing and moving. My absence would have been carte blanche to make use of the Cadet. With shaking fingers, I searched through the list of contacts on my cellphone, trying to remember how I had listed the sheriff's office telephone number.

"Hello, this is Doris Flynn. I'd like to speak with Sheriff Neddel, please."

"I'm sorry," said the young man, who answered the phone. "The sheriff is not in the office today. Would you like to speak with the officer in charge?"

I gulped. Shane had said Neddel was going to Dannemora prison, hadn't he? Had Shane said exactly when the sheriff was going? When he would be back? Was that why Neddel had called asking if I was coming into town? I wanted to kick myself. If I hadn't been on my high horse and all attitude that day, maybe I'd know where he was.

"No, I'm good. Thank you."

Neddel had given me a second business card, and I'd taped it on the fridge. That one had his private cell phone number on it. I stood on the worn linoleum facing the squeaking, creaking appliance, wondering what to do. Should I call? Leave a message? What good would that do if he was out of state somewhere? Then again, the idea the key and the tractor were right there, and the fact that I'd been far away, might be a solid fact, but how on earth was I going to prove who might have used it? Might, being the pivot word. Not only had Juan Noche's body ended up on the mountain behind my home, but it could have traveled through my yard, ridden in my trailer. Somehow, I was feeling responsible. It was stupid. My feet felt ice cold.

"What are you doing, Mom?" Melanie asked.

"Trying to decide between iced tea or lemonade?" I asked, keeping my face averted.

"Go with green iced tea. You look a little stressed." With a bag of chips and a bottle of water in hand and the black pug dancing on her heels, Melanie went back to the serenity of her office.

When I was sure she wouldn't come sneaking back, I headed into the bathroom and sat on the closed lid of the toilet for several minutes. I couldn't think. My brain refused to work. In the end, I went outside with my cell phone and made the call. It rolled over to voice mail.

"Hey, Sheriff Neddel. Everett. Uh, sheriff." I blew out my cheeks. "Listen, this is Doris Flynn. No emergency, but can you give me a call when you get back into town, or tomorrow sometime? Thanks. This is Doris Flynn."

I was repeating myself like a confused old woman. I broke the connection, so embarrassed I knew I was flushed like it was a hundred degrees outside, and I was staked out to fry. My shoulders curled around, and I felt exposed, unsafe. I wanted to lie in my bed wrapped in a heavy coverlet and feel like I was being comforted.

Instead, I settled for getting back to the housecleaning I hadn't finished. Eventually, thoughts of calling Neddel to explain about the key in the tractor evaporated because I became fixated on cars—only this time, it was due to the fact they *weren't* driving by. Melanie and I were out here all alone at the end of a dead-end dirt road where normally there was practically no traffic, where we couldn't quite see the nearest neighbor's house. I'd never felt afraid of living here, even during the dark nights. But right now, I wanted Melanie to walk by with her car keys and purse in hand, telling me she was going into the city to visit a friend for a few days. I locked the doors and closed the windows, shutting the warmth out and the chill inside. By mid-afternoon, I was dusted out, and my brain was too tired to come to any coherent thought. I needed a long, hot shower to rejuvenate my stinky self.

* * *

An unmarked file was on the kitchen table when I came back down from my shower. Either Melanie had left it for me, or I had just had an alien encounter. Inside, I found several pages of notes. Each page covered police encounter incidents of different people I knew. Some were the same guys Neddel had made right-sided marks for on his cove party participant list, but there were others as well.

"Melanie, did you leave this file for me?" I asked, walking into her office.

My words were followed by my daughter wildly waving her hands over her head.

"I'm sorry," she said, "can you repeat that, Mrs. Shaw?"

I backed out and returned to the kitchen. This time, I found Sheriff Neddel seated at the table. I almost screamed.

"Where did you come from?" I demanded.

"You called and left me a message earlier. I wasn't able to answer then, so I drove over. It sounded like you needed me to. I got here about ten minutes ago. I was outside looking for you and finally decided I'd come in and leave you a note. The file was gone, and I heard you talking to Melanie, so I sat down. Would you rather I went back outside and knocked?"

"No. So you're the one who left me the file?"

"Yes. There are things in it I wanted to talk to you about. And possibly Melanie."

We had only a short wait before my daughter was able to take a break and join us.

"You let the sheriff in and never told me he was here?" My question was sharp.

CHAPTER TWENTY-ONE

Melanie responded in kind. "You were in the shower. Why was the door locked?"

We frowned at each other across the expanse of the oak table. Neddel cleared his throat.

"I'm going to ask you to keep this confidential," Neddel said.

Melanie held up her hand, fingers in the Girl Scout pledge, and said, "So help me, God."

"Great," he said.

Ignoring his sarcasm, she grinned widely. I gave her the *behave yourself* look, which, of course, she ignored.

"Rather than canvas everybody in the valley, I thought I'd start with you two. I'd appreciate it if you would look at the notes, see if there is anything there that you might not have known, or maybe heard a reference to, that might shed some additional light on these offenses."

"What do these have to do with Juan Noche?" I asked.

"Murder usually isn't spur of the moment. There's a lead-up," Neddel explained. "I'm looking for that small incident that might have brought this on."

Melanie and I both nodded and read and exchanged pages.

"I knew Zoe got caught shoplifting," said Melanie. "I was with her."

I nodded. It had been a tense couple of hours, mostly because Zoe's father and Ian were arguing about whose child was responsible.

"And who knew Russell got so many parking tickets? He must get at least one every time he goes to Portland." Melanie was still perusing the pages.

The outlier was Noah Deyak. That was because, right up until the time he and his father left town, he was a regular customer of the sheriff's department.

"Alleged," I said, reading the notes. "Alleged. Alleged. Alleged. Noah was never convicted, or as near as I can tell, even charged with anything. Just questioned, or held for questioning, and eventually released. That makes no sense."

Neddel gave a tired sigh. "That's because, where it says 'as reported by a witness,' or 'witnessed by,' most of the names that are removed are his father's."

"His father turned him in? Repeatedly? Why was his name removed?" I could have been knocked over by a chicken feather.

Melanie's alarm went off, calling her back to work.

"I have to go," she said. "But I don't see a lot that I didn't know, except maybe on Noah's."

After she left, I held up the page, frowning. "I don't get this."

"Neither do I. Every time Noah was involved, the witness pulled out at the last minute. There doesn't seem to be a way to prove he was guilty of anything," said Neddel. "All the witnesses' names are removed. His is the only one where you see a witness referred to repeatedly. That's probably why you picked up on it. I went up to see his dad at the prison in New York and got nowhere. According to the warden, Mr. Deyak is a regular in the infirmary because he can't keep his big mouth shut. He's got eight more years. May be lucky to live that long.

"This type of report in front of a judge would put Noah behind the eight ball. He may deserve to be there, but it's a hell of a note when a long list of maybe's takes precedence over an actual."

"What do you mean?"

"A smart lawyer is going to point out all these alleged as being possible. Then he's going to build a case on the theory that this was the beginning, and it finally escalated into murder."

Neddel was curled in his seat, not sitting straight up. He had his legs crossed, and one lower arm on the table. He looked relaxed, but there was something there that reminded me of a coiled snake.

"That's ludicrous. Any of these guys could have any number of things hidden in their pasts that you didn't find." I pointed out.

"Oh, believe me, I've looked hard. If someone had, let's say, been arrested at a sit-in during the eighties, I'd know."

My ears went beet red. I knew that, because I could feel how hot they were. Why had he been checking the eighties? Or rather, why had he been checking on me?

Chapter Twenty-Two

For the last few nights, my sleep had been a patchwork quilt of bizarre dreams mixed with frequent trips from window to window, searching for alien lights. That left me exhausted in the mornings, but finally a night of uninterrupted slumber had me awake at dawn and ready to go.

After breakfast, Melanie went into her office to work. Rex, Buttercup, and I crossed over to the orchard and took a hike along the riverbank. It was early. The day was just unfolding, and our outing was beautiful. Even after that long walk, I felt like I had plenty of energy.

Releasing Rex to play in the yard, I let myself into the garden plot, intent on correcting the minor damage that had been done by the rain. Overall, I was pretty pleased. All the seedlings seemed to be reaching toward the sun. I could almost hear their happy giggles.

"In a few days," I whispered, "your cousins will pop their heads out of the soil. All of you together can grow, grow, grow!"

At the gate, Buttercup gave me a soft *scree* to let me know she'd like to come in, too. However, her days inside the garden fence were finished until after harvest. Rex and Royally gave her a little yip, inviting her to play, but she ignored them. The tender young greens were what she wanted.

A pickup truck screeched to a halt in front of the driveway barrier. Shane jumped out, leaving the door open as he ran towards me. I knew something was wrong. Picturing his elderly parents, I rushed to the gate.

"Mrs. Flynn!" he yelled out. "Where's Melanie?"

"Calm down, Shane, before you stroke out," I said. Young people can be so melodramatic. "She's in the house. She has to work today."

"No, she's not there." He was panting. A long trickle of sweat ran down the side of his very red face. "I saw her in the car with Noah. They were driving out of town."

Laughing, I clicked the garden patch gate shut tight against the persistent pig. "You're wrong, Shane. If Melanie was going out, she would have told me. We just had this long discussion last night about our new safety rules. If one of us leaves, we let the other know where we are going and when we're coming back."

Amazingly, it was Melanie that proposed we set up some type of protocol. When I pushed her, she responded that me locking all the doors during the day, and Neddel showing up and acting all Jack Reacher had jangled up her nerves.

"You're wrong. I'm telling you, I saw them." He was almost wailing, so much so that the dogs had come over. They watched him closely, his agitation cueing them into a problem. He was even making me a little edgy.

While Shane was talking, I started walking to the house. I didn't move quick enough for him, because he sort of jogged in the same direction. A hint for me to walk faster.

"Melanie?" I called, walking into the house. No answer, but if she was on a call, I shouldn't expect one. Motioning Shane to stay in the kitchen, I went down the hall. Melanie's office door was open, Lilo was lying in her pink Hello Kitty bed, and the computer monitor was a blank screen. I checked my daughter's bedroom and the downstairs bath. Even though she didn't usually go upstairs unless she wanted a tub instead of a shower, I checked up there, too.

"She's not in there, is she?" asked Shane, a stark look on his face.

"No," I said, brushing past him.

"Where are you going?" he asked.

"To check the yard." My teeth began to grind together. I wanted to yell at him to back off.

"We were just out there two minutes ago." He followed behind me. Rex and Royally followed him. Buttercup abandoned the infant greens and joined the conga line.

"There are other places to check." I tried not to snarl, failing miserably. "She could be in the barn, or even over in the orchard." Standing on the edge of the deck, I called, "Melanie? Melanie!"

This time, my steps across the yard were faster. I didn't find her in the barn, or collecting eggs in the hen house, or even out at the pig wallow. My chest tightened.

Damn you, Shane, for scaring me to death, I thought, rushing back to the deck.

He was right on my heels, almost stepping on me. Whirling around, I pointed across the street.

"Go check the orchard. She wouldn't have gone far. If she's there, you should be able to see her if you stand on the wellhead."

He took off running across the grass. At the ditch, he stretched out in perfect high-hurdle form, clearing the open space, landing, and sprinting out of sight.

I went inside and searched the house again. This time, all three dogs followed. I had barely gotten back to the kitchen when Shane came in. The screen door slammed behind him. He was talking, but I didn't hear the words because I was focused on a fluttery pink Post-it stuck on the refrigerator.

Gone with Noah. There was some squiggle beneath that, but it wasn't readable. Melanie has tiny, cramped handwriting. The barely humped line at the bottom of the note would have been indecipherable even to her.

Pulling the note down, I crushed it in my fingers, demanding it tell me more. I tried to get my emotions in check, but control was slipping away fast. I was mad at Melanie for not being right where she should be, and at Neddel for throwing fear into our lives, and at Noah and Shane because they weren't who I thought they'd been, and I didn't have the nerve to ask who they were. And finally, I was furious at Ian for leaving us, proving I was not capable of taking care of myself and our daughter. And, I was afraid of what could be happening to my little girl at that moment.

"Mrs. Flynn?"

"Shut *up*, Shane." I grabbed the handheld receiver for the landline and dialed Melanie's cell. "Come on, come on." The urge to shake the small piece of plastic was almost overwhelming.

After an eternity, her phone rang. But my brief sense of relief burst like a water balloon. Why was the ring echoing? Receiver still pressed to my ear, I circled the kitchen table. Hanging on the back of the chair was Melanie's purse. I could see the lit-up screen of her cell phone peeking out of the top.

My daughter was indeed gone, and I hadn't seen her leave. The cryptic note only told me something I didn't want to hear, but it catapulted me into terror.

"It could have been written by anybody," I whispered, and immediately I was sure that was so.

I dialed the sheriff's office, only to be told Neddel was not available. His private line went to voice mail. I wanted to scream into the recording and might have done exactly that if I hadn't turned slightly and seen Shane still hovering.

"Sheriff Neddel, this is Doris Flynn. When you get this message, please call me back right away. I'll be home all day." I very carefully replaced the handset on the charging base.

"We have to go out and find her." Shane's voice was barely over a whisper.

"No." Ripping a page off the grocery notepad, I sat down. According to the clock on the wall near the hall door, it was eleven-oh-seven. "What time did you see Noah's car?" I asked.

"About forty minutes ago, maybe longer. I don't know." Shane's voice shook a little.

"Take a breath, sit down," I said. "If you're going to be any help at all, you had better get your act together. We both had better get it together. Treat this the same way, you would an accident, if you were with Burt. Now. Where were you when you saw Noah and Melanie? Consider the time range."

Shane bowed his head, rubbing both hands in his hair. "I was on my way back from the hospital. Doctor Kennett and I responded to an accident this morning where a man on a motorcycle hit a deer. They both died."

I blinked hard. Shane dropping the fact he'd just attended a double death scene made me gulp. I had told him to look at the issue like a professional.

He was a kid, a young man. He'd made the leap, but I couldn't.

"Okay, what time did you respond?"

"It was just getting light. Uh, four forty-five or seven, I heard Doctor Kennett talking to dispatch. We were there about an hour. The guy and the motorcycle were all messed up together. It took us a while to get ready to go. Oh, so at six ten, I punched the ticket for the autopsy suite."

A slow, trembling breath helped me try not to rush the kid.

"At nine-thirty, I submitted the tests Doctor Kennett asked for. He told me I could go home, but I would need to be back by two. He was going to stay and finish up. I took a shower there and left."

His head was still bowed. I watched his right-hand creep into his front pants pocket and re-emerge with a tiny scrap of paper. "I stopped and got a coffee. When I was waiting to pull into traffic, I saw Noah's car drive by." Shane offered me the scrap of paper. A receipt for an order that was placed at nine fifty-five. Allowing for the time to drive to the next window and pay, Shane would have been in place by no later than ten-oh-three or ten-oh-five.

"Perfect." I glanced at the receipt again. "You stopped at the Dunkin's on Route 16, north of Calwin Mountain Road." I made a note.

"Was Noah headed north or south? Could the rider have been someone else?"

"North." Shane raised his head. "Melanie had on her oversized Hollywood sunglasses and a vertically striped top."

Yup. When I had seen her that morning, she was wearing a navy and white nautical top with small red sailboats floating in the stripes. I added that to my notes.

"What good is writing all this down?" Shane demanded. He wanted action, not words scribbled on a grocery note.

"Right now, the facts are fresh. Later, they may become less so, or even forgotten. Her being gone could be an innocent coincidence. Maybe Noah doesn't have to go in early, and they went to breakfast." Was I trying to calm myself or Shane? I didn't know. But Melanie's purse still being here, was a red flag.

"You just said she wasn't supposed to leave without telling you. Her phone is here, her purse. She is with someone I don't trust at all, and you probably don't either, or you wouldn't have tried to call the sheriff."

As Shane listed the same facts that raced through my brain, I wanted to open the door and shove him outside. He was like lightning striking a tree. I was trying to be solid. He was splintering me apart.

I didn't answer.

"If they were driving north, Mrs. Flynn, where were they going?"

"I don't know, Shane." I bit my lip before admitting, "You're right, I am nervous."

"I'm going to go out and drive around." He stood up. There were large circles of sweat under his arms. I was willing to bet the humidity was not entirely responsible. "I can check parking lots."

"No, go home, Shane. You have to go back to work at two." I walked with him to the door, laying my hand on his arm. "If I hear from Melanie, or she comes home. I'll call you right away."

"Even after I go to work?"

"Absolutely. Set your phone on vibrate. I'll send a text. That way, Burt won't give you a hard time if you're working and I call."

"You promise?" His sad eyes held mine.

"Have I ever lied to you?" I gave his arm a squeeze, and he walked down the drive.

I only stopped long enough to make sure Buttercup was still in the yard before I opened my laptop and brought up the bank's page to get the telephone number. It was the world's longest hold while I waited for the bank manager.

"I'm looking for Noah Deyak," I said as the manager came on the line. I gave my best confused old lady giggle. "By the time I realized I'd asked for you, I was on hold."

"I'm sorry, Mr. Deyak isn't here today. Is there something I can do to help you?"

"No, thank you for your time," I said. The back of my throat felt dry and gritty.

No matter what I had told Shane, I was fast losing the small amount of perspective I had. I didn't know Noah's cell phone number, and I'm not proud to say I started going through Melanie's private things, looking for it. I knew it was saved on her cellphone, but I didn't have the password.

Calling Noah's friends looking for him could very possibly work against me if Shane was right about there being a problem. Someone could alert Noah to my search.

But I could call Zoe and Heather.

That was easy. I told them I was looking for Melanie, so I wouldn't have to make a trip into town. She had forgotten her phone. No big deal, *if* you hear from her. Thank you.

"If that was so easy, why am I sweating bullets?" I asked Lilo.

Her little pug face looked up, trying to please and hoping for a treat.

I spent the next couple of hours circling the kitchen table, adding more wear to the ancient linoleum. At one o'clock, I called Neddel again. Still no answer.

"Just where the heck is he?" I shrilled at the dogs, standing with my back to the portable telephone. I screamed and jumped far enough to ram into the kitchen table when it rang.

"Are you looking for me, Mrs. Flynn?" Sheriff Neddel drawled.

"Melanie is missing!" Every tiny iota of self-control vanished. I was babbling, then sobbing into the phone. "My daughter had to have been taken against her will, because she would never have gone off and left me worried out of my mind like this. There's a note, but I don't think she wrote it."

"Okay," Neddel said. "I'll be there in ten minutes. Make yourself a cup of tea and sit down. Do not leave. I am on my way."

Tea was in no way near strong enough. That left only the big guns. Black Cherry Chunk ice cream. Sheriff Neddel pulled in to find me prying the cherries out and leaving the ice cream.

"I'm not sure that's the way the company expected you to eat it," he said

I thrust the ice cream back into the freezer, then sat down at the table. "Okay," I said. My bottom lip was quivering.

"I want you to start with what happened earlier, and I don't mean when you got up this morning," he said when I opened my mouth. "When did you see Melanie last? What was her frame of mind? Did she tell you what her plans were for the day?"

"We had breakfast. She told me she had hours of work to catch up on." I spread my fingers on the table, pressing down on the wood to ground myself. "She seemed fine. I don't usually get worked up like this. It's just that... Melanie?"

The screen door opened, and my daughter, cat carrier in hand, walked into the kitchen. I jumped up and ran around the table, grabbing her in an enveloping hug and jostling the carrier, which gave out a tiny, plaintive meow.

"Mom, what are you doing?" she demanded. "What's wrong?"

"Where have you been?" I was sobbing again. "I was so worried."

She pushed away, righting the carrier and glaring at Neddel as if my reaction were his fault. "So, you, what? Called the cops?"

Before I could answer, Neddel stood up. "Have a seat," he said to Melanie. "let's figure out what happened here."

Melanie gave him another dirty look before she opened the cat carrier to let Spitball out. Sitting at the table, she said, "Doctor Rhoades' office called. They had a cancellation and asked if we wanted to bring Spitball in. I said yes. You were on the trail with Rex, so I got Spitball in the crate. While I was chasing the cat around, Noah showed up. He had taken the day off and offered to drive me. I didn't realize I didn't have my purse until I had to pay the vet. When we got there, a dog that had been hit by a car had just arrived. It looked bad. Doctor Rhoades and most of his team were working on the dog, so I sat down and waited. Eventually, they got to us. When we were through, we drove through Burger King and ate in the car. I didn't want to leave Spitball alone. He didn't do well at the vets."

"Where is Noah now?" Neddel demanded.

"He took the day off because he had a dentist appointment. He's gone to that." Melanie shot a look filled with barbs at Neddel. "If you're going to arrest him for giving me a ride, you'll find him at Doctor Sawyer's office."

"Why did you leave here going north if you were going to the veterinarian's office?" I asked.

Melanie looked at me funny. "How did you know we went north?"

When I didn't answer right away, she said, "Noah had just come up Route 16. The road crew was working on the lights in front of the Chinese restaurant, and everything was backed up. We went around to the North-South Road and bypassed the construction."

I looked at my hands, took a peek at Neddel, and went back to scrutinizing my fingers.

The sheriff cleared his throat. "Well, as long as I'm out here, I wouldn't mind a cold drink."

Jumping up, I offered lemonade or iced tea.

"I'm sorry if I upset you, Mom," said Melanie. "I left you a note."

Taking it out of my pocket, I spread it out on the table. "I found it. I just couldn't read it."

From the look on Neddel's face, he couldn't read it either.

"It's okay," I said, handing Neddel his tea. "I shouldn't have let myself get all riled up."

Dogs and cats that had been loose in the house were hovering around the Glenwood. Once free of the carrier, Spitball had crawled underneath to hide. He was going to need some downtime to recoup, so I got down on my belly, pushing dogs out of the way, and reached underneath. Once I had him in my arms, I held him close until I got into the cattery. I had an empty crate, clean and ready for whatever. I placed him there next to Tiny. She gave a little meow. I told her I would be back.

Neddel went out, remarking how one day I might call him when I wasn't all wound up. He kind of smiled, while I was feeling embarrassed. I had been hysterical and called him. He came right away. When Melanie arrived, she'd been on the cusp of rude. It was clear she wasn't pleased to see him. I knew I owed him an apology, and on top of that, there was something else I'd wanted to tell him. I knew there was, but I couldn't remember what.

"I'm sorry you couldn't read my note," Melanie said. "But when I walked through the door, it felt like you and the sheriff were jumping all over me." She looked away, shoulders drooping.

"And I'm sorry. that's how you felt. I didn't know you'd left while I was out walking with Rex," I explained. "I came back, went right into the garden, and then Shane showed up and he was all hysterical about seeing you and Noah."

"Shane?" Melanie turned back towards me; brows drawn together.

"Yes. He was all wound up. Working with Doctor Kennett, he's hearing a lot of gossip. He thinks Noah is dangerous. To be honest I have my own questions. Anyway, he was running around like a wet chicken, squawking about you being in danger. I'm afraid I let his angst get under my skin."

"I told you Shane is, like, falling off the deep end," Melanie said. "And why are you so down on Noah? Is it because of Neddel's investigation? Is there a reason he thinks one of my friends killed Juan?"

"Yes, you did tell me about Shane. I'm thinking I need to have a more serious conversation with both him and Noah." Even though I wanted to avoid Neddel's questions and investigative notes, there was a look on Melanie's face that forced me to add. "It's not that the sheriff knows one of your friends killed Juan, I'm sure. But rather, that they were where he was last seen and perhaps saw something important."

Melanie shook her head. When she headed into her office, I sent Shane a text telling him Melanie was now home. Then I shut my cell phone off in case he texted back. From the amount of dinging of Melanie's cell phone, which was still lying on the table, we should have shut hers off as well. Eventually, it got under my skin. I was worried Shane was going to come through the back door and I was going to blow up at him. I was chewing my thumbnail when I looked up and saw the landline. If it had been Melanie who was going off the rails, I'd want someone to give me a heads-up. Days ago, I had this same thought when I listened to Neddel's taped conversation with Noah. It was time to let Shane's parents know we were concerned about his behavior.

"Hi, Mrs. Davis? This is Doris Flynn. Do you have a few minutes?"

Chapter Twenty-Three

My conversation with Mrs. Davis started off with me thanking her for the rhubarb sauce she'd sent down a couple of weeks before. Then I said something idiotic about Shane being so much help, such a nice young man.

"Yes." Mrs. Davis sighed. "There have been some rough times, you know. He's so sensitive and not physical, like most of the other boys he went to school with. Fortunately, he always has Melanie, and his cousin comes up to see him every couple of weeks. It's nice." After a pause, and with a lower voice, she added, "All the traffic going up and down the road lately is frightening. In today's paper, they identified the remains found on the mountain. I didn't know who that young man Juan Noche was, but Shane told me he was dangerous. I don't know how we could get along without Shane here."

I said something inane and hung up. When Mrs. Davis had spoken so gratefully about Melanie, I had been caught unaware, leaving me speechless. Then, she'd switched over to the increase of cars brought on by curiosity seekers. Until then, I hadn't considered the neighbors were noticing. My whole pre-planned conversation dissolved.

"Well, that didn't go as planned," I told Royally and Argyle.

Opening my laptop, I brought up the local newspaper, which was a give-away. The news was always a day or two behind, both locally and nationally. There it was on the front page, just as Mrs. Davis had said. Without a doubt, the drive-bys would pick up again.

Next, I called Rose Ann. "Is this a bad time? Are you at a site?"

"Actually, no, I'm administering a test to a class of grad students. What's up?"

When I hesitated, afraid I was interrupting her, she said, "Go ahead. They're fine. I just gave them a packet with four photographs taken in situ. They need to write up a conclusion, and they only have a half hour."

Laughing, I said, "You obviously don't know the new generation. They have Google."

"Ha," she said. "You underestimate me. All cell phones need to be turned in prior to testing. The room has overhead cameras. I have four senior grad students who are monitoring this group. Believe me, they will be diligent. I select only two field assistants a year. This is the last question for the students being tested today. They can leave when they finish, turn in what they've got done at the buzzer. So, like I said, I've got plenty of time."

"I've had a couple of conversations with Sheriff Neddel. I thought we were getting along all right now, but I'm guessing I was wrong."

"Because?" Rose Ann asked.

"He periodically stops in, tells me things, you know, like updates. But nothing that really matters. It's more like he's checking to see what I'm up to. And we had an incident here that puts me under the umbrella of a highly hysterical female."

"So, he's just fishing. You haven't broken any laws, or messed up any evidence, right? There are two ways people might typically react to the discovery of remains on their property. Some might close down and not address it. They don't want to think about it, or talk to anyone they don't have to, like the cops. The other way would be for the property owners to demand something be done to clear the whole incident up. Immediately. This minute. That would be classified as hysteria."

I started to respond, but she stopped me.

"Hold on, there are also several levels in the middle. More like thorns to the authorities because those people aren't just communicating with the cops. They're the folks who grab their fifteen seconds of fame on the evening news. Or the social media wanna-bes, or... those who are out gathering information, looking for an answer, all by themselves."

"You mean, like me," I said with a sigh.

"Yes, my new and dear friend, like you." She chuckled. "If truth were to be told, I'd have to give myself the same advice I just gave you. It seems I might have been the Bonnie to your Clyde at one point."

I didn't think it prudent to tell her I had lied to her on the occasion when she thought I had already called Neddel, but I hadn't pushed the send button.

"So, you think I should stop?" I wasn't sure how I felt about that.

"I could say yes. I bet the sheriff would like me to tell you to stop, too. But I'm worried that if I do and something else happens tomorrow, and you aren't able to stop yourself from getting back into it, you won't have anyone to tell what was going on. I think it's better for me just to say you shouldn't be doing the sheriff's job. If you think of something, consider if he should be there before you, or even with you. Not after you."

"Okay," I said.

"Good. Remember, I'm your compatriot, your friend. Nancy Drew had Bess and George. Whenever she took off into the wilds, she called them first. That's what I want you to do. Call me. If you're not going to contact Neddel, or tell Melanie, call me." Her voice got more serious. "The closer this case gets to resolution, the more dangerous it could be. I may not be able to ride in the shotgun seat. But I will know and be ready."

I grinned all over. "I like the sound of that."

"Awesome," she said. "So, is that all you came up with, listening to Neddel?"

"Actually, that's not what I was going to say at all." I sighed. "I've been watching him work, listening closely to what he's saying, not just the words. Neddel is like Melanie. They both work in a black-and-white world. It is, or it isn't. Any segues are very minute sections of gray. Me? I'm all over the color wheel. I'd jump into the river on a dare, am willing to change my plans in a heartbeat, and I'm open to about anything. It's a trait Melanie is used to in me, but Neddel is not. It's like he expects me to be more, I don't know, staid or structured."

I heard the medicolegal death investigator sigh. "What you're describing is one of the job qualifications for what he and I do. At any given site, I have to be able to see the black and white, the absolute facts. Then, I have to find the hidden slivers that take me to Wonderland and introduce all the oddities and fantasies that a perpetrator might have. People who orchestrate bizarre crimes live in the kaleidoscope world. Neddel might get there eventually. A lot of police personnel do, but for some people, like you and me, we're already headed there from square one. It's not a bad thing. You just have to make your own safety number one. Do you understand?"

"I believe so," I said.

"Then go, grasshopper. Spring forth, but use restraint."

In the background, I heard the test timer go off, and she was gone.

Chapter Twenty-Four

I t seemed like I spent the rest of the day going back over conversations that I'd had with Neddel, starting with the one where he showed me the videotape. I kept looking for little innuendos I might have missed. I had to get space ready for the new dogs the animal control officer in Berlin had called me about. Being bad-tempered housemates, they would have to be separated. I'd put one in kennel one, the other in kennel three. In between, in kennel two, I hung plastic tarps. That way, even though they could still hear and smell each other, they'd be out of each other's sight. Most of my time I spent fussing in the garden patch or working with Rex and Buttercup. My friend from the Humane Society told me they had found someone, a man named Leslie Rollins, who was interested in Rex. They would bring him out later in the day for an initial introduction. It was exciting to know there was already a home for Rex. He was a good boy and deserved it. I knew he was ready, and I kept telling him so.

I wandered down into the open space of the orchard. It was a different world, sad because it was deserted. The stunted trees, which had suffered long years and hard frosts would never grow another leaf, or offer a ripened apple to a happy child, yet the wild growth among them was beautiful. The sun shone down, highlighting flying grasshoppers and yellow butterflies. The already tall shoots of new grass waved in the breeze. Beyond the field, sparkling water flickered from the bed of the small Saco River. A picture-puzzle-perfect scene.

I sat on the bowed trunk of a downed apple tree. Chickens clucked around my feet. Grass that hadn't been mowed in forty years offered a thick bed, which would muffle the sound of footsteps of any walking closer.

I must have heard the jingle of his equipment belt because I turned and saw Neddel coming towards me. Seeing him startled me, I jumped up and gasped. He smiled, raising his hand. There was a heavy rustling as a strong body surged through the grass, rushing Neddel from the left. He looked up, probably expecting to see the thundering bulk of four-hundred-fifty-pound Buttercup Belle. Instead, Rex, the gray and white pit bull, tawny eyes aglow, came crashing at him.

"STOP!" Neddel yelled, holding up his left hand. "Sit."

Rex, still fairly new in his training, seemed confused. I could see him trying to figure it out. He stopped, but remained standing in place, eyes on Neddel. His tail, did a slow wave, which said he was unsure. Unfortunately for Rex, Buttercup had been chasing him, and she never slowed down. The dog yelped with surprise and pain as he was cast aside. The pig slammed on the brakes and stopped inches from Neddel's knees.

"Ha, are you lucky," I said, unfreezing at last. "Coming at you at that angle, she would have broken your kneecaps in a heartbeat."

Neddel nodded, but didn't take his eyes off the pig.

"Pig, pig," I called. "Rex. Here. Come on, my lovelies. Here."

The dog skulked through the long grass. The pig trotted away from the sheriff like the diva she was. I gave both a dog biscuit while I ran my hands over Rex, cooing to him.

"Did he get hurt?" Neddel asked.

"Only his feelings." I sat back on the tree trunk, and Neddel perched nearby. "I heard your car pull in a while ago. Thought you were a friend of Melanie's."

"I stopped in to tell you I've been out doing more canvassing on Melanie's list of names. You know, the people who were at the bonfire party at the cove? I even went down there and checked out the area."

"What did you learn?" I asked, once again rubbing Rex's head.

"Well, the cove is definitely a good place to party. And it seems pretty clean. Just a couple of beer cans lying around."

I couldn't help smiling at Neddel's lame attempt at humor. "What did the kids say?"

Pausing for a heartbeat, he looked me straight in the face. Assessing, I think.

"Is there any possibility Melanie might have seen Noche through starstruck eyes?" Neddel asked.

My brows tightened. "You mean, like possible boyfriend material?" At his nod, I said, "No. At first, I thought maybe so, especially when she started meeting him for coffee. He came here once for supper. But he was all about his girlfriend back home. And Melanie referred to him as 'interesting,' in the manner you would talk about a new NOVA episode. When he left, she felt bad he didn't say goodbye, but she wasn't anguished."

"What do you know about the girlfriend in New Mexico?"

"She had a name like Ariel Hacienda." I blushed. "I'm not good with names, but I remember thinking it sounded exotic."

"Estella Hernandez," said Neddel.

Gaping, I went from surprised to irate in the flash of a neon moment. "If you knew who she was, why did you ask me?"

"Curiosity." Neddel shrugged. "I located her through channels in the Forestry Service. Next of kin. She said Noche had stopped calling or writing. He didn't answer his cell phone. She thought he had found someone new and left her behind."

"How horrible. For both of you. I don't envy anyone having to make that call."

Neddel nodded. "It's never a good one. It's worse when you are thousands of miles away and you need to ask some hard questions. My local conversations didn't seem to go any better. People remembered John Noche, not always positively. When I asked about the possibility of drugs, no one seemed to have any real knowledge, or recall where they had heard Noche was pushing."

I thought about Mrs. Davis. Shane had given her his take on John, and she had just accepted it. How many others had done the same thing?

Neddel looked down toward the river, where Buttercup was wandering in the grass. A parade of chickens followed her.

"The biddies follow her because she always raises a mess of insects," I said.

"There's also the chance she will start rooting and uncover juicy grubs."

He nodded. "If more people knew what chickens ate, egg consumption would fall radically."

"I agree," I said. "So, what's your next step, Sheriff?"

"Everett." He spoke softly, without taking his eyes off the meandering pig. "Call me Everett."

Chapter Twenty-Five

I pressed my lips together to keep from smiling. Palm against my chest, I said, "Doris."

"Doris," said Neddel.

He ducked his head slightly, but I saw the little curve of a smile on the edge of his mouth. And it made me happy enough to blush slightly. Rex wiggled. I looked down at him to give both Neddel and me a moment to get used to what we had just done.

He gave the type of heavy sigh I would have thought had been surgically removed at the police department. Our moment was over, and he was back in uniform.

"During the course of my investigation..."

I cut him off. "Okay, if you're going to go all professional cop on me, let's take this conversation somewhere else. This is my happy place."

"Actually, I was going to suggest that we pool information and work together," Neddel said. "It feels like we're running up the hill on either side of the road. We could meet in the middle and move ahead together. But I'm perfectly willing to go somewhere I won't have to deal with buzzing insects or the possibility of a tick bite."

"Let me alleviate your fear of ticks," I said and called the biddies to me. It didn't work. I laughed. "They know Buttercup is going to be flushing out more insects than they can catch, so they aren't interested in a couple of measly ticks."

Sheriff Neddel had the good grace not to laugh at me.

"Let's go up to the house," I said. When I stood up, Rex, who was lying at my feet, rose with me. In the tall grass, I could see the long black and white stripes that were the top of Buttercup's back. "Pig, pig," I called.

Immediately, the tips of her ears came up. She didn't search out a path but came towards me through the tangled brush. I could hear the clucking of her poultry pals behind her. Neddel looked astonished. By the time he, Rex, and I reached the road, Buttercup had caught up, and the first of the hens were already running across the packed dirt.

In the distance, a cloud of dust traveled toward us.

"Come on," I said, moving faster and hustling my broodies along. "There's a car coming. Let's go, Buttercup. No dawdling."

Traveling down the Calwin Mountain Road, vehicles always raised a roiling mass of dust, even if they were only moving twenty miles an hour. A car could be obscured by its dust trail if the prevailing wind was moving the same way as the vehicle. So, it was with this car. It got really close before we actually saw the vehicle.

"Holy cow!" I cried out. "It's the red Audi." I slapped Buttercup on her rear end so she'd pick up speed and counted the chickens ahead of us to make sure they were all safe. Neddel, however, was still in the road. He held up his wallet badge in one hand and, with his other, motioned the driver to pull over.

The man did exactly what Neddel had instructed him to do. I came out of the driveway, bent on giving the driver a piece of my mind—and demanding to know why he had been cruising by my house on a regular basis.

Neddel pointed to a spot on the side of the road towards the rear of the car. "Stay there," he ordered me.

I cussed on the inside. The biddies had continued hurrying up the drive, but both Rex and Buttercup had stopped midway and waited.

"License and registration," Neddel said, eyes on the driver.

The driver complied. I heard him asking what was going on. He hadn't been speeding.

"Both hands out the window where I can see them," said Neddel. "It's been brought to my attention that this vehicle has been recorded traveling on this stretch of road several times over the last few days."

"Recorded?" The driver sort of laughed.

"We've got cameras set up," I said loudly.

Neddel gave me a look. I took a step back.

"So, Mr., ah…" Neddel studied the license. "Ryder. Why have you been out here multiple times?"

"Can I get out of the car?" Ryder asked. "I'm sitting on my company identification."

Neddel nodded and stepped back. He held Ryder's license and registration in his left hand, but his right rested on his service weapon. From where I stood, I could see the safety strap had been unhooked, flapping back off the holster. I think my mouth was open, as I was inhaling copious amounts of residual dust. I took another step back. Now, I was far enough behind the Audi to see the license plate. Orange and black. New York State. Noah's cousin lived in Boston. Her plate would have been from Massachusetts. When I'd first recognized the car, I had thought it might be Noah. I felt a little foolish, but still, why had this guy been going up and down my road?

"I'm a real estate developer," the man said. "Can I get something out of my wallet?" He pulled out another plastic square and handed it to Neddel. "I was tipped off the undeveloped property across the street might be coming on the market. I've been down here a couple of times to look it over. The area is supposed to be quiet, but there seems to be a lot of traffic. I was looking for property markers, but there aren't any. I asked around and found out that a body had been found here."

Neither Neddel nor I reacted to Mr. Ryder's statement.

"To be honest, that was a turn-off. The people I represent want a quiet place for their more, ah, elegant vacation homes. I don't know if this is it."

I wanted to agree that it wasn't, emphatically.

"Mostly, what I've seen is other cars and a lot of dust."

Neddel said nothing. I stayed quiet, too, but I wanted to cut in and tell him we didn't want that type of people out here. Folks with lots of money and city attitudes, building outrageous houses and, thinking if they were out of the city, they could do whatever they wanted with no regard for the locals.

"This entire area," Neddel said, "is zoned agricultural. That means people around here are farmers or woodsmen. And I believe that side of the road is considered part of the floodplain. The river is restricted from power boats, docks, and the like. No fishing. You know, really low-key."

Neddel was painting with a wide brush. In a few more words, he'd have my neck turning red and one of my front teeth falling out.

Mr. Ryder cleared his throat. "It's a really pretty area."

Right on cue, Rex came running back into the road, with Buttercup trundling after him. As soon as she saw Mr. Ryder, she swerved. Here was somebody she didn't know. She wanted an introduction.

The man from New York couldn't take his eyes off Buttercup. The closer she got, the bigger his eyes grew. She was only about four yards away when he considered finding a safer place to stand. While the New Yorker had been staring at the pig, Neddel had also moved. Now he was blocking the driver's door.

Mr. Ryder took a step backward; Buttercup kept advancing. Soon, the man was backed up to the front fender of the Audi and appeared to be trying to crawl up onto the hood. There was some squawking noise that must have been coming from him, because none of my animals had ever made that sound.

"Stay," Neddel ordered the pig.

Buttercup hesitated. When it looked like she would ignore him and take another step, he used his big cop voice. "Buttercup. Stay."

"Buttercup?" Mr. Ryder sounded like he was strangling. "It's a hog. Why isn't it in a cage somewhere?"

"No," said Neddel. "It's a pig. She and her friends live out here. They free-range. You know, wander around loose in the yard. Across to the river, up in the woods." He spoke like it was a normal thing. "They've been here a while. I guess you could say they're grandfathered. As a developer. I'm sure you know what that means. They've got rights."

"Rights?" Ryder looked at Neddel, then at me, and finally back at Buttercup. "I'd like to get back in my car, please."

"Mrs. Flynn, could you have Buttercup move back a tad?" Neddel asked.

I crossed back to the driveway. Rex moved with me. "Buttercup. Heel."

Nope, she wasn't having any of that. Her disk was snapping back and forth; her tail was keeping time. Something about Ryder, maybe his fear, was holding her attention. She wasn't done with him yet.

"Buttercup. HEEL!"

Still nothing. I didn't care about Ryder, but she was making me look bad in front of Neddel. I did the only thing left for me to do.

"Peanut butter," I whispered under my breath.

I'm sure neither of the men heard me, but the pig certainly did. Her ears and tail came straight up. She made a tight U-turn and sashayed toward me. I hustled up the driveway, and she trotted right along behind, asking when-when-when in her precious little piggy woofs.

When Neddel came up to the house a few minutes later, I was smearing peanut butter on the outside of Buttercup's rolling ball. She tried to help, licking off as much as she could before I let the ball go. With the toe of my boot, I sent the ball rolling across the lawn. The little purring woofs changed to excited grunts and actual oinks.

"How long will that keep her busy?" Neddel asked.

"A while. The ball is too hard for her to get a bite and too big to hold down. It cost a pretty penny, but it's the best enrichment toy we found for her."

Rather than swatting at black flies, we went back inside the house. When I left the peanut butter container on the counter, Neddel looked at the black magic markered "PIG" on the side of the three-pound institutional plastic tub and laughed.

"No mistaking hers for yours, I guess."

"No, even I found a place to draw the line," I said, motioning him to the table. Once I had two glasses of iced tea poured, I sat down.

"Getting back to our previous conversation," he said. "I'd like to see everything you collected for information so far."

"I'll show you mine if you show me yours," I said without a smile.

"Alright, but I have to warn you there are a few things that I have to withhold." He wasn't making eye contact, and his grin was more of a grimace.

That wasn't what he had indicated earlier, but nonetheless, I went to get my notebook. Showing just a hint of self-consciousness, Neddel pulled out a pair of cheaters. With the glasses balanced on his nose, he sipped tea and read over my notes. I wasn't sure if he was being thorough or a slow reader, but I sipped iced tea and munched on cookies until he sat back.

"Well, most of what you have is information I also collected," he said. "There are a few things I find interesting. With your local knowledge, your observations come from a different place than mine."

He had brought a thin manila file in with him. "There are a few things in here I would like you to take a look at. Mostly in the hopes that if you think they're erroneous, you can tell me so."

I accepted the file and pushed the plate of pecan sandies closer to him.

"Sheriff Neddel," I said, closing the file after I had read through it, and pushed it to the side. "Where do you stand with any suspects other than young men from this area? You made a quick reference to Target B. What's that?"

He looked pointedly at the fridge. His glass was empty, and I didn't want to offer him more. I knew I was being petty. With a sigh, I poured us another round of iced tea.

"I stand behind my belief that John Noche died the night of the cove party that Melanie attended with her friends. It's a keystone in all of your own reasoning," he said.

"You must have a solid reason to believe that," I said.

"I think my feeling as to the possibility that the killer was a local individual is clearly shown in your own research." He opened my file, blunt finger traveling from bullet mark to bullet mark. "Everything I read here travels back to the conclusion that John Noche was somehow involved in a drug trade that got out of control."

I nodded.

"However, I believe some of your findings are flawed," he said.

"What? No, they aren't." I immediately got defensive.

"Yes, I can say unequivocally, you are wrong." He held up his hand to silence me when I opened my yammer to argue.

"Let me explain," he said. "From what I am seeing here, you believe the night of the party, after Melanie left and probably before Ian returned, someone approached Noche. There was some type of altercation, and he left willingly with that person or was forced to leave. After that point, he was taken to the ridge, part of the National Forest, above your home and murdered. But through technology and Doctor Lombard's expertise, we can prove he was not murdered there, that the site on the ridge was a dump site."

When had Rose Ann deduced this? She hadn't said anything to me, but Neddel had said there were things he couldn't share. Was the medicolegal investigator under the same restrictions?

"Okay," I said, "So, I believe that what happened to hurt Melanie somehow spilled over and caused Noche's death. Maybe he saw something, and when he spoke up the killer panicked. There is also the chance these were two separate events instigated by different people. However, ultimately, that was the place where everything went south for both Melanie and John Noche."

I sat back, considering what I'd just said. How was Melanie going to take this news? My thoughts were already looping on to what I was going to say to convince her she was in no way responsible or should suffer from guilt.

Neddel pulled his file back and placed my notebook inside. I knew right then my notes were gone from me forever.

"Initially, I believed, as you did, that whoever was out to cause trouble for Melanie had either showed his hand or done something else to alert Noche that something was wrong. I also believe that after Mr. Flynn collected your daughter and took her home, Noche approached the perpetrator and maybe accused them. Then, at that point or before Noche was seen again, there was a fight, an argument, or something that got out of hand, and Noche lost his life, but not there. Everything I have heard leads to the fact that Noche walked out of that party alive. If he had been attacked or there was some other altercation, the people there would have noticed. As Melanie's mother, your main concern was for your daughter. Noche's disappearance didn't surface in your world until months later. And when it did, it was only logical for you to assume the two events were not related."

"Right," I said slowly, as I tried to remember exactly when I had connected the two.

"When I was first given the information relating to the cove party event and then learned about Melanie's mishap, I tended to agree with what you did. As time went on and I talked to several others, I realized that, even though most people knew Melanie left early, few knew she wasn't well. No one I talked to knew she was incapacitated by the punch. We can't ignore that someone might have lied."

"Where are you going with this, exactly?" I sat back and crossed my arms. I had the urge to stand up and punch him in the mouth. That's what Ian would have done.

Neddel sighed. "The lion's share of people we interviewed from Melanie's list who attended the party associated Noche with drugs. The odd part is that he didn't provide any, had no history of selling to any of the other partygoers, and most people described their knowledge as a rumor. They had heard, someone told them, yet not one person could point a finger at who had spread the word."

Not good. I'd known this, but somehow, I thought I was just missing a connection.

"Now, don't misunderstand me and think we didn't learn anything about any drugs at all, because we did. Most of the local kids, those from the villages to the north, and the kids who came up from Tamworth are all getting their supplies from two sources. One is actually located in Tamworth. The other is just south of town here, and we've been watching that place for a while. We want to take these people out, but we'd like to be able to hit their supplier at the same time. There was a small contingent of local young people who referenced another person who, we believe, is local and able to supply prescription drugs. This person has been successful thus far in keeping a low profile, but eventually, they will slip up."

Now, I was on my feet.

"Are you accusing Melanie?" My voice was rising.

Neddel reached out a hand, but when I pulled back, he gently waved me down.

"No, Doris, that's not what I'm saying at all."

I was starting to get even more impatient. Like Buttercup smelling peanut butter, I knew a tantalizing morsel was coming. It was all I could do to not demand he get on with it.

"Eventually, my investigation took me to Noche's supervisor at the forestry department. We did a few date comparisons and discovered Noche reported to work for ten days after the keg party."

I think my jaw might have bounced off the table. A simple thing, but I had totally overlooked it. I had talked with one of his co-workers, but never approached his supervisor or the person in charge of his unit. On top of that, I had been confident I knew his last day, and never asked anyone if it was right.

What an idiot, I thought, meaning myself.

"The supervisor, of course, kept written records. We also had a number of witnesses, and finally, we also had Mr. and Mrs. Otis. They positively identified the last date they had seen Noche as three days before he stopped reporting for work. That would be seven days after the keg party. At that point, we started doing an hour-by-hour timeline of Noche's last few days. Besides the forestry department records and my conversation with the Otises, we now have John's cell phone records. He spoke with his fiancée at least twice a day. He ate regularly, at the diner. His credit card places him there, at gas stations, at the movies one night. We have a pretty tight record."

"Oh." It was all I could say. My brain was racing from one piece of Neddel's information to another.

"My investigation also took me to looking into Noche's life beyond this town." Neddel took a napkin and wiped up the wet circle left on the table from his iced tea glass. "We needed to learn if there was anything, or maybe any*body*, from his past who might have resurfaced and done him harm."

"Did you find somebody?"

"Actually, no. That doesn't mean he never did anything wrong, or that he didn't have an enemy somewhere, but overall, he was pretty innocuous."

"Okay," I said. "If Noche's past is out, what have you got?"

"On Noche's last night, he was working the evening shift with a partner covering Crawford and Pinkham Notch. Around ten thirty, they were called to a moose/truck collision."

I nodded. Unfortunately, these types of collisions are common in our area.

"Noche's report says they found the moose crippled and struggling. They had to dispatch it. Rescue used the jaws of life to get the driver out of the pickup truck. He was taken to the hospital here, where a decision would be made whether he should be taken by a Medivac helicopter to Portland. The injured man didn't live long enough to make it to the hospital. The last notes I have from Noche were from his meeting with the medical examiner. When Noche finished at the hospital, his shift was over. We assumed he went home. However, unlike every other night since he has been here, he did not call his girlfriend."

"Would it be safe to say," I asked, "that you believe something happened to Noche either at the hospital or after he left there and before he got home?"

"I personally called the girlfriend. Normally, Noche would shower and call her before he retired for the night. I have spoken to Noche's partner and the EMTs that responded to the accident. I've also been able to reach all the emergency room personnel that he may have been in contact with that evening. I need to leave in a few minutes because I have a meeting with Doctor Kennett at the hospital. He's the last person I have to talk to. I've met him a couple of times in other cases. I believe he may be able to answer my questions."

Neddel had raised the thought of Burt Kennett, who fell into the category Rose Ann referred to as having overstayed their abilities. I knew Burt, and I knew Shane, who worked for Burt; both were gossips. Because I had access to Rose Ann Lombard, the medicolegal investigator, I had ignored any chance to speak to either Doctor Kennet or Shane. Neddel had pointed out my investigative incompetence twice in the last fifteen minutes. This sounded like another situation in which I had failed.

"Everett, Noche's skull was caved. Can you tell me if he was struck or something else, maybe hit by a car?"

"Yes." Neddel got to his feet, ready to leave. "Juan Noche was struck from behind by an irregularly shaped circular weapon."

* * *

After Neddel left, taking with him my notes as I knew he would, Melanie found me still sitting at the table, pondering all the sheriff had told me.

"What did he say?" she asked. "Don't leave anything out, because I'll know if you're being evasive."

I recapped the conversation. "I feel so stupid," I ended. "There's so much I didn't look into."

"Why are you feeling that way?" she asked. "You're not a cop. The guy's been trained to do that job. He has a whole network of law enforcement types. And he has actual authority to question people. That doesn't mean he can do everything. Let him try to figure out how to trim the fingernails on a four-hundred-fifty-pound pig."

Melanie's irritation with Sheriff Everett Neddel was rising again. I decided not to tell her about the moment he and I had shared in the apple orchard, but that brought to mind the red Audi.

I smiled. "You're right." I put more cookies on the plate and poured her an iced tea. Then I told her about the red car. Down the hall, Melanie's cell phone dinged in her office.

"For the love of cat fur! There's Shane again." Taking her glass and the plate, she left. Royally and Lilo followed the plate.

Chapter Twenty-Six

The stress of the last several days was weighing on me, and the need for normalcy was as tangible as the weight of a heavy winter coat. Instead of dusting or vacuuming my messy house, I went to the place where everything seemed so much simpler.

I stood in the barn door with the bright sun's rays lighting up all but the highest, furthest corners. Looking down the broad central aisle, past the feed barrels and the cat sleeping in the straw, I could see the back wall where Ian's tools hung neatly over the workbench. The top of the bench was stained and spotted with paint and oil, but clear of debris. If you excluded the barn dust, anyway. Above the workbench, nailed between the four-by-four supports, were a myriad of odd shelves constructed from bits of lumber left from other projects.

There was a shelf with Ian's tackle box, another with trophies from high school and college sports. Boxes of nails and screws. Ian had been a bit OCD about this stuff. The pieces of scavenged lumber had to be standing in the wood bin just so. All the cardboard boxes on the shelving were lined up, left to right. Tallest to shortest, labels facing out. Looking particularly out of place was the battery-operated drill Neddel, and I had used. We'd left it lying on the wood surface of the workbench.

I pulled the red plastic case out from under the bench. The drill and battery pack had pre-formed pockets they fit into. It took only a small amount of effort to press the drill bit into its case, where it snapped into place.

While I slowly set Ian's things to right, I thought about my late husband and his somewhat fussy ways. Touching his tools made me smile, taking away some of the loneliness that crushed my heart and left a dull ache.

Wait. What was this? His tackle box was right in front of my eyes.

"Ian," I whispered, "*you* put something away wrong?"

Neither Melanie nor I fished. The workbench wasn't all that wide, and before I knew it, I had hold of the tackle box. Instead of turning it around and replacing it on the shelf, I unsnapped the latch. The lid rose, lifting the three tiers of lure trays with it.

Instead of neat rows of single hook or treble hook spinners and bobbers, I found a jumbled mess. No one had been in here, and I hadn't touched this. That left only Melanie to have shaken the contents into chaos.

"No, that can't be right," I told myself.

Melanie referred to her father as Mr. Triple-A. When she first started doing chores, Ian had taught her how to GI-fold underwear and socks. She still folded ours the same way.

"I ought to make her sort this out," I muttered.

More than once, Ian had come into the house with bloody fingers because he kept the hooks so sharp. Very carefully, I emptied the box, intent on putting everything back where he had kept it. Underneath a snarl of fishing line, which had worked free from its packaging, was a small plastic bag. Lifting the snarl and packaging out in one handful, I uncovered more packets. Each was three-quarters filled with white powder. My brain slowed down as I fixated on the bags, and I suddenly felt dizzy. Dropping my hand to the workbench to steady myself, I felt a sharp jab and yanked it back.

"Ow!" I cried out. "Ow, ow, ow."

Flipping my hand over, exposed a deep gash on the outer side of my palm. Like the novice I was, I had gotten it caught on a big hook attached to a large-mouth bass lure. Deep red blood was already running down over my wrist and curling around the back side of my arm. The workbench swayed. I felt dizzy again, and my stomach rose in revolt.

"What are you doing?" demanded a masculine voice behind me.

I turned, releasing my grip on the lid to the tackle box and shielding it behind me. Shane stood in the door, dressed for a day off in jeans and Nikes. Not the young man I knew, but a tall, wiry guy whose face was twisted darkly. Then, like a traffic light, it changed to concern, and this stranger became Shane again. I held out my hand. A drop of blood dripped off the point of my elbow to the floor.

Shane's concern deepened as he stepped closer. "I'm sorry if I sounded rough. Doctor Kennett has a meeting with the new sheriff. He's getting a little weird, and I'm worried about how it will go. For him, I mean, you know? Anyway, Melanie sent me out to check on you. She said you were acting a little hinky, and she's concerned." He reached out his hand to steady me.

I drew in a breath. It seemed to go only to the top of my throat, yet my chest was rising and falling at an accelerated rate. I knew him, Shane, right? I knew him. His mother said he was a good boy. But what about Shane, the man? I started babbling.

"I got cut." My mouth was dry. "Some of these hooks…"

I stopped cold, almost reaching out to Shane, before pulling my hand back in to cradle it in its sister as I remembered. Glancing down at Shane's hand, I saw instead Noah's. I remembered, could actually smell the white first-aid tape on the big white bandage Melanie had wrapped on his wound to hold it in place. *I was going to do a little fishing,* he'd said. *I wasn't paying attention, and I caught myself.*

What was right? What wasn't? Inside, I had a visual superimposing Shane onto Noah. It almost locked together, but not quite. Noah was there, but not Shane. I couldn't figure it out, and trying to was making me feel a little sick.

My legs felt wobbly, but I needed to call the sheriff. What were the chances Sheriff Neddel would find Noah's blood on Ian's hooks? I looked up. Shane was watching me. His face had always been an open book, easy to read and understand. Right now, he looked hard and… nervous. Really nervous.

No, not Shane, I thought. *He's a young guy, an innocent.*

My thoughts were tilt-a-whirling like one of those old-fashioned horror movies where the girl goes into the garage with the chainsaw-toting madman. This was Shane standing in front of me, the kid who worked with the medical examiner's office. His boss, Burt, was no innocent. But he couldn't have corrupted Shane, right? How much would Shane have done for Burt?

Rose Ann had said the old-timer had no respect for the changing of times. That, beyond the physical body, he wasn't interested in the clues the dead shared with those trying to decipher their last moments. She had remarked on how Burt was out there destroying evidence because he couldn't take the time to look for it in his rush to get done. Shane had said Burt gossiped all the time.

Gossip grew with the telling. Wasn't that like destroying evidence? I mean, if Burt was maliciously spreading rumors, implanting erroneous thoughts in the minds of others, wasn't that a backdoor way to alter the facts? To destroy evidence that was held in memories?

If I said anything about that to Shane, I was sure he'd tell Burt, hoping to win a little praise. The kid was eager and, I'm sure, wanted to please his boss, just like Rex wanted to do what he thought I asked him to. Shane would be calling the medical examiner's office before I was across the yard. And I didn't want Burt anywhere near here until I had talked with Neddel. Maybe Rose Ann, too. I needed to get into the house where I would have some privacy.

Shane held his head slightly sideways, looking at me. Like Rex, he was trying to figure out what I was thinking.

Waving Shane away, I tried to give off a little laugh. "Rusty nail. Need Mercurochrome, I think." Head down, I hustled past him, leaving a wide space between us. I was sure every thought showed on my face.

Out in the sun, I picked up the pace, believing he would follow. Behind me, I heard the tap of his shoes on the barn floor.

"No, wait!" he called out. "Stop right there."

Then I heard the barn door shudder as something solid hit it. Like the wooden panel had been slapped. The metal slider rattled hard on the steel roll bar. The white powder-filled plastic bags were still lying out in the open. It wouldn't take a genius to figure out that I'd found them, and I knew what they were.

I started to run. Suddenly, I was falling through the air, landing with a hard thump. As soon as my cheek mashed into the grass, I flipped over. A man gripped my foot.

It wasn't Shane, but he looked familiar and was dressed like Noah in business casual. His tie was navy blue with little red flags the same color as his face. The white line around his mouth reminded me of the white powder. It grew as he pulled me back towards him. I was terrified.

Lashing out with my other foot, I caught him in the side of the face with my barn boot. The soft rubber was no deterrent.

"Let me go! MELANIE!" I screamed.

The man gave a nasty laugh. "Melanie is deep in la-la land. She missed out the first time, but this time, we got her good."

The center of my fear morphed into anger.

"Don't you dare hurt her!" I kicked and swung out with my fists, splattering my own blood all over both of us. Then, I recognized my attacker. Derek, Shane's cousin. The one his mother had just told me days ago had such a great job, made so much money, and came up every two weeks with his girlfriend, who was from the valley, to visit her young son.

In the kennel, Rex was barking furiously.

"Take it easy, you old bitch." Derek flipped me back onto my belly.

I looked for Shane in the barn doorway, but he was gone.

Even though I struggled like a fish tossed to the stream bank, Derek was younger and stronger.

With a knee in the center of my back, he pulled my hands together behind me, trying to get a zip-tie in place. The blood still seeping down my arm made my skin slippery. Derek grunted with the effort.

I needed to get to Melanie.

"ROYALLY!" I screamed.

Because there was no one left, I let out a wordless wail, hoping the heavens would open and drop a hero to my rescue.

In the time it would take a hummingbird to flutter, the pressure on my back disappeared. I actually felt the slide as it left. I sucked in air, trying to move, and felt a sharp jab as a hoof dug into the back of my thigh.

Lifting my head, I dragged in a ragged pant. Five feet from my nose and inching closer, Buttercup's dancing hooves ripped up the turf. The pig jerked around, snorting and squealing in porcine cuss words. Her long body twisted like a gator's; her angry sounds roared like lion cries on the savannah. My beloved baby girl had morphed into everything people had warned me about, but I was not afraid.

Buttercup had hold of Derek's arm now. She shook him like a rag doll. The man was on his knees, trying to get up and pull away. I couldn't tell if he was screaming in rage or pain. Finally, he got free and tried to run. Buttercup mowed him over. Switching back like a well-trained tight end, she caught hold of his calf. This time, his cries were definitely pain.

"Get her off of me," he yelled, pounding Buttercup's sides and back with his fists.

Buttercup stood over him, one leg still in her mouth, daring him to move. I did the only thing I could think of.

"Buttercup," I ordered sharply. "Down."

The four hundred-fifty-pound pig dropped straight downward, pinning Derek's legs beneath her. His screaming ratcheted up, even though the pig had released her bite on his leg.

I turned to the barn again, but still did not see Shane. Down the road, I heard the rising noise of a police siren.

"Stay." I tried to struggle up on my feet, and finally sat while I pulled my hands free of the zip-tie which Derek hadn't gotten fully tightened. All the while, I commanded. "Stay. Stay."

The noise of the sirens increased as the cruisers broke out of the tree covering. Buttercup raised her head, looking toward the flashing red and blue lights.

"Stay," I said. "Right there. Stay."

I was still on all fours when the lead cruiser screeched to a halt, sending gravel in all directions. Sheriff Neddel was beside me in a heartbeat.

"What happened? You're bleeding."

"Melanie," I cried. "She's in the house. He attacked Melanie. Drugged her or…" I couldn't verbalize the terrors in my mind.

Scooping me up, Neddel ran for the house.

Behind us, Derek screamed. "Help me. The pig is crushing me. My legs are broken."

Neddel paused at the top of the steps. I tried to speak, but it was more a moan. "Stay, Buttercup."

"Stay, Buttercup," Neddel ordered. "If she moves off of him," he told the deputy, "Shoot that scuzzball, and I don't mean the pig."

Noah ran up, yanking the kitchen door open. I had no idea where he came from. Neddel looked startled. I don't think he did either.

"Noah." My fingers reached out. "Melanie is in here. That guy Derek,Shane's cousin, drugged her."

Noah ripped past us. "MELANIE?" he yelled. "Where are you? Melanie?"

I struggled free from Neddel's grip and followed Noah down the hallway to Melanie's room. She was lying on the floor beside her computer chair. Her face was colorless, and her legs were entangled with the chair, but she was breathing. Neddel ran back down the hallway.

"I need a medic in here, right now!" he bellowed.

The next several minutes were pure chaos. While the medics worked to revive Melanie and get her ready for transport, a second ambulance arrived. I sat on Melanie's bed as one of the new EMTs kept poking at me, trying to make sure I didn't have more injuries than the cut on my hand. Out the window, I watched as a second EMT knelt on the ground, trying to shove Buttercup aside. No matter how hard the poor guy tried, she wouldn't move off Derek. The EMT finally gave up when the pig swung her massive head around, little piggy eyes glaring, and issued her version of a growl.

Melanie was on the stretcher. They were wheeling her out. I followed behind. Just as I got to the edge of the deck, I looked back. Noah walked out of the kitchen door. Under one arm, he carried Lilo, who was shivering in fear but still yapping and howling. Under the other arm, he carried Royally. The very concerned-looking young man held the corgi in such a way that the dog's broad chest was supported in his hand. No amount of squirming, growling, or snapping seemed to faze Noah.

"I'll put them in a kennel to keep them out of the way," he told Neddel and me. As he passed by the EMT who was trying again to shove Buttercup off Derek, Noah said, "Come on, Bon-Bon, let's see how much damage you did

216

this time. Heel. To home."

In a move that astounded me, the pig responded instantly. It was evident she remembered this guy and thought he might be good for a treat. Trotting over Derek, stepping on him only once, she sniffed at the squirming Royally as she kept step with Noah's long strides.

Neddel and the EMT watched them go.

"My legs!" Derek whined. "They're both broken. I was only trying to help. The pig attacked Mrs. Flynn. My legs! I'm going to sue. I'll see that brute butchered. My legs!"

"GUYS!" Noah yelled from the barn. "I need help here. Shane is on the floor, unconscious and bleeding."

Neddel and the only unattending EMT ran for the barn.

As the EMTS and deputies ran back and forth across the yard, Neddel returned to where I was standing beside the ambulance. He told me that Noah was locking up the dogs and Buttercup and that Shane was being loaded onto a stretcher. Just as I was climbing in the first one to ride with Melanie to the hospital, Shane was wheeled up.

"Mrs. Flynn," he whispered. "I tried to stop him, I did. Don't let him hurt my mom, okay?"

Behind him, the EMT told Derek he would have to wait for transport. Shane was in more serious condition, and neither of Derek's legs was broken.

"You're wrong," Derek cried. "My legs!"

"Shut up, asshole," Neddel said.

The EMT who was helping me up into the ambulance said to Neddel. "We're taking Melanie to the hospital. They'll be able to bring her out of it there."

My heart hurt.

Neddel looked up at me and said, "That's for the best."

Before I could say anything, Noah ran up, cell phone in hand. "I've got a friend coming over with some two-by-fours. Buttercup took the gate off the hinges. As soon as the cops are done collecting the dope in the barn, we'll get it fixed up. I'll stay here until you come home. Call me when you're ready to leave the hospital. Either Zoe or Heather will come and get you, okay?"

"Thank you, Noah," I said. "I'm so sorry."

"It's okay," he said with a smile. "She busted it one time when you were gone, so we know what to do."

I didn't have time to explain before the door was shut that my apology was for doubting him. We were ready to leave when I heard Neddel talking.

"Dispatch? Don't rush the next ambulance. I want the ladies out of the way before this dirtbag goes into the ER."

Behind Neddel, I could still hear Derek moaning about his legs.

"What a loser," the EMT sitting beside me said. "He's going on about his broken legs and hasn't even realized yet the pig got a good bite on his calf."

"Oh, no!" I gasped. "Is he bleeding?"

"Some, but I got it wrapped up. Don't worry about it. But you might want to get the pig a tetanus shot."

Out the little window on the side door, I caught a glimpse of Noah and Buttercup sitting on the stoop in front of the barn as Neddel and his deputy went inside.

I held tight to Melanie's hand.

Chapter Twenty-Seven

Though I only got a butterfly bandage and a tetanus shot, Melanie had to stay in the hospital until the next day. I didn't want to leave her. Right about the time I thought I would have to go home, Noah called. He and one of his buddies had been able to fix the gate Buttercup had torn down on her way to rescue me.

"We didn't want to put metal into it in case she needs to escape again," he said. "But we made it double thick, so it will be more of a challenge for her. If it's okay, I'll stay the night, because when I went in to feed the cats, the new one attached herself to me like Velcro."

"That's Tiny. She's new and nervous," I said.

"Speaking of new, the black one that spits had babies. I don't know how many."

"Double her food ration, Noah. Then just leave her be. She'll be fine until tomorrow." I paused for a minute; then I had to tell him. "Listen, Noah, I need to tell you that during this entire mess, well, I thought a few times you might be involved. I don't know if you can forgive me, but I am truly sorry."

There was a pause before Noah answered. I thought he was going to hang up, tell me to take care of my own damn animals, or maybe I'd come home and find my place ransacked.

"If you promise not to squeal on me," he said. "I'll tell you that I've been avoiding my friends because I thought one of them was guilty. I probably need to apologize as well. See you when you get home."

As I was saying goodbye, Neddel walked in. We went down to the family room to talk, so we wouldn't wake up Melanie. It felt awkward, he and I together. Our relationship had changed and neither one of us quite knew how to address it. People talk about teenagers having issues speaking their minds, it doesn't get any better.

"She's going to be okay," he said, addressing my fears.

"I know," I whispered. There was a coffee machine on the table, and I put a pod in the basket.

"I have to say…Doris," Neddel began. "There were some things you were pretty right on. A few others, though…"

"Can you tell me?"

"Can you keep a secret?" Neddel laughed, dropped a dollar into the contribution jar, and popped a pod into the coffee machine.

I had already tasted my coffee. He was going to be sorry, but who was I to tell him? While the pressurized cup spit and spat, he started laying out the facts.

"As I told you earlier, we knew there were a couple of small-time pushers around here, and their supply came from out of state. It seems Derek Davis and his brother, Gary, have been bringing in dope. Started small. A little weed, then the business grew big time. It worked for them, that they had a couple of insiders. One was Derek's girlfriend, a local girl named Jenna White. The other was Shane, who for years was innocent of what they were doing."

"I know Jenna," I said. "She went to school with Melanie. They were friends. Jenna even dated Noah for a while."

"And that's where the doping of Melanie comes in," Neddel said. "Noah dumped Jenna, who held Melanie responsible. When she and Derek showed up at the cove to make a drop, Melanie was right there. Jenna had one of those fruit smoothies with her. She doctored it up and just passed it to Melanie on her way by. Shane told us the two girls were smiling, and it was all nice. Jenna handed Melanie the smoothie she had just gotten in town. When I questioned why Melanie would accept it. Shane said Jenna had brought it for a friend who wasn't there. It was something Melanie could drink without affecting her meds."

"So, Jenna pretended to be Melanie's friend, but doped her out of spite?"

My eyes narrowed.

That didn't sound like the Jenna I knew. But it had been a while. *If she was running with a pusher, was she using?* I wondered.

"Jenna knows what Melanie does for a living and that if anyone was going to set the brakes that night, or any other, it would be Melanie. Derek said they got such a rush out of seeing Melanie having to be carried off, they decided to do it again. Jenna and Gary were at your house. When they saw Derek tackle you and Buttercup jumped him, they took off in the car. We put a BOLO out on them. They were picked up on Route 25 in Tamworth."

"Are you kidding me?" I put the nasty coffee down. "Jenna was Melanie's friend! She has a child. She's from here. I know her." His words were shocking.

"I'll be getting statements from both Melanie and Noah, though they probably don't know any of this. I haven't questioned Gary and Jenna yet, but I got a photo of them being cuffed. She's big time into junk. All skin and bones. From the looks of her, she's never going to be really straight again."

Neddel took a big swig of the coffee concoction. His shoulders rolled up as he gagged. With no qualms, he spat into the trash and threw away what was left.

I laughed behind my hand. "Go on, Everett."

While he was looking for something to rinse his mouth out with, he said, "On the night Noche investigated the truck and moose fatality, he came out of the hospital and saw a couple of guys rummaging around the trunk of Shane's car in the hospital parking lot. I don't know if Noche was parked near there, or if he was just curious. They had been using Shane as a mule and were looking for a package of drugs. When Noche asked the guys, Derek and Gary, for ID, Derek picked up a broken piece of curbing and beat Noche. It was dark, the trunk of the car was open, they shoved him in. Later, when Shane got home from work, the brothers were waiting for him."

I was backed up against the wall, one hand over my mouth, the other on my roiling stomach.

"How did they get Noche's body up on the ridge?" I asked. Had they been in my driveway? Used my tractor? I remembered thinking that before but forgetting to tell Everett.

"I don't have all the details yet," Neddel said. "Shane said when Derek and Gary told him about Juan, Shane tried to back out. The brothers threatened Shane's family. He's the one that took Noche's things up later on. That's how come they were so well hidden. He knew the rock openings were there. Derek had stashed the drugs in your barn. He wanted it back. Shane said he'd come over. He tried to keep Derek and the others away, or at least keep you and Melanie safe. It didn't work out for him. When he tried to stop Derek from running after you, he took a heavy hit to the side of his head. Even as he was passing out, he was trying to call 9-1-1. He's still going to be in trouble. I just don't know how much."

"What about Melanie? Did he know she had been doped?" I didn't want to ask, or rather, I didn't want to hear the answer.

"He says no. That he thought only Derek went into the house. We're not done trying to figure this out. I have to go. I just wanted to make sure you were okay and give you what I had."

"It's nice that you came here to tell me," I said shyly. "You could have just called."

Everett pinked up slightly. "What? And missed that awesome cup of coffee?"

While I sat next to Melanie in the hospital, I had plenty of time to consider a lot of things. She was still sleeping, but I've heard even asleep, you can hear what people say.

"You're going to be okay," I spoke softly. "The doctor was just here. He said the last blood test showed the flushing is working and the drugs are leaving your system. I don't know what Derek put the drugs in, but when I get home, I'm going to throw all the cached food in your room away. Probably everything that's open in the kitchen as well. There's still a lot of information to be sorted out, but Everett, Sheriff Neddel, is working on it. Oh, and I'm sure you'll be pleased to know I apologized to Noah. Did you know he has a pet name for Buttercup? He calls her Bon-Bon. Who knew?"

I rubbed her fingers. They still felt chilly to me.

"I can't help wondering about the serendipitous arrival of the sheriff and his men. Or Noah, who was right behind them."

* * *

It was close to midnight when I finally left the hospital. Noah was asleep on the couch in the living room. The animals were tucked away, but none of them stayed that way. I had to go out to the barn, with Lilo and Royally tailing me to pass out peanut butter snacks. Back inside, I paused for a moment, looking at Noah, sprawled on the couch, Tiny in the crook of his arm, and my two gregarious ring-tail females lining the top of the sofa.

"Thank you," I whispered. Upstairs with Lilo, Royally, Rusty, and Argyle on the covers, I fell right to sleep.

Chapter Twenty-Eight

First thing in the morning, or as first, as 9:00 A.M. was, Noah and I drove back to Memorial Hospital. After what felt like an eternal wait, we left with Melanie.

The resulting hangover from the date rape drug Jenna had slipped into Melanie's iced tea had left her with a terrible headache and some confusion,

"I'm okay," Melanie snapped. "Just give me a minute. Stop babying me."

She was lying on the couch with Lilo, who patiently waited to cuddle with her human. I knew Melanie didn't mean it and that in a few minutes, she'd probably be sleeping again, so I stepped out into the hall. Lilo crawled up close to Melanie's chin, nuzzled her, and waited. So much patience in that little black-haired pug.

In the evening, Zoe showed up with a pot of chicken noodle soup her mother had made. While it heated, Neddel and Noah, who had both shown up to check on Melanie, competed for the supreme male right to explain.

"Good thing Melanie's medic alert activated when she fell," Neddel said. "The alarm went off at both the rescue barn and in my office. As soon as the alert was issued, we were moving out. Shane's call rang in, but he was already unconscious."

"Ian got the alert for her, thank heavens," I said. "He was worried she might be alone and have another bad episode. She wears it under her shirt, so Jenna may not have even known she had one. The alarm would have sounded. She doesn't remember, though. But what about you, Noah? How did you get here so fast?"

Noah blushed all the way down to his fingertips. "I knew she had a medic alert. She'd told me about it when she first got it. I have to tell you, she kept taking it off and leaving it on her dresser. We had some, ah, heated discussions about it. It wasn't until after Mr. Flynn passed away that she started wearing it all the time. I remember her crying, blaming herself for his heart attack."

He looked down the hall, where Zoe was spoon-feeding Melanie soup.

"I got a little tough on her about that. You know, sort of semi-tough love. I told her, instead of being angry with everything that was happening around her, she should be focused on how much she loved her dad. And how much he loved her. After that, I never saw her without it.

"One day, when I was over here, I downloaded an app that allowed me to sync my phone to the frequency of her personal alert. When it went off, I knew something was wrong as soon as rescue did. The sheriff came racing out of the parking lot across the street, and I was already running for my car."

My jaw dropped. "You ran out of the bank? Without telling anyone? Wait, you were cyberstalking Melanie?"

"Yeah, no! Sort of." He rubbed the back of his head. "The app only lets me know if the alert is sounded. Nothing else. I was worried you might be outside or training. Or, I don't know, in town, and you wouldn't know. I'm sorry. I'll shut it off. After you left to go to the hospital, I called the bank manager and tried to explain. We're probably going to have a talk about this."

I wasn't sure how I felt about Noah activating the app without our knowledge. But I was going to have him synch my cellphone to it. He was focused on the edge of the table, hands clasped together. I reached over, laying my hand on his.

"Don't worry, Noah. If he gives you a hard time, I'll go in there and tell him I'm taking my twenty-seven dollars out."

We all laughed and slurped our soup.

It didn't take a lot of effort for Sheriff Neddel to wear Shane down. The process might have been sped up by the sight of his elderly parents holding onto each other and weeping in the corridor outside the room where he was being interrogated. Neddel told me the couple had been strategically placed, so every time the door opened, Shane could see the havoc his actions had wrought in their lives. He willingly told the authorities everything he knew, which gave them an edge in dealing with his cousins. I heard his lawyer told him it would help his case.

"John Noche was killed because he was in the wrong place and just trying to do his job. Technically, up here, the forest wardens work with the same capacity as the sheriff's department. He should have called in before engaging, but from what I hear, he probably felt no need." Neddel stirred his soup. "You know, the way these things work out, it wouldn't have been long before Shane's cousins started pushing Shane to pocket drugs from his job, or the houses he went into with Burt."

Melanie, sans makeup and a hairbrush, came in from the hall with Zoe behind her. I noticed there was still soup in her bowl when she sat down.

"And," said Melanie, who was offering noodles to the hounds, "how long would it have been before they had him casing places, for items they could lift and sell back in Massachusetts? There's a ready black market for almost anything there."

She rubbed her hand over her forehead. Zoe put a glass of iced tea in front of Melanie. I could see her fingers trembling slightly as she reached for it.

"I think you're right. Derek figured he and Gary controlled the drug market in the valley. Eventually, they would have decided they could spread their fledgling organization into other fields." Neddel pushed back from the table. Royally had moved to sit in front of him. Even though the sheriff held up his hands, showing they were empty, the corgi stayed in place.

"I find it hard to believe," I said, "that Shane would have allowed his cousins to dictate what he was going to do. Shane knew it was wrong. I've known him for a long time. It's just not the way he was raised."

Neddel's face twisted for a moment. Then he said, "Shane had a lot of stuff going on in his world. Things even you, his neighbors and friends, didn't know about. A lot of them sprang from money issues. Did you know his job with Burt is not classified as full-time? That means there are weeks he earns less, and he doesn't have any type of benefit package. He has some big-time tuition loans, though, and his parents were struggling financially. He has other siblings, but they all have their own families. Derek loaned him money a couple of times to help out his folks. Knowing Shane didn't have the money to pay back the loan, Derek leaned on Shane, saying he was ready to expose that the elderly Davis family had accepted drug money. Shane told us that if he hadn't done what Derek wanted, his cousin said he would go to his aunt and uncle and demand they transport the drugs."

"We were all right when we surmised killing Noche wasn't planned. But once the deed was done, the brothers circled back to Shane and where he lived below Calwin Mountain.

"Derek said he'd come over here a number of times in the past and remembered the keys were always in your tractor," Neddel said. "He and Gary backed in, loaded Noche's body into the trailer, and drove up on the ridge to get rid of it. They thought they were pretty slick. Then, when you were gone, they decided that might be a sweet place to stash some of their stuff. They either came right up the road, or entered the trail system behind Shane's house and came out near the barn. When you came back, it threw a wrench into what they were doing, because now Melanie was here and working from home. They were still using the barn. Shane was here practically every day. Derek sent Shane over to pick up the drugs hidden in the tackle box. Shane came by foot through the woods so no one would see him, and for whatever reason, Derek followed him in the car on the road. Maybe he thought he'd scope out another hiding spot. Who knows?"

"I was working," Melanie said. "I didn't hear a car. I turned around, and Jenna and Derek were right behind me. I told them I was working. He left. She sat on the edge of my desk. My cup of tea was right there. She had a drive-thru coffee she was sipping. I think I reached for my cup." Melanie rubbed her forehead again. "I just don't seem to remember."

"It's okay, Melanie," Everett said. "We're working on it. You should take it easy for a few days. If you think of something, call, but don't worry about it."

"You don't have all this sorted out yet?" I asked. It sounded to me like they knew all they needed to.

Neddel guffawed. "You're kidding, right?"

"No," I said. Beside me, both Noah and Melanie shook their heads as well.

"If it weren't for Shane, we'd still be at square one," said Neddel. "I mean, we had a lot of the main pieces of this puzzle, but we'd still be sorting out why and where. Shane's story is keeping us near the center. But don't get me wrong, what he did was not right, and there will be a price to be paid. Derek, Gary, and Jenna are all out there trying to screw each other and cover their own heinies. None agreeing about who did the deed or masterminded the whole scheme. Unfortunately, Shane's cousins have acquired a slick lawyer who is already shoveling blame onto Jenna. She's part of the equation, but from what Shane told us, she wasn't there when Noche was murdered, or when his remains were disposed of. Unfortunately for her, like I said before, she doesn't have as much where-with-all as she did at one time." He scooped a cracker off the table and offered it to Royally, who grabbed his prize and ran away with two or three cats trailing him. "And I'll tell you upfront, the lawyer has his sights set on Shane taking the fall as well."

"Is Shane in jail?" I asked.

"No. Thanks to Burt and Noah, Shane has been released to his parents' custody. He can stay there or go to work, but that's it. Jenna is in protected custody in a high-security dry-out. Her folks were devastated. They got her a lawyer, but this was the best the judge would give them. The other two are being held in Concord. I'm just not sure for how long. There's so much legal shuffle going on; you need a scorecard to figure out which charges are tacked on to which of the four players. Their arraignment is tomorrow."

It got quiet around the table. We were all thinking the same thing about how this horrible event had happened right here in our backyard. How people we knew had been drawn in, and the suffering had spread like fungus. If it hadn't been for the advent of the squealing and snorting of Buttercup, we might not have known someone was on the back deck, trying to get into the house unaccosted.

I had to push hard to get Buttercup's butt out of the way and the screen door open. Rose Ann was trying to squeeze around the rotund pig, who had an interest in the pastry box my friend was holding over her head.

"No," Rose Ann said. "Sit. Lie down. Stay."

"Is any of that working for you?" I asked.

"No," she said with a laugh. "Not any of it at all."

I finally got both of them into the kitchen, which was pretty full at that point.

"I brought a lovely three-berry pie and some good news," Rose Ann said. "I have to tell you, though, I expected Buttercup to be wearing a Superman cape."

"Hold on," said Melanie. "Let's see if we can drown out some of the confusion."

She got down the pig peanut butter jar. Then she and Zoe, who had spent most of our discussion with her mouth open, took turns making little peanut butter and Cheerio balls while I started making coffee. Buttercup happily stayed in place as the treats kept coming. Once everyone had a mug in hand, I dished out pie.

"Well, you missed all the rest of the gab," I said, "but feel free to tell us what you know."

"Don't worry, I'll see it when it comes out in the theaters." Rose Ann reached for a fork and the first plate offered. "Right from the start, I started running the DNA samples from everything that was collected. I put in an order to bypass Burt Kennett. Everything came directly to my office. To be honest, the results will take a while, but we have some preliminary findings you might consider useful." She took a big bite of her pie. We were all sitting there watching her chew.

"Swallow," Neddel ordered. "And tell us what you got."

Rose Ann did as she was told but looked pained. "First, the sample I took off the kitten appears to match the swab we took from the pig." No one laughed. Then she said, "The initial swabs I took off of Noche's belt buckle, which had been protected by the jacket and the body, and then from the rock left right beside it, are a match to one of the samples Neddel's officers took from the local suspects."

"Which one?" asked Melanie.

"Derek Davis."

"That means Derek touched the belt buckle, right?" said Noah. "It's not really clear what you're saying."

"It is if you're a cop," I said. "So, basically, you can prove Derek had contact with the belt buckle and the rock, but not that he killed Noche?"

"Did you discern if the rock was a piece of the same curbstone from the hospital parking lot?" Everett asked.

"Exactly. This is really good pie, isn't it?" Rose Ann tried to look innocent, but there was a naughty gleam in her eyes, like maybe she was talking about something she shouldn't, and now she was done.

I had more questions, and from the looks of some of the others, they did as well. But Everett cut in.

"Time to stop the shop talk," he said.

We did well keeping to mundane topics for a little while, and then I said, "Just think where we'd be without Buttercup. Not only did she find Noche's remains, but she found his stuff as well. She may not have known anything about drugs, but when push came to shove, she knew who to bite." I sat back in my seat, both hands wrapped around the warm mug.

Buttercup was lying on the floor next to my chair. On the other side, Royally was tight up against me. Though Zoe hadn't been around a lot since we'd acquired Buttercup, she and Melanie had been tight friends for a long time. She knew how things worked around here and just accepted it all. At that moment, she had the jar of peanut butter in front of her and a pile of Cheerios. After applying a smidgeon of peanut butter to each round O, she hand-fed the treat to her porcine friend. Royally only got about every sixth one.

"Aren't you afraid of losing your fingers?" Everett asked.

Zoe scoffed. "Listen to you, Mr. Big City. Did you know a horse will do anything it can to avoid stepping on you? Well, it's true. And this sweet girl is not going to bite me just for the heck of it. Are you sweet-cheeks?" She made a smooching noise at Buttercup. Both Royally and Everett whined, but for different reasons.

I was still thinking about the case, and I needed someone to help me figure it out.

"Shane didn't come back around here after Melanie got doped because he was concerned about her, did he?" I asked. It hurt me to think that he would have used our feelings for him to do Derek's dirty work. "All that time, he was so helpful, so friendly. Was that all an act? Was he just checking to make sure I didn't get too close to the truth and that Melanie didn't remember anything about Jenna giving her the spiked drink?" I felt my chest seizing up. "Melanie and I believed he was just kind of going off the rails. Derek could have made that work for himself as well. He could have killed me. He or Jenna could have hurt, even murdered, Melanie." I heard her take a sharp breath at my words. It was a fact we needed to get into the open to get past. "Then made it all look like a robbery gone bad, or Shane having finally lost control. There have been so many weird things going on around here lately, the story would have sold itself."

"That's true." Everett reached across the open space and took my hand. "He may have had that plan hatching in his head. But he never expected Buttercup to tussle with him on the back lawn. Of all the scenarios he could have concocted or thought of, I bet having a four-hundred-fifty-pound linebacker take him out was never one of them."

"She's such a good girl; yes, she is." Melanie kissed the top of Buttercup's head.

Noah paled.

Long after Rose Ann went flying out to the next site that called for her attention, and Noah went home for a good night's sleep before his meeting the next morning with his boss, I was still walking around wringing my hands. Zoe offered to sleep in the spare bedroom that night, but we laughed her off. But later, I would have welcomed an extra body. Melanie had taken a sleeping pill. But I would lay down, get up, lay down again. My legs were restless, and my brain felt shocked. Everett had said I was right on this and that, but I had been horribly wrong in other places. Now, I argued with myself about my decision-making abilities.

In the wee hours, I got up to check on Melanie and make sure the windows were all locked. Down at the end of the driveway, I could see Everett's cruiser. Standing in the window, watching, I smiled and asked Ian if it was all right for me to be interested. Finally, my nerves settled, and I took that as a yes.

"I should make him coffee," I said to Royally and received a little chortle for an answer. "You're right. If he's sleeping out there, he won't be happy to be caught at it."

I would have liked to say I slept well after that, but it would be a lie. It would take a while to feel safe in my own home again.

* * *

Noah and Travis had done a good job fixing the damage caused by Hurricane Buttercup. The new, heavier door came with a solid latch. On a subsequent visit, Noah arrived bearing pizza and hot wings. I think maybe he and Melanie had their first real conversation since grade school. Melanie told me later that together they discovered a lot of interests they hadn't shared before and that Noah was not really crazy about mudding. He sat down one evening and just started talking about his father's mental illness and the horrible things the elder had said about his son.

"He used to beat Mom and me up on a regular basis," Noah said. "He wasn't a big guy, about my size, and he was really good at acting like he had suffered a grievous wrong and should be pitied. He told my teachers and counselors at school how my mother had a breakdown, or cancer, I don't know which. And that she had been sick in bed for years. There was this long story about us having gone to counseling and how I lied all the time, stole things, and got in fights. The teachers seemed to believe him more than me, maybe because I didn't dare open my mouth. When I got some real size, my father laid off smacking me around, but he'd still wale hard on my mother. Then he'd let me know while she was lying bleeding and crying on the floor that it was my fault."

Noah paused. Melanie inched closer to him.

"He used to accuse my mother of fooling around with other men, leading them on, making him look like a fool. A couple of times, he got involved in some bad fights when he was drinking because, even if she'd been home for days, he was sure she was guilty. When he was drunk, he'd blame some poor guy who didn't even know what was going on. He never drank here in town.

There was a tavern just across the Maine state line he used to go to, down on Route 25. I knew where it was because sometimes, he'd get home without his truck, and Mom would borrow the reverend's car so we could go get it.

"One night, he came home, and he was in a real tear. The next day, my mother packed our stuff up as fast as she could. I had slipped off to school so I could pick up some stuff in my locker I needed. While I was there, the sheriff showed up. He was looking for a guy in a letterman jacket who had beaten a man into the hospital over in Maine. It was my jacket, but my father had been wearing it."

This time, when he stopped talking, I heard Noah swallow wetly.

"My father was waiting when I got home, and we took off. That's when we went to Peabody. He was all broken up, crying and all. Told me how my mother had just walked out on us both—that while I was at school, her boyfriend had pulled in and the two of them were gone like scalded cats. I think somebody helped her get away. Maybe the reverend, or her friends from Eaton. She just walked out the door, leaving everything behind, and was gone. Sometimes I wonder if I hadn't snuck off to get my stuff at school, if she would have taken me with her."

"What did your mother say the next time you spoke to her?" I asked.

"I never heard from her again." His eyes drifted out to where Buttercup and Royally were playing tug of war with a bath towel off the line. "I never found my letterman jacket when we unpacked, either." He kind of hiccuped away a sob. "One day, I know, one day she's going to come through the door and hand me that jacket. I just know it."

He was silent. Melanie wrapped her arms around him. I slipped away.

Leslie Rollins came down and picked up Rex. Though he and I hadn't had a chance to meet before he came for Rex, he called often over the next couple of days, telling me how happy they were together. Several times, he thanked me for the work I put into his new friend to make him obedient and well-trained. I didn't get much of a chance to miss Rex, because the next day, the animal control officer from Berlin arrived with Fred and Ethel, both a pit bull and lab mix. Even though they had been fixed before they were transported, they were suspicious, not trusting, and, as a team, a real handful. I suspected they were going to take a lot of work before they could be homed out.

On the upside, the couple who were transporting were used to Buttercup, so when she walked up to them, they didn't pay her any attention. Even though Fred and Ethel couldn't see each other because of the drape, when I walked around to the outside of the pen, they charged the fence. I don't know if they saw Buttercup at first. She waited half a beat, then jumped forward, snarling right back at them. Now, the newbies knew who the Queen Pig was.

Though I'm still not quite ready to move on after all my years with Ian, I was taken aback when one of the waitresses from The Rough-Cut Diamond Café remarked on how often Sheriff Everett Neddel seemed to bump into me on Main Street, after which of course, we'd come in for a cup of coffee.

"Sure takes a long time to get through one cup sometimes," she said with a knowing smile.

For Buttercup Belle, the happy hours spent with Noah and Travis feeding her as much as she wanted while they were doing piggy repair work are a memory that was followed by several days of a more rigorous diet. We do, after all, need to maintain her svelte figure.

Acknowledgements

How could I have gotten this far without so many others not lined up behind me, but standing arms linked together and creating my solidarity?

Thank you, Glenn, my life partner, my children, family, and friends who listened to me rant and rave, and babble on about what I was doing.

My friends on the written page who speak to me in the dark of night, when I'm cruising the back roads, or trying to concentrate on Sudoku.

Level Best Books. Verena Rose, Shawn Simmons, and Deb Well. Where would I be without you answering my hysterical questions and providing the awesome cover art?

Lisa Matthews, Kill Your Darlings Editing. She knows my worst faults.

Ellen Byron and Darlene Dziomba, who willingly blurbed.

Joshua Prior and the people at Northwest Public Access TV, Donna Howard at The Eloquent Page, and my Northwest Farmer's Market family, all of whom help me get the word out.

The readers who follow my words, big hugs and kisses.

Did I forget to mention you? I am sorry. But know, every one of you, that I am so very, very grateful.

Until the next page is ready, all my love, DonnaRae

About the Author

In true New Englander fashion, DonnaRae Menard has her fingers in a lot of pies. It doesn't matter if it's trying out some new and odd job, rescuing animals, or selecting the best from the side-of-the-road thrift store. She's in it. She brought the same excitement to writing, insisting always that the best part of the read is the smile it leaves you with at the end. Drop in for a cup of coffee, a little gossipy chatter, and maybe you'll find yourself on the pages of something yet to come.

Visit her new and updated website, donnaraemenardbooks.com. Soon to come will be character sketches about people in her books. Sign up. Maybe you'll come away with a bit of free fun.

AUTHOR WEBSITE:
donnaraemenardbooks.com

SOCIAL MEDIA HANDLES:
Facebook: DonnaRae Menard Author

Also by DonnaRae Menard

It's Never Too Late Series
Murder in the Meadow
Murder on Eagle Drop Ridge
Murder in The Village Proper
Murder on The Small Farm

The Woman Warrior Series
In the Shadow of Pharaoh
Strength of the Mayan Leopard
Wu-Lee

Shorts
Dreams of a Mad Woman
It Takes Guts

Children
Willa the Wisp

Fantasy
The Waif and The Warlord

Detective Carmine Mansuer Series
Patterns
Hunters

The Courier of the Dead Series
The Morality Issue

Lynn Steeves Series
Beneath the Fountain

Gwen Hanson Mystery Series
Dopped from the Sky

www.ingramcontent.com/pod-product-compliance
Lightning Source LLC
Chambersburg PA
CBHW020621110726
47899CB00002B/600